CINEMA LOVE

CINEMA LOVE

A NOVEL

JIAMING TANG

DUTTON

DUTTON

An imprint of Penguin Random House LLC
penguinrandomhouse.com

LIBRARY OF CONGRESS CATALOGING-IN-PUBLICATION DATA

Names: Tang, Jiaming, author.
Title: Cinema love : a novel / Jiaming Tang.
Description: New York : Dutton, 2024. | Identifiers: LCCN 2023050381 (print) |
LCCN 2023050382 (ebook) | ISBN 9780593474334 (hardback) | ISBN 9780593474358 (ebook)
Subjects: LCGFT: Novels.
Classification: LCC PS3620.A68455 C56 2024 (print) | LCC PS3620.A68455 (ebook) |
DDC 813/.6—dc23/eng/20231218
LC record available at https://lccn.loc.gov/2023050381
LC ebook record available at https://lccn.loc.gov/2023050382

Printed in the United States of America
1st Printing

BOOK DESIGN BY DANIEL BROUNT

For Mom and Dad

CINEMA LOVE

PART I

THERE HE IS: hiding in the basement and waiting for love. Upstairs is a cinema. The movies on rotation are old, and to outsiders it's a wonder there's any business at all. They joke about the place over cheap beer. Money laundering is a popular theory. So's human trafficking, except the people who frequent the theater are small, nervous men. The only woman anyone has seen there is the box office clerk. You know, the stern one who limps. She's here now, shuffling from hallway to box office with a dustpan and a broom. A customer waits outside, his hat pulled low. Their exchange is wordless. The woman's eyes lick like a tongue while the customer gestures with his finger—*One ticket, I don't care for what*—before a larger-than-normal bill moves from hand to outstretched hand. Woman and customer exchange nods, and the latter enters with the gait of a bandit.

The customer knows the cinema like the lines on a lover's face. There are two wings, each with a screening room, a toilet, and, in the left wing, a staircase disguised as a closet door. These stairs lead to a basement, where the customer walks down a dark hall. Past graffiti, past cigarette butts, over torn-up movie tickets, and into a cloud of smoke. There aren't any strobe lights down here, but he imagines that there are. No music, either, or alcohol. Just a lone mattress on the floor. A lightbulb with a hanging chain. And sometimes, like now, a man waiting for love.

"Are you . . . ?" the man asks.

Yes, the customer says with his eyes.

"Ah."

There's no more communication between them. Only a slow movement forward. Thumping heartbeats and surprise. *I can't believe this is going to happen*, the customer thinks. *I can't believe I'm about to . . .*

Afterwards, shuddering.

The groans of an ancient mattress.

ONE

I N NEW YORK, in Chinatown, a man named Old Second remembers. He has freckles all over his face. Burn scars and blackheads, like barnacles on a whale. Trembling hands attached to long, hairless arms pick up and light a cigarette. A ceiling fan spins, and the open window offers a view of people marching. He watches them. They are mostly quiet, but sometimes they chant words he can't understand, hold up signs he can't make out. Still, he knows what this is for. They've come to him in the past, with cameras and notebooks and sputtering words.

Hi, my name is . . . We're here to get your signature . . . Do you mind if . . .

And so on, until Old Second says, in broken Mandarin:

"Sure."

Old Second grew up in the mountains, missing all but a year's worth of school. It was the same for his siblings. The girls went for longer while the boys went straight to the fields. They preferred it, anyhow—they claimed it gave them freedom. Especially in the hot, damp, sticky summers. Instead of Mandarin, they learned how to fish. How to transform old shirts and water bottles into river traps. They'd wait in the stream with their buckets, their eyes gleaming and their bodies completely still. Then, suddenly, a shout. *There! There's one!* Old Second remembers a thrust of the body. Gold, sinewy skin; the muscles taut and firmer than steel. He remembers, too, the weight of his brothers' limbs as they leaned against him, not quite hugging but almost.

Now, decades later, he watches a similar kind of love outside his window.

He may not understand the words or the signs, but he's aware of what's going on. A rent strike. The marchers are trying to save Chinatown. Like the mall on East Broadway with the Fuzhounese kiosks and the decades-old restaurants on Eldridge Street. The marching started three hours ago—small. A trickling of Chinese protesters walked down the street like shoppers. Then a woman with a loudspeaker arrived, and youngsters in lion dance uniforms. Passersby joined in, and soon it became a crowd.

From above, the marching resembles hugging. It moves Old Second, causes him to remember. Not just childhood and brother-love, but also the time he stood with thirty-seven men outside the Mawei City Workers' Cinema.

That was a long time ago, Old Second thinks.

In August, it will have been thirty-five years.

BUT FIRST WE MUST VISIT AN EARLIER TIME. NOT THIRTY-FIVE years back but forty. This is where the story begins, where a boy from the mountains learns that the wrong kind of laughter can kill. You've already met Old Second, but there are other characters, too.

Family members and neighbors who will remain in the background, like cardboard forests in a play. Mother and Father. Big Sister, Little Sister, Old Third. The brother named Eldest matters more to our story, but only by a little. He's the oldest son and works at a welding factory in Fuzhou. He's also the darling of the family, the one destined to be killed, and he dies in a factory accident in 1980. The other important characters are Old Second's youngest brother, Spring Chicken, and a neighborhood boy, age sixteen, who goes by the name One Meter Sixty-Five.

None of the boys resemble their names. Spring Chicken has matchstick arms and medium-rare cheeks. Instead of tanning, his skin burns under sunlight. Blushes pink, then red, and the boils that form resemble the bumps on a plucked goose. He's ugly, and that's why people love him. Then there's One Meter Sixty-Five, loved for the opposite reason. He's had his nickname since childhood. It represents the height of every man in his family except for him: a giant with a voice that sounds like a stroking hand. Its cadence approaches your ear like a curious cat. Then it romps, playful, before boredom sinks in, leaving with a piece of your heart.

Which is what happens to Old Second.

SUMMER 1980. A VILLAGE WITHOUT ELECTRICITY OR HEAT, and whose name literally means High Mountain. One morning, Eldest will leave for his factory job in Fuzhou, never to come back. No roads connect High Mountain with Fuzhou, so the journey will take an afternoon and an evening. Spring Chicken will watch Eldest leave. His dark, round, curious eyes will stare until his brother dips out of sight. There are so many trees up here, so many places to hide. You can climb up a tree and disappear for hours. There's a reason High Mountain kids don't play hide-and-seek, and it's not for lack of imagination. It's simply too easy to vanish. Too easy to climb into the leaves and forget that life exists.

Today is Old Second's turn to collect firewood. He's already tied a bundle with rope and packed it into his basket. There's more to be gathered, but for now, he'll rest by the stream his brothers call River. In two hours, morning will have passed and the sun will have reached its highest peak. Sweat on his skin, under his arms and between his legs, gets splashed away in the water. Nearby, a river trap is laid—one of Eldest's. The scene is quiet aside from the water sounds, the rustling of leaves. Old Second assumes it's an animal until One Meter Sixty-Five falls, crashing to the forest floor.

"Shit," he says. "You scared me."

"*I* scared *you*?"

"All that noise you made. I thought you were a bear."

"A bear in these parts?"

"I've seen them. They look just like you."

"Where'd you see a bear?"

"Right now. He's talking to me."

"Don't be funny with me. I know where you live—I'll kick your ass here and I'll kick your ass there."

The play in his voice burrows under Old Second's skin. It's not merely the sass and the teasing. There's also a look in his eyes. A curling of the lips that makes Old Second's cheeks burn with anger. The boys consider each other friends despite running in separate circles. Most days, their interactions are brief. A distant nod or glance, neither of them smiling. Yet here they are: joking, grinning, the heat rising in Old Second's belly. He's fifteen and tends to experience every emotion as anger. Now is no exception, though this time he doesn't feel the itch to strike. He stays and listens, observing the knots of muscle like tree roots running along One Meter Sixty-Five's legs. The straightness of his torso, bare under a lifted flap of shirt. Most aggravating of all: his laughter, beckoning and beckoning.

"You always come to this stream, bear?"

"Why? Do you own it?"

"Sure. But you're welcome here anytime. No fee."

From that day on, the boys claimed each other. One because his oldest brother and best friend had left High Mountain, the other because he was bored. Curious. *If I ask, will he come? He does in the day, but what about at night?* They look at each other in the darkness, examine bits of face illuminated by moonlight. An eye here and a smile there. No words, because they don't want people to hear them. Neither says it, but they know their friendship is strange. Rumors would form if they were caught. Yet all they do is silently embrace. This is what Old Second tells his mother when she finds out. He omits the part where they sneak away from home at two, sometimes three in the morning. He doesn't talk about the waiting, his anger and impatience at always being the first to arrive. Nor does he mention the part where he performs twice the amount of work the previous day. No one will miss him if he gathers extra firewood, digs up all the sweet potatoes.

No one but Spring Chicken, who's baffled by the extra work Old Second does.

Nine years old and curious, he snoops around like a dog. He's too young to work, too sickly. All day and night he watches his siblings live their lives. At the first sign of suspicion, he'll follow them: through brambles, under trees, across the stream called River. And recently there have been strange behaviors. The first is Old Second's sudden productivity. A sibling doing extra work for no reason? Not in Spring Chicken's world! Second, his brother's frequent trips to the stream, all yielding zero fish. Not even a single croaker, his favorite. When Spring Chicken asks, Old Second says nothing. Instead, he darts his eyes. Where is he looking? Because it's not here—the boys' shared bedroom contains nothing but mats and blankets.

Maybe his behavior has to do with exhaustion. He's been yawning a lot lately, sometimes before the sun has even set. At the dinner table, too, and while cleaning himself. A yawn followed by lip smacks, sometimes a burp blown into a sister's face. At night he's the first to fall asleep, and often he forgets to lower the mosquito blinds. Spring Chicken has to do it for him. He doesn't realize that Old Second is trying to escape quietly. That's why he sleeps with his clothes on, and why, after dinner, he leaves the kitchen door open.

But all of Old Second's efforts go to waste because, one night, Spring Chicken wakes up. Not due to any noise—he simply has to pee. And while walking to the latrine, he sees Old Second sneaking off in shadow. Spring Chicken follows him down the mountain path, into the forest. Minute after minute of twigs snapping underfoot. Eventually, they reach a clearing. Spring Chicken is far behind, but he can hear the water, the croaking of bullfrogs. Thin shafts of moonlight are everywhere. And with the glow of fireflies, he can see his brother standing with another figure: a feline boy with skin that shines like polished metal. He's frightened but knows better than to yell. In fact, all three boys are silent. Even when Old Second touches the figure, and when the figure touches him back.

Tenderly, like a mother stroking her child. But then the figure turns and sees Spring Chicken, and begins to laugh.

OH, THE MOUNTAINS. THE MOSQUITOES AT NIGHT AND THE rabbits nibbling behind trees. You can't see them, but they're there. Always. This is the kind of place where words don't matter. Only the language of bodies, and the sound of machines. Can you hear the machines? They approach slowly, but to the villagers it's too fast. Way too fast. A road is paved; a telephone pole goes up. Then another, and another—giants obscured by gravel dust. The stream Old Second calls River becomes a puddle, and his bottle traps with the croakers still in them are buried in mud.

Old Second is no longer there, and neither is the lover with the inaccurate name. Their friendship ended the night Spring Chicken watched them hold each other.

The precious secret that once belonged to two boys now belongs to others. To Spring Chicken, who will tell his mama, who will tell her husband, who will clench his fist when Old Second approaches the dinner table. The other villagers will know, too. Try telling a nine-year-old boy not to share a secret. By the following morning, even the trees will know the truth, with their own embellishments to boot.

Did you hear about Old Second?

With Old Guan's boy at that.

I always knew he was funny. Too pretty for his own good.

In later years, Spring Chicken will reconsider what he saw in the clearing. At the time, he told his mama that Old Second and the other boy were kissing, but age and distance have sharpened his memory. He will conclude that he was wrong. The two silhouettes, entwined like vines, were merely touching. One stroking the other's back with a golden hand, the other sighing and sighing. It wasn't the dirty seduction his mama had made it out to be. It didn't justify the beatings. Nor did it justify the way his baba forced Old Second to kneel outside their home. For hours and hours his brother kneeled, and if anyone dared to help him, they'd get a smack across the face. He remembers his mother: how she refused to speak to Old Second and pretended he wasn't there. Even after Eldest died and Old Second left to work in Mawei, the siblings were forbidden to speak to him. Forbidden to say goodbye.

TWO

D O YOU SEE her? The limping woman with the shopping bags. She walks slowly and stares with hatred in her eyes. Maybe it's the heat. The sweat dripping from wrist to sidewalk as the carp she bought spoils in its plastic. A shiny tail pokes out from behind a bent bundle of chives, and the ice cream in her other bag is melting. The marchers crowding the streets smell the fish, or at least some imagine they can. Anything to dismiss this glaring woman whom they believe to be an enemy. There's something haughty about her. An expression matching the crinkling of a nose, like when you see a beggar on the street and decide to cover your face. In the words of one of the youngsters, "You never know with people nowadays." He's not wrong, but he's not right, either. It's true, this woman doesn't care for the marchers. She'll believe in rent cancellation when she sees it, but right now she's got a carp spoiling below her wrist and all these people in the way. The white ones she pushes, especially if they're posing for pictures. She's kinder to the Chinese marchers, but her sympathy lies solely with the old men and women.

A few are her neighbors, two of them illegal. To her, their courage is stupid. What if the cops get you, and what if you are infected with the new illness? It's better to be safe than sorry, especially in this part of the world. She shakes her head and walks up the stairs of her building. The steps haven't been swept in weeks, and scraps of paper are scattered everywhere. Receipts, lotto tickets, scratch-off cards, and a child's drawing—ugly. Her apartment is on the third floor, a one-bedroom, and the door opens the moment she shakes out her keys.

"Did you get the shrimp paste?" Old Second asks.

The woman doesn't respond and instead places her groceries in the fridge. They've been married for thirty years and rarely address each other by name. A grunt is greeting enough for them. Instead of calling her Bao Mei, Old Second clears his throat and glances in his wife's direction. It's the kind of communication you see in very old couples—ones who've gone through things together.

"It's a million degrees out, and all those people," Bao Mei says.

"Did you remember the shrimp paste?" Old Second asks again.

"No. Out."

"Are you sure? They always have it at the big store. Near Canal."

"Why don't you go yourself if you have all the answers?"

"It's one block over. Doesn't take more than five minutes."

"Okay," Bao Mei says, thrusting her shopping bags at him. "Why don't you go now? Walk through all those people, I dare you. God. It's so sweaty out there, so sticky. You touch someone and you're stuck to them like tape."

"Next time go the other way. The crowd is gathered on one end of the road."

"I don't have time to talk to you anymore. I'm going to lie

down. With all those people out I haven't been able to sleep at night."

"The protests only started this morning."

"Yeah, well." She blinks while lying on the futon. "Let's hope what happened to us doesn't happen to them."

TOGETHER, BAO MEI AND HER DREAMS REMEMBER EVERY-thing. Not just her own memories, but those of others. Asleep, her body twitches and so does her mouth—choking on silent words as they fail to enter waking life. Today, however, a scream exits her lips, mixing with the thick August air. When she wakes, it's to the loathsome sound of Old Second running from the bedroom. They perform their usual routine. He asks if she's all right; she tells him she's had a dream. No, she doesn't want to talk about it; yes, she'll take a bowl of water. The warmer, the better so she won't taste the tap flavor like blood in her mouth. She swishes it. Looks around at this apartment they've built together as husband and wife.

It's a one-bedroom apartment, and the bedroom has no door. Instead, there's a curtain that's too short and a little cumbersome. Feet and the bottoms of old furniture are visible from the living room. A bedpost, scratched. Table legs—you can tell that they wobble. The things unseen include a dresser draped with a dust cloth, an old TV, and a mattress too solid for Bao Mei to sleep on. Napping on it could break bones, and rolling over in the night feels like an hour on the rack. No, no. Not good. Let the old fart sleep on it if he wants. Bao Mei prefers the futon. A table sits in front of it, so she sleeps facing the cushions, soft as belly meat. On the table are items that make her feel protected. A wallet with pictures of herself and Old Second. A phone and a TV remote. She grabs one or the other when waking from bad dreams. With the push of a button, she can play a video to keep the nightmares at bay. But before that, she always reaches for the most important item of all: an ancient ring of keys older than her grief.

Standing at the window, Bao Mei clutches the keys. The marching continues outside, but there are no more speeches, no more shouting. Just the steady one-two one-two of many dozen footsteps and the fluttering of banners. They have slogans and hashtags. "Cancel rent." "Save Chinatown." "Please donate." Search online and you'll find links to mutual aid funds and Venmo accounts. Artists have collaborated with restaurants to sell T-shirts with—as Old Second would say—hideous designs. A black polyester shirt with three smiling buns is not worth twenty-five of his hard-earned dollars. But Bao Mei buys them. Secretly. Not because she wants one but because the East Broadway Mall is too important to fade into a dream. Lately, she's been fantasizing about a fund that would've saved her friends and her brother's spirit thirty-five years ago.

What if, she thinks. *What if, what if, what if.*

THREE

N 1984, A priest gives a list of numbers to a teenage Bao Mei. He explains that these dates are for the burial of her brother. He also tells her the best time of day to move the body. When to break ground and when to cremate—if that's what her family wants. Bao Mei accepts the list with a grateful nod, sniffling. She's sick from days of running around, asking for favors. It turns out death isn't merely sad. It's obnoxious, too. Relatives must be notified; workers must be hired. Grief has rendered her father useless, and all day long he sits in the field, watering crops with bloodshot eyes. At home, he stares into space or at his son's coffin, left open the smallest crack. When he thinks he's alone, his breath catches. Becomes a gasp, then a sob, then a wail.

Bao Mei hears it often. Her father's footsteps and his endless sobbing. He repeats the same words over and over: "Hen Bao . . . bloodlines . . . my boy, my heart." She listens, sleepless, and feels something like anger harden in her chest. The anger turns out to be phlegm, and the phlegm will later turn into illness. Right now, however, she walks from the temple to her home with a bag of funeral items. Afterlife money, joss sticks, a little white grieving cap. It's November, which, in this part of China, means a lot of wind and even more rain. Trees shake with a noise resembling a young boy's speech. Bao Mei believes that this is Hen Bao trying to contact her. Since childhood, whenever they were apart, he'd send her dreams. It happened the day he left to work at the pants factory in Mawei, and it happened the day he died.

The dreams are so mundane, they feel like memories. In one, Bao Mei and Hen Bao sit in their shared bedroom, talking about what they ate and what they plan to eat. In another, he gives her a tour of his apartment in Mawei. It's attached to the pants factory, and Bao Mei sees the factory floor in yet another dream. The cafeterias with their migrant workers and lunch ladies appear to her, too, and sometimes she eats their twice-a-day bun meals with a man Hen Bao introduces as his "friend." "We met at the cinema," Hen Bao says, and Bao Mei knows not to ask for details. The final dream, the night before her brother dies, is burned into Bao Mei's mind. She sees the outside of the cinema, ruined and lined with litter. When she looks closer—at the creepy, too-familiar woman working the box office— Hen Bao suddenly pushes past her, sprinting. His last words are: "I have to go inside, you don't understand yet, I have to . . ."

That morning, Bao Mei wakes with a feeling of dread. Her father does as well, and so do the chickens—eggless. They know. Before the man comes to their door with bad news—"Sit down, uncle, sister, I need to tell you something"—they know.

IT'S INTERESTING: HOW DEATH IS DIFFERENT IN REAL LIFE. Bao Mei's gone to the movies many times, and there, death is a grand, dramatic, and heroic event. It's waterworks and fists against the chest. Soldiers wailing and a wife-mother-sister collapsed on the ground. When the man comes to her door, she wants to cry, but her eyes are dry as chalk. Sadness more vicious than monsoon winds lash at her throughout the mourning period, but not one tear escapes her eyes. She pretends to sob in public, however, because people look at you funny if you don't. They'll judge you and spread rumors.

Bao Mei remembers how her father negotiates the price of Hen Bao's coffin with an artisan who insists that he's selling at a loss. How that artisan points at his three daughters, dressed like royalty by comparison, and says that they need to eat too, your dead son be damned. How her father kneels in that same artisan's shop, begging yet full of dignity: "Please help us, mister. We're poor. Come, daughter, come. Kneel with me."

Then there's the morning she sees Hen Bao's body. He's but a face inside a cheap coffin, the interior lined with fabric scraps. Anger like a sickness spreads through Bao Mei, and the first thing she does is fight her brother. His face is calm, looks ready to wake up. His is not the kind of dead body you hear about from elders. The kind that dies without wanting to, whose eyes have to be weighed down by coins. No, Hen Bao's body is like when a child goes to sleep. The only difference is the lack of breathing. The lack of movement in the chest, which Bao Mei decides, in a moment of rage, is a trick. *Why does he get to rest? Why does Father have to kneel, and why must I as well?*

She decides to pinch him.

Pinching is what she used to do when they argued, and the act used to bring her great satisfaction. But now the only thing she feels is terror. The texture of Hen Bao's face is nothing like she imagined.

She expects the limpness of a cheek. The oily texture of pores. But what she doesn't expect is sawdust on her fingers. Coarse and hair-raising. Nothing prepares her for the raised welt that doesn't bruise; nothing prepares her for the raised welt that doesn't go away.

BAO MEI STARES INTO SPACE WHILE HER RELATIVES SING AT Hen Bao's funeral. She sits in the back of the room, annoyed and holding back her rage. Grief stuns her like a knife against her neck. She's barely able to tolerate her family's death pageant. The sobs of her father, the chanting of the priests. The loud prayers of her uncles: dancing and pretending to throw themselves against the casket. Bao Mei knows that these actions are customary at a funeral. But the boldness of them—the wildness that could be confused for joy—causes her nostrils to flare. What do these people know about the death of a sibling? About Hen Bao, who will never sew another garment, never tell another joke? At the end of the day, they'll go home and pat themselves on the back. But for the rest of her life, Bao Mei will sit with her brother's absence: scrambling but failing to fill it with ghosts.

Two priests signal the next segment of her brother's funeral. As is the custom, his loved ones will carry the casket to a burial spot determined by shamans. But it's storming today, and the wind lashes Bao Mei like a whip. She refuses to acknowledge how her father has to be dragged like a drunkard behind the pallbearers; ignores the whispers of a neighbor seeking gossip. Trying to suppress her fury, Bao Mei shifts her thoughts to the question of money. Bao Mei's never had much of it, and her job isn't enough to support her family.

What's worse is the irregular nature of her father's labor, seasonal and dependent on his health.

These days he doesn't wake with the energy to move stones. Not in middle age, and not when he's grieving his only son's death. He can only do that kind of work twice, maybe three times a week—if he's lucky. Manual labor is difficult and low-paying, and the government has plenty of men to recruit. Bao Mei sees the signs everywhere. "Help China expand, help China modernize!" The mountains with names like Stone and Drum are the first to change. Mountainsides are carved, bored into, and dynamited into tunnels. Roads are built. Poles are erected; temples are renovated. If you're unlucky, the government will take your land. Their notices promise payment, but it won't be enough. It's never enough. To say no, however, is to risk your life. Bao Mei's heard of this happening before: the government sending thugs to beat those who refuse their offers. *Stupidity*, she thinks. At this point she'd gladly take any money she could get.

Because here's the other thing she learns about death: It's expensive. Death means paying for a funeral and losing income. Hen Bao used to send a portion of his paycheck home every month, and now Bao Mei has to make up the difference. Nobody suggests this to her; nobody tells her to do anything. But while marching at her brother's funeral, she decides that this is what she must do. Inside, her mind is a complete and total calm.

HEN BAO'S GHOST FLOWS LIKE WARM AIR AGAINST THE mourners' shoulders. He floats above and sometimes beyond the trees, watching as dirt is piled over his body. Gravel falls into the coffin his sister had to beg for—dirtying his face and the suit that once belonged to his father. It's not one he liked in his waking life. The color is ghastly, and the fabric is cheap. He used to joke that he "wouldn't be caught dead in that thing." But look at where he is now: He's both dead *and* in that thing, and the realization causes him to erupt in a tantrum. For days he goes around blowing out fires. His father lights firewood under a stove, and Hen Bao tries to knock out every ember. But a ghost is not quick enough and can't compete with a human's ability to pile on coals. Even if the ghost stomps his feet, cursing, the human will always win.

Like how Bao Mei always wins when lighting candles in her room. Hen Bao blows them out to get her attention, but she lights them again and again, each time in a haze. She doesn't notice that these candlewicks are strangely weak. She doesn't notice, either, that there shouldn't be drafts in her bedroom, which is windowless and without cracked walls. Her brother's death has shocked her into a state of numbness. She walks everywhere without a jacket despite the wind and the November rains. Days ago, at the coffin-maker's house, Hen Bao saw Bao Mei kneel with their father in an outfit as thin as it was ugly. His hatred rose when the coffin-maker rejected their offers for a reasonably priced anything. He had to intervene by dropping into the artisan's head and knocking things around like a hammer on thin wood.

Hen Bao can only play tricks in places where people believe in ghosts. Elsewhere, his presence would be explained away. Dismissed. For instance, Bao Mei's blown-out candles aren't so strange when you consider the age of the wicks. There's also the way her father, unscrewed by grief, keeps opening, then shutting the door. November winds enter their home and blow everything out—the stove fires first. Believers, on the other hand, will interpret these events as the work of a spirit. They'll light incense and burn afterlife money and leave bowls of rice on altars painted an austere red. Cold against the arm is enough to change the direction of their route. Finally, this happens to Bao Mei as she marches down High Mountain after burying her brother. A redness starts to spread in the breast of her funeral robe, and upon reaching home, Hen Bao's last words reenter her head.

I have to go inside, you don't understand yet, I have to.

Hen Bao watches her from a corner of the room. He's sitting on a dresser made of bamboo, his legs dangling above a clump of dirty clothes. There's the funeral robe. The white headband and the fabric shoes—ragged and frosted with mud. Red socks pass through his kicking legs when Bao Mei throws them against the dresser. He doesn't care because excitement and relief wash over him like a tide. He's sure that he'll be able to communicate with his sister again if she goes to the cinema. Within those walls exists a force that allows the hidden parts of people to be seen. Come alive. Like the first time he went, and a man offered him a cigarette, and Hen Bao learned that sweat and saliva and piss were the smells of love. Or the second time, losing his mind, when a man said he had a husband who worked at the bank.

"A what?" Hen Bao asked.

"A husband."

"A husband?"

"A husband."

The cinema is a place where a certain kind of reality pauses. Where, if a sissy's hand brushes against another man's knuckle hairs, his first reaction is to grab it. Hard. Then harder, and harder again, until that nameless, scentless flower blooms. In the cinema, you don't have to worry about your parents' demands. The pressure of a father wanting to further the bloodline (for what purpose?), a mother obsessed with grandbabies. Hen Bao smiles, watching his sister, and the smile becomes a calmness in her mind. She's lying in bed, worrying about money, when the image of the Mawei City Workers' Cinema flashes into her head.

FOUR

A YEAR AND SEVEN months later, Old Second leaves his apartment to buy food, mess around, and—he tells himself—do nothing at all.

It's a warm day. Windless, with knee-high fog blanketing the ground. The men who offer tricycle rides rest in tea shops or under the eaves of markets. They wear their shirts open, baring brown chests with jutting ribs and, if they're eating, noodle bits on their collar. It's 1986 and Mawei's new roads are already dirty. This is fine, maybe even preferable. It feels comforting to have the streets smell like overripe fruit. And with the stalks of unsold vegetables everywhere, the city looks more like home. A crowded one, if you ignore the side alleys: empty and full of insects. The one that leads to the Workers' Cinema has nothing but a pay-per-use toilet and its bored attendant.

Old Second walks to the cinema for the second time in his life. The first time was last week, and he had lost his composure, running out in the middle of a war film. Not because of anything on-screen but because the men in the audience were touching each other. He could see it from the aisle. Sissies sitting in dark corners with contorted bodies and wandering eyes. There were sounds, too (Old Second heard one man ask another for money), and smells. The moment he entered the Workers' Cinema, its love-feeling quickened the pace of his heart. The ticket taker could sense the change in him through the box office window.

"Are you sure you're in the right place?" she asked.

"Yes."

He's sure because he's looked for it his entire life. A place where men like him meet. He tried the parks before, the public toilets, but whenever someone approached him, he freaked. One time he grew so angry that his fists came out. He only stopped himself when the man shrank back, crying. He was as old as Old Second's father, but his face wore the urgent grief of a child. Wordless, Old Second left the man in the park. He wanted it, but every time he got close to someone, the memories came back. Not just of his father's anger, or the disgusted look on his mother's face. Their beatings had hurt, sure, and so did the hours of kneeling. But worse than both was the belly-up tone of One Meter Sixty-Five's laugh. When Spring Chicken found them that night, the first thing Old Second thought was: *Deny it. Fake it. We'll return in two weeks and nobody will follow us then.* But before a word could leave his mouth, One Meter Sixty-Five began to cackle. He slapped his knees, rolled on the ground. Cried and cried and cried.

Old Second knew then that it was over.

The laughter is what Old Second remembers when he meets a man in the park. He wants love—there's no question—but fear always returns like a reflex. It's such a problem that he prays to the gods for help. For strength, too, and courage, and a prosperous year without illness. This time, when he returns to the Workers' Cinema, it's after a long night of deliberation. The ticket taker notices the bags under his eyes. Chuckles.

"You sure you're in the right place this time?"

"I'm certain of it."

"Sure, sure. Don't run out again."

Flushed with embarrassment, Old Second says nothing. Glares.

"It gives us bad attention. I have to spread rumors and tell people the place is haunted."

"I'm certain I'm in the right place."

"I didn't ask for all that." She slides him his ticket. "Enjoy the show."

ONCE AGAIN, HE'S IN THE DARK ROOM. ONCE AGAIN, THERE are cigarette butts in the seats and burns from fallen ash on the floor. Last week's war film continues to play on the big screen. A grenade goes off, and the sound shakes the seats of the three men in the screening room. Two sit together; one is alone. This last man is Shun-Er, and Old Second sees him looking from a corner of the theater. There's no fluke here, no act of the imagination. His pock-marked face, angled to the left, stares like a Roman statue, its expression one of appraisal. *Is he? Does he want to?*

A courtship begins.

A slow, "accidental" movement toward the other man is the first step. If he doesn't pull away, or if he glances back at you, you can move closer. Sit behind him, offer a cigarette. Look closely. Is he watching the movie, or is he feeling the space around him? Either way, accepting the cigarette means he wants you. If he doesn't, move on. It's no big deal in a city like this.

Old Second doesn't smoke, but he accepts Shun-Er's cigarette. He puffs on it and coughs so wildly Shun-Er has to pat him on the back—*rub, rub, rub*—while the other men in the theater laugh. The touch is tender, reminds Old Second of One Meter Sixty-Five. It calms him. Soothes him, even though Shun-Er stares with bewildered eyes.

"Why'd you take the cigarette if you don't smoke?"

"Seemed like the right thing to do."

Like children, they giggle. The kind that hurts the chest. Old Second laughs so hard he doesn't notice Shun-Er's ugliness. He also forgets about the night in the forest clearing. He just laughs and falls forward, nudging Shun-Er a little. They're intimate without meaning to be, and they move like a pair of drunks. Hands snake toward wrists, then arms, then shoulders—all of it smelling like sweat and cigarette smoke. When, finally, Shun-Er leans forward to give Old Second a kiss, it's to the sound of death on the movie screen. Nobody watches, but a soldier, running into a battlefield, is destroyed by a mine.

FIVE

THEIRS IS THE kind of love that can change the weather. A radio forecast predicting rain switches its tune the moment Old Second sees Shun-Er. Clouds part, a breeze picks up, and the sun becomes so yellow it looks *delicious*. Just peel the skin, remove the seeds, and bite. Not hard but soft, the way Shun-Er touches Old Second. Hand-holding is forbidden, so their fingers and palms must find each other in creative ways. One day at the beach they discovered they could touch forever if it looked like they were brushing sand off each other. They took turns doing this for hours. One man rolled around; the other patted his back. Switch. Rinse and repeat. Once, they hiked up a mountain and snuck sweaty kisses in front of a folk god's altar. If the god saw them, she was merciful: The men were left alone. And of course there was the Workers' Cinema. The place where they first met, and where love became more than words and gentle touching. It was a thickness in the air. A taste, too: of sweat and saliva, blood in the mouth.

They were young, so their love was intense. It continued for weeks. Then months. A year passed, and their feelings were fresh as spearmint. It was like sucking a lozenge that never lost its flavor. Theirs wasn't a jealous love. Nor was it angry, paranoid, or afraid. Each man was lightened by it and moved through the world with new eyes. A thing Old Second kept saying to Shun-Er was:

"I can't believe this is happening."

"What?"

"This." He pointed at himself, then at Shun-Er. "Isn't it weird?"

"No, not at all."

Some days they talk. Share stories. Old Second doesn't cry when he revisits the past. Instead, he laughs. Crying is too simple, he feels, and too loud. More than anything, his emotions are like whispers. After his father punched him and his mother saw, in place of her son, a roach, Old Second was forced to kneel outside his home for hours. But worse was the nonchalance of his neighbors. They walked around him, whispering among themselves—yes, even One Meter Sixty-Five—and not daring to meet Old Second's eyes.

"Only my youngest brother cried. The idiot who caused this mess. He cried when they beat me, he cried when I kneeled. Then Father beat him, too. *Harder.* Not only for the tears, but for following me in the first place. That's my suspicion, anyway. People like us, we're not a problem until *they* catch us doing something. Then it's blood and fury and all eighteen levels of hell. My theory is that Father was mad at my brother for confirming something he already knew. Because he wailed while hitting me. He wailed and beat his chest like he was at a funeral."

"That's the first time you were caught?"

"What do you mean? I was a teenager. My balls had just dropped."

Their laughter is quiet, personal. Nobody hears them in the

Workers' Cinema. The men cruising are too busy with themselves. They walk in circles around the screening room with nervous, bloodshot eyes. Some of them, regulars by the look of it, are jovial; they crack jokes and buy food for anyone who needs it. Old Second was once the recipient of this charity, though normally, it went to a pair of nomads—penniless but beautiful—from Sichuan Province. They, like everyone else, are built into the tapestry of the cinema, made up of fat men, thin men, ugly men, beautiful men. Some are destitute and sell plasma to come here. Others are fathers, *grandfathers*, who mask their poor behavior with thoughtless generosity. But regardless of who they are, they all ignore whatever it is the Projectionist plays on the big screen. Which is sometimes disappointing for Old Second because today's feature is his favorite: a supernatural cop film set in Malaysia.

Old Second and Shun-Er gossip about the projectionist in a lazy, contented way. *Is he, you know? Not when he looks at the ticket taker like that. Such a shame, he's pretty good-looking.* They consider his eyes, his shoulders, the width of his arms. Old Second likes the projectionist's belly, but Shun-Er doesn't. He's tall, though, towering over everyone. And they can't forget those hands. "Punching glove hands," Shun-Er calls them. "Get hit once and you're flying across the room." They wonder, giggling, if he and the ticket taker have kissed. If they've hit a home run or spent the night together. Old Second makes a comment about her being lucky. The Projectionist is as gentle as a grazing bull, he notes, and kind, too. Shun-Er smiles in silence. When his breathing deepens, Old Second senses that a switch has flipped—one that signals a return to seriousness. It's often like this with them. Jokes, followed by anger. Sadness. Then jokes again, and gossip, too.

The cycle repeats.

"My wife caught me once," Shun-Er says.

Old Second's body tenses. He does this whenever Shun-Er brings up his wife.

"It was two years after our wedding."

"You said it was arranged?"

Shun-Er nods. "Like everyone else. She worked during the day, and I worked at night. Sometimes I brought men home. If people saw us, I'd say we were work brothers. This one guy, he looked like you. Almost identical. He was skinny. Buzzed head and monolids. The only difference is he was a bit older, and"—grinning—"a lot uglier, too. It was one of my first times with a man. I was so hungry for it I didn't take the proper precautions. I left the front door unlocked."

"Like two dogs in heat."

"We were in the bedroom. Neither of us heard my wife coming. The footsteps up the stairs, her taking off her shoes. It was only when she called my name that I remembered. By then, there wasn't much we could do. I locked the bedroom door. Told the guy to put his clothes on while I did the same. When her hand twisted the knob, I was in a shirt and underwear. She shouted my name and asked what the big idea was. I told the guy who looked like you not to say a word. When we were both dressed, I unlocked the door."

"So she didn't see anything?"

"No, but she's not stupid. Two people in a locked room with the bed in that state? Plus, there was a smell."

Old Second nods. He's familiar with that smell, and blushes at the mention of it.

"She burst into tears. She never said one word to me about the incident, but right then and there she burst into tears. A crying that wouldn't stop."

"I'm sorry."

"She was twenty years old."

DAYS LATER AT THE NIGHT MARKET, THEY LISTEN TO MER-chants shout their slogans with machinelike regularity. Loud-speakers block faces that have long since tanned into leather. Sometimes Old Second and Shun-Er hide behind sunglasses, or under hats labeled with improper English. Not "Nike" but "Mike" and, at lower-quality kiosks, "Aike." Playboy hats with rabbit logos are sold alongside flip-flops and underwear and—oh, what the hell—floor cleaner, too. There are lightbulbs and roach spray, the superstrong kind that's illegal in Europe. Be sure to open the win-dow before each use, and if you get light-headed, you can say you bought it at the other kiosk. Or the other one. Or the other other one, because they all sell the same things.

It's not like anybody cares. The Mawei City Night Market is where merchants test their mettle, go from poor to rich without ever touching middle class. The best ones have names related to their merchandise. Hat Man sells caps in every color and style without once having haggled with a customer. Same thing goes for Melon Lady, who looks exactly like her name, and Undergarments Uncle, who invented the first bra that unsnaps from the front. He chats now with Shun-Er, who walks the night market. Old Second trails behind.

They're on a date. From morning to night, the two have clung together like flies to raw meat, walking past noodle stands, barbecue shops, crowds of gamblers, and a drunk man yelling about God. A distant radio blasts music from Hong Kong, and the smell in the air is dock-like: salt water mixed with sewage. Most days, Shun-Er wouldn't be walking around like this. He'd be eating dinner or running errands with his wife, a woman named Yan Hua whom Old Second knows through word of mouth. She's a small woman. Quiet, but with a hidden temper—crying alone and never shouting. From the picture in Shun-Er's wallet, Old Second can see that she's lived a worse life than him. All three of them are from the provinces, but she's had to bear the brunt of fieldwork. She's had to attend school in private, learning arithmetic and how to read on her own. Her job as a seamstress at a pants factory is a blessing, an escape, and it's also why she's not home.

"Business trip," Shun-Er tells Old Second.

But Old Second knows it's because the couple got into a fight. For starters, what kind of factory sends a seamstress on a business trip? Where would that business trip be? What's more, there's a dreamlike expression on Shun-Er's face. It disappears when he argues with the night market merchants, but Old Second sees that something heavy is weighing on his heart. A seriousness that signals they'll have a personal conversation later. For now, though, it's all fun and games as they haggle with the merchants with food in their hands. Sauces spill onto shirts and pants, clinging like sap to bare, hairless skin. The men discover that this is an opportunity to sneak touches.

Others like them are here. Old Second can tell who they are, and they can tell who he is—all with a glance. Sometimes perfume in the air or a gasp when you walk by is indication enough, but for the most part they find each other with their eyes. Whose hands rest too long on whose shoulders, whose eyes flit to or stare at the bareskinned men. The merchants can tell, too, and poke fun at the customers with lilting speech. They'll call a man "auntie," and the man will skip over, laughing. It's all in good fun because, as one merchant says, "a wallet's a wallet." Unless the wallet is empty, in which case nobody pays attention to you. Not even the mosquitoes, which ignore Shun-Er and Old Second, walking now to the dock with peanut noodles in plastic bags. They listen to the sound of footsteps, the rattle of construction, constant since last summer.

"My wife's not on a business trip."

"I know."

Shun-Er laughs. "Because nobody sends a seamstress on a business trip, right? That's what you're about to say?"

"It's the dumbest thing I've ever heard," Old Second says. He smiles, though, and rests his left hand on Shun-Er's knee. Rubs it until Shun-Er stops trembling.

"The truth is we fought. Same shit as usual."

"She's mad you're not with her?"

"What doesn't make sense is why she's suddenly upset about it now."

Shun-Er pauses, gazing into the river. A passing fishing boat appears as an opaque sheet against black, crinkling water. *Like a roll of film*, Old Second thinks. There's moonlight and stars and, across the water, the provincial capital: Fuzhou. The changing skyline, with its unfinished tall buildings and finished short ones, is a government project. Bungalows from the previous century—maybe older—still stand, lights blinking in their paper windows. These will get torn down within the decade, as officials expand and redevelop the city. Skyscrapers will rise. Shopping malls, hotels, a building with a sign that reads "Fuzhou: The City of Fortune."

"You think she knows?" Old Second asks.

"I don't care that she knows."

"But you suspect she knows about *us*."

"Kind of." Shun-Er throws a rock in the water, watches it skip. "The problem is, Yan Hua's like my mother. She's clueless about gay people. I used to act the way I do now, all through my childhood, and not once did my mother suspect man-love. Not once did she think I was different from my father. She couldn't imagine that a person like me could exist. The possibility never crossed her mind. She ended up tossing a village girl at me when I became of age, told me to marry her, and . . ."

"And what?"

"Do you know what she asked me the other day? She asked who 'the other woman' is."

Old Second laughs, but the noise is hollow.

"Even though she saw me with a man in our bedroom. Even though she cried about it for days and nights and weeks. She said a neighbor's name and wouldn't listen when I told her no, that I wouldn't have an affair with someone who looked like that (seriously, our neighbor has the face of a horse). In fact, I was extremely offended that she would accuse me of such a thing, and—"

"She left?"

"We fought because she didn't believe me, and the next day she packed her bags."

Another pause, another rock thrown. *Skip, skip, skip, splash.*

"My eldest brother," Old Second says, "was like that. He didn't know what a sissy was. A man in the town below our village, he was gay. His mannerisms became his nickname. Sissy something, I can't remember exactly. He made pants and could sew better than anyone else in the region. My brother was friends with him but had no clue that they weren't alike in love. Sissy was just another nickname to my brother, like Backwards Foot or Does Not Speak. He'd say to me, all the time: 'I introduced a girl to Sissy, but it didn't work out' and 'I saw Sissy with a girl today, the bastard.' He never considered that people like us existed. That same-sex love was a possibility."

Another pause.

"What are you thinking about, Shun?"

"I don't know. I think I miss my wife."

SIX

OLD SECOND TAKES pictures with the "Save China-town" organizers, but he doesn't join the protest. Something about his health, his high blood pressure. Bad at Mandarin, he shows the organizers a bottle of pills. They ask if he can take a picture with them anyway. *Sure, sure. In front of the door? Yes, if you don't mind.* He poses the only way he knows how. Straight as a stick and unsmiling, his shirt buttoned up to his neck. The photo is posted on WeChat along with pictures of other people, their stories. *This man's rent is $800, and he can't find work in a shut-down city. This man hasn't received unemployment, state or federal, and his part-time job barely covers the bills. This woman's been let go from her nail salon job and now collects recyclables to make ends meet. This man's savings are almost used up—can anyone help him?* Face after face in a WeChat album of thirty-seven. Near the end is Old Second, and the caption is half about him, half about Bao Mei.

He and Bao Mei used to work at the Golden Unicorn six days a week until March, when business slowed and their schedule shrank to four days. Then three, then two, and now "whenever you're needed"—which clearly is never. He doesn't tell them about Bao Mei's nightmares. Her migraines upon waking and the fact that only Eastern medicine, not covered by insurance, helps. You don't reveal that sort of thing to strangers. Like how he doesn't talk to his American friends about the nature of his marriage.

Theirs is a world that exists outside the pictures posted on We-Chat, outside the protests that run from morning to sunset to morning again. The "Save Chinatown" organizers are aware of this but try to capture as much as they can. Along with photos of people on social media, there are pictures of places.

For example, the East Broadway Mall: a hub for immigrants who return to Chinatown from their non-Chinatown jobs. Next to it are the work agencies, now closed, where job listings are scrutinized by people without papers. There are the bus systems with names like Panda that take these same paperless workers across the country. Temples sit beside churches beside apartments with folk god altars, quiet and fragrant with smoke. All are in danger of being lost; all are in danger of becoming a conversation between two people who've grieved for thirty years.

One night, while eating dinner, Bao Mei asks Old Second if he's ever heard voices. Old Second spits a fish bone into a napkin in response.

"Some days I heard one," Bao Mei says. "A woman's voice, or a boy's. But then I'd look around and see nobody there."

"Where'd you hear it?"

"Everywhere. In the village, in China, in America. And don't"—she points her chopsticks—"say that I'm crazy. My eyes are bad, but my mind is sharp, sharper than yours."

"Maybe you're blessed."

"It's not a holy voice. It's just a voice. I used to think it belonged to my brother. But now . . . Now I don't know. I used to think it was him. I'd talk back like it was him, too."

"Why are you looking at me like that? I believe you."

～

HEN BAO'S GHOST STARTED FOLLOWING BAO MEI THE DAY after he died. She believed it was him when she began to hear voices at the Workers' Cinema. When the owner's son, a burly projectionist who hated his name, explained the unusual nature of the moviegoers, a whisper entered Bao Mei's ear. Afterwards, a pressure on her shoulder, the sensation of a too-weak massage. Even then she was wise enough not to mention anything. As her father used to say, "Nobody knows you're stupid if you don't speak." Nobody knows you're crazy, either, and so she listened to the Projectionist describe the moviegoers while her brother's ghost whispered in her ear. *Don't look around*, she thought. *Don't make it seem as though you hear something.* An unneeded precaution, because what Hen Bao whispered were words that made Bao Mei feel calm. Calm as she listened to the Projectionist explain the cinema's cruising rooms, calm as she learned about the space dedicated to *them*.

It's nothing Bao Mei didn't understand already. Her brother was a sissy—designated, then self-proclaimed. A proud one, too; she figured it out by the way he posed for pictures. An arm over a swung hip, the face girlish and tilted to the left. Shirts colored with stolen dye flowed across his body like river water. He loved a shade of blue he called eggplant, and another, darkness. He wore them all the time, even in the pants factory where he worked six days a week. People in town knew he was a sissy. They treated him like one, calling him "auntie" and "girlfriend," and using his childhood nickname, Sissy Bao. His behavior was regarded with curious eyes, and his lovers—older men with bellies—were accepted with amusement or a friendly swat of the hand. Naysayers who spat knives under their breaths were immediately shut down by neighbors: old men and women who remembered Hen Bao's eager kindness. The way he would, even as a child, stretch himself thin with errands, at the same time dancing in the street just to be smiled at. He learned people's voices, aped the mannerisms of elders. For example: the schoolteacher, who didn't mind the jokes, and the police chief, who did. But regardless of what these two men thought, everybody liked Hen Bao—so long as he prostrated himself before the village. His love could be seen but not spoken about, and village elders tolerated his queerness so long as he understood that he'd have to marry a woman someday. He could do whatever he wanted within that marriage, but it had to take place. As the only boy-child, he needed a son to pass on the family name. That was the way things worked in his village, and his life would've continued down that path if the truck going sixty kilometers an hour hadn't struck him.

Hen Bao died in the hospital and returned to life in the Mawei City Workers' Cinema. That's what Bao Mei believed. She also believed his ghost allowed the place to operate the way it did for so long. The ghostly pats on her shoulders felt like the light touch of her brother's hands. Delicate and with a note of laughter in the fingers. She listened as he insisted that the Projectionist was cute. Not just cute, but good. Gentle. Bao Mei had to narrow her eyes to pay attention to this man who preferred to be nameless. He was more Hen Bao's type than hers, but she liked the sound of his voice when he asked if she could start working that very day.

"Right now?" Bao Mei asked.

"Why not?"

"Take it," Hen Bao's ghost whispered. "Take the job."

"I'll do it," Bao Mei said.

She set aside her bags and entered the box office that would soon become hers. The broom, too, with the dustpan, and the paper scraps that the men used as movie tickets. Boxes of playing cards, perhaps belonging to previous ticket takers, sat in stacks on an old desk, which was moved to give Bao Mei more space. Hen Bao tried to fix his sister's limp by barking posture advice: "Stand up straight. No, not like that. Straighter. Too straight now. That's good." The same advice he gave her in childhood, which never worked, since Hen Bao wasn't strict enough. The sight of his sister's tears stopped him every time, even if they were fake. Like him, Bao Mei hid her deepest emotions with clownery. And Hen Bao knew how fake tears could express a hurt that real tears couldn't. Bao Mei couldn't help her feet. She hated them and kept the hate to herself, but Hen Bao's ghost understood. So, after a while, the furniture was arranged to make walking easier for her. Meantime, Hen Bao talked endlessly about the Projectionist and the nervous men who came to "watch movies."

They wore cheap laborers' rags and were courageous as mice. On any given day, Bao Mei saw faces that were sad, fearful, excited, or expressionless. She sold movie tickets to men who didn't want to be seen. Who wore hats pulled down to their chins and oversized coveralls. She'd protect them by keeping "outsiders" away and would ignore the pleas of wives searching for their husbands. She was a barrier to policemen who wanted to start trouble, and a friend to the homeless who wanted to stay out of it. But despite her best efforts, in the beginning, the cinema men viewed her with suspicion and annoyance. If she went to sweep the toilets and there was a sissy inside, he'd leave, sometimes running out of the cinema without a shirt on. Same with the screening room, where men loved, and loved, and loved. The cinema was open ten hours a day, but the loving felt endless. Infinite. And until the men cozied up to her, discovering in Bao Mei a good but sarcastic friend, she had to learn their stories through her brother's ghost.

"This one"—he points with invisible fingers—"loved a mother who didn't love him back."

"That one sews dresses from fashion magazines and sells them at the night market."

"That one with the sad face. He has a son who goes to university in Beijing."

"This man beats his wife because she doesn't hold him like a man."

So on and so forth, a silent parade of sorrow.

By the time Old Second arrived to look for a love he didn't understand, Bao Mei was already a fixture at the Workers' Cinema. The men there called her Sister Bao, Madame if they were close. She was a source of advice for everyone. Jokes and gossip and comforting words. "Leave that man," she'd say. "Leave that man and find someone who won't take your money." Most of the words came from her brother, who—outside the cinema—was nothing but a grave on the side of a mountain. But here he was a protective spirit. A folk god who played Solitaire and never won.

SEVEN

THE MOVIEGOERS COME from Chang-Le District. From Fuqing. From Guangzhou City, Sichuan Province, and a nameless village outside the Yunnan border. Town names, unknown and unspeakable in Mandarin, sound like music when uttered in the cinema. This isn't merely a place for lovers and lovemaking. It's also where men from faraway towns come to laugh, joke, and gossip about their previous boyfriends. Pictures of parents, wives, and children are shared in a darkness punctuated by movie sounds, sentimental and booming with gunfire. Afterwards, love-drunk and wearing their emotions on their faces, they go to the night market eateries, where everything but the atmosphere is criticized. Scallions get picked away from oyster cakes along with sprigs of wilted coriander. Eggs scrambled with tomatoes are sent back for having too little sugar, or sometimes too much. "It's better how my wife makes it," a man says. "We don't eat this kind of stuff where I'm from," another adds. Each word is spoken with a tilted head and quiet affection, the cadence of a bragging mother. You hear calmness in the air when these men speak about home. A calmness like when someone holds their finger out and a bird lands on it, gentle.

The atmosphere changes when they leave for the night, returning to their apartments and factories. At work, the talking may continue, but for the most part everyone is focused on the garments on their table. There are pants, more pants, dresses, skirts, and shorts. Next to the men are local women with their snoring toddlers, restless but asleep under harsh overhead lighting. Too poor to afford childcare, the women bring their children to work—some even help their mamas by snipping loose threads away from buttons. Factory managers forbid this, but few check or criticize. As long as the work gets done. As long as quotas are met and sales are strong. The mothers aren't likely to be fired, but the men sure are—if they're discovered to be sissies.

It's happened before. Someone in the work-unit apartments, after a long night of alcohol and soul-searching and cries of *I want to be free, all men should be free*, decides to bare his soul to his roommate. In a trembling voice, he says he believes there is something wrong with him. Or maybe not something wrong but rather something different *inside his chest*. Hen Bao, Old Second, and Shun-Er have all witnessed these conversations, most of which result in the same outcome. An airless room with racing thoughts, cigarettes on the floor, and silent, uncomfortable men. Afterwards, a report from his roommate (citing "discomfort and indecency") and the man's eventual dismissal from work. Maybe it won't happen that week, but it'll happen the next, or the one after that. A packing of bags will be followed by the purchasing of a train ticket. Then, from the factory manager, a final paycheck that will be tucked into shallow pockets like a losing lotto ticket.

OLD SECOND REMEMBERS THESE CONVERSATIONS WITH something like fear in his heart. He sees, on nights when his brain won't shut off, the frantic, giddy, sunburnt faces of the men desperate to reveal their souls. If he had the power to travel back in time, he'd beg these men to stop. The risk isn't worth the reward, and besides, there already exists a place where you can freely make love to men. Why not go to the Workers' Cinema and relieve yourself of your urges? But he understands that every sissy must endure his ten seconds of wanting to speak; of wanting to release the pressure weighing on his spirit.

Because the urge also struck him at times. Decades ago, when his roommates at the pants factory bragged about girls, he'd wanted to join in with stories about boys. These feelings that the other men experienced—shyness, terror, lust, and couple-love—matched the ones he had for Shun-Er. He wanted to talk about himself and his feelings. How, upon seeing the bare shoulders of laborers, the bile in his belly would roil. But he'd stop himself when he remembered the punishment meted out by his parents. The hours of kneeling, the hot summertime sun beating over him like a hammer. And he'd swallow the words that floated to the surface like scum. These words would have to be transformed before they were spoken, to match the desires of normal men.

"I don't know," Old Second once said to Shun-Er, "why my roommates keep talking to me about girls. It's always at an inconvenient time, like when I'm cooking noodles or brushing my teeth. 'Hey, have you met the new girl in So-and-So's section?' 'Hey, brother, come look at this magazine I found . . .'"

They were in the Workers' Cinema, holding hands and staring at the screen. No movie was playing. It was Saturday morning, and the Projectionist hadn't yet arrived. This was normal. The Projectionist didn't drink beer except on Friday evenings, and every Saturday he arrived to work late, hungover, and moody. Not that Old Second cared. He loved these quiet moments at the cinema; loved the way Shun-Er's fingers danced around his palm.

"Just talk about girls the way you would me," Shun-Er said, grinning. "It's simple."

"No, no, no. It's not. First of all, these assholes talk in disgusting ways. Second, I'm not used to lying. Third, I'm not perverted enough to talk about girls in that way."

"Okay, okay, I get it. You're chaste as a monk, and I'll die and go to hell."

"If the ancient imperial exams had been about women's bodies, every single one of those assholes would pass with top scores."

Shun-Er shrugged. "They'd probably do better than the toupees leading us now."

The next week, Old Second described how someone in his building tried to "come clean."

"Was he blackmailed?" Shun-Er asked.

"I don't think so. It was a guy we'd seen here before. You called him Ugly Mulan."

"Ah," Shun-Er said. Apparently, he couldn't remember who Ugly Mulan was or why he gave him that nickname, but he seemed proud of his wit.

"It was nighttime, on Thursday. Some guys on my floor decided to drink together to celebrate So-and-So's birthday—don't ask me who, I can't remember. Mulan's one of those talkative drunks, and his mouth gets going the moment he empties a can. Everything comes out: his favorite foods, his family background, why his wife left him . . ."

Shun-Er, knowing what would come next, gripped Old Second's hand.

"After the third can, something strange happens to his face. I see it and feel sweat forming on my brow. Something's coming. I always know when something's coming."

"So you say."

"He starts talking about love. The philosophy behind male attraction. I'm glaring at him, trying to get him to stop. But he keeps going. He keeps going and starts waxing poetic about the difference between man- and woman-love. 'Man-love'"—Old Second imitates Mulan's voice: deep and with a northerner's accent—"'is the rough and unpredictable affection of a friend, a teammate. You fight and cause each other pain, but at the end of the day there's always a beer and a hand over your shoulder.'"

"Bullshit," Shun-Er said.

"'Whereas woman-love is like the love a grandmother provides. All-encompassing, but it's not exciting. It's not enough. I'm the kind of man who needs something more in life, even if it hurts me.'"

"I should've called him Stupid Mulan."

"Yeah, well. The room fell silent when he finished speaking. He knew he'd made a mistake."

SHUN-ER CALLED HIM UGLY MULAN, BUT HIS PARENTS NAMED him Dollar. He was born after the famine and lived a simple, vegetarian life in the provinces of Sichuan. If his parents, laborers from a mountainside village, had access to a camera, you'd see the difference between his body and theirs. His mother was small. Narrow, full of bones, and, because of that, perpendicular. Like the cross on a flying kite. His father was an inch shorter than his mother, and his face was tinged with an unusual darkness. It wasn't the brown of naturally dark skin, but the brown of a spreading bruise. And this bruise had spread everywhere. Patches appeared on his face, his neck, his elbows, his legs. Sometimes on his fists, too, when he became angry and shouted for a switch.

He made his children (three girls, a tombstone, and Ugly Mulan) pick out the switches themselves. It was how they discovered that different types of sticks whipped differently. Each one hurt, but the kind of hurt was defined by the age, length, and thickness of the stick. Young sticks slapped and stung. Older ones were sharp, then dull, then sharp again. The shortest sticks—twigs picked to outsmart their father—snapped in half. The old man would use his fists then, and he used them indiscriminately on his children. They'd run and sob, sometimes seeking help from their mother.

"That's enough," she'd say, in a pinched and useless voice. "The neighbors will hear."

Except there were no neighbors. Just chickens, rabbits, pigs, and an ancient woman with cheeks the color of rotten apples who traveled past with a wagon. She sold vegetables and spoke an unusual dialect. A hat covered the shiny baldness atop her head, and the first time Ugly Mulan saw it, that shocking revelation of skin, he gasped, causing the ancient woman to laugh. She laughed with narrow, rain-soaked eyes. Her laughter was a shock because the people in his life never laughed like that. They made jokes, they argued, they fought, they simpered. But they didn't laugh with her freedom—with her back arched, her head tilted to the sky, her lips unpinched.

It was like seeing a new color. Not only seeing it but feeling it.

Something between red and blue and purple (and yet it wasn't violet). Thereafter, and for the rest of his life, Ugly Mulan sought out this feeling. Passively, because he didn't understand that emotions could be worked for, like food and clothes and money. So he waited. He waited as his sisters married men as poor and mean as his father. He waited as his father's left eye clouded over, and he waited as his mother, asthmatic since childhood, became sickly, then bedridden, then dead. In all that time, he went on with life as before: eating sweet potato slices like candy while he worked, napped, made little money, and felt nothing at all.

A woman from a neighboring village married him by arrangement. There was no love between them. He tried to sleep with her, but she became impatient because it took thirty minutes for Ugly Mulan to finish tugging between his legs. Thirty minutes of boredom while he rubbed his unmentionables to the point of rawness. There was no joy like the men in the village had promised. No pleasure, either. And when this woman left him, he felt no sadness or embarrassment, and continued as before. Eating sweet potato slices and preparing food with the temple monks on holidays. A quiet life, until one day a friend told him to go to Mawei.

"You'll make better money there, you'll have a better time. Plus, it's not like you have a wife to hold you back."

So Ugly Mulan left. On the last day—that dark and early morning before he rode in a neighbor's truck to the train station—he cooked noodles with his father, whose eyes turned deep as wells. Neither spoke, but Ugly Mulan called the old man Baba in his head. Understanding had bridged the gap between the two, and father and son stared at each other like dogs at a mirror. Their faces echoed, repeating features. The same jowls. The same puffy eyes. The same overly thick eyebrows like the horns of an owl. This was his father, a man like any other, but if he looked closely enough, he could see his own smile. His own body hidden under a shirt, his own voice, even his own sadness.

"I'll write to you," Ugly Mulan said.

"I can't read."

Ugly Mulan looked into his father's eyes and discovered that they were rain-soaked, like the ancient woman's.

"I can't read," his father said again.

"I'll write to you anyway."

And he did. Once. Ugly Mulan sent a short letter home and his father sent one back. His sister helped compose it, but Ugly Mulan recognized the grotesque and sloppy characters that were his father's handiwork at the bottom. It was his name—Nanjing, like the southern capital—and, seeing it, he felt the colors of his childhood well up in his eyes.

Dear Son. I am eating every day. The sweet potatoes are good this year, some of the vines have flowers. The fish at the market are cheap. I am doing well because there is food every day. Remember to eat, remember to shower. Your sister's boy is very fat and another one is on the way. I want your son to be the same when you have him. A plump and well-fed boy . . .

"WHAT ARE YOU READING?"

It was a man Ugly Mulan had met in the cinema. They were lying together in the man's apartment, Ugly Mulan's head in the crook of the man's arm.

51

"Nothing," Ugly Mulan said.

The feeling in his eyes spread to his chin, then his neck, then his heart.

"What's the matter with you?" the man asked. "Why're you crying?"

"Nothing," Ugly Mulan repeated. He wiped his eyes with the outside of his arm, then the inside. The outside again—a back-and-forth movement until only the redness remained.

He never wrote his father again.

EIGHT

BAO MEI REMEMBERS her brother to be a trickster, a busybody who hides in dark rooms like a bug. Bored in death, he's developed a habit of floating around the Workers' Cinema, searching for men with stories to tell. These men experience his ghost in various ways. Some are skittish and run the moment they hear his whispers. Others are oblivious and treat him like the voices that live in their heads. A third group, gregarious and full of prayers, treat the encounter like a meeting with the gods. In each case, the men who reveal their stories exit the cinema with a lightness in their steps. Happy (though they can't explain why), awake, and more interested in life. The effect is like that of forcing open a kitchen window. Cooking smoke billows out and a breeze comes in, sweet as sugar water. And because their stories can't be told in a single sitting, the men come back. They come back to love and be loved; they come back to hear and be heard.

Hence the story of the sissy named Ugly Mulan, a background character in the grander scheme of things, but one whose life echoes like a village elder's hymns. It's not a unique life and Ugly Mulan is not a unique person. His tale is that of a thousand other migrant workers, all of them leaving home with their lives dangling from fat bundles. If you close your eyes, you can see them, too. Their firm backs, their tanned cheeks, the stern slants of their eyes. Concentrate harder and you'll see how they sleep on the floors of trains, each silent and with a hand under their cheek. Sometimes, a mouth will move, and you'll hear the smack of a lover's name. In Mandarin, in dialect, in the REM-cycle language of forgotten dreams.

"That man," Hen Bao tells Bao Mei, "is a 'one.' He does the penetrating. And that man"—he points with an invisible finger—"is his 'zero.'"

"I'm eating!" Bao Mei cries. "I don't want to know this stuff!"

Despite the bad hours and the low pay, Bao Mei takes her job at the Workers' Cinema very seriously. She befriends the sissies and stays true to her promise to protect them. She lies on their behalf; turns away petulant family members. They can stomp their feet all they want, but the girlfriends of her customers won't be entering the screening rooms, not on her watch! Nor will their mothers, their fathers, their siblings, their children—all of whom Bao Mei placates with brazen lies. "Your husband's not here," she'll say. Or: "I've never seen that man before" (meanwhile, he's hiding under her desk in the box office). She doesn't think about the implications of her lies. Her fidelity, after all, is to the theater men and their stories. To their lives and their forbidden loves.

Hen Bao tells them to her. These aren't fairy tales. There's no "once upon a time" and there's no "a long, long time ago." Everything happens today, right now, with the urgency of a bullet wound. The smallest of details—who cooks, who doesn't, who gives to beggars, who considers himself a beauty—are given to Bao Mei, who shares them with the Projectionist.

According to Hen Bao, "everyone and their mother" knows that the two are a couple. It's easy to tell if you have eyes, if you have ears, if you smell their breath and realize they've been sharing meals. For the first time in the history of the Workers' Cinema, the Projectionist has been sloppy in changing the reels between films. Ten minutes might elapse before the same cop or war film restarts because he's busy following Bao Mei as she sweeps the halls. He stops her to share canteens of lukewarm soup, oranges with varying levels of tartness, and offers—despite staring rudely at her dragging leg—zero help at all. Meantime, the moviegoers grow confused and embarrassed. One day, a man with the redness of love still on his cheeks leaps out of the screening room to curse at the Projectionist.

"Hey, brother, what am I paying you for? To flirt with your employees?"

Later that evening, the Projectionist tells Bao Mei: "I didn't know they cared about the movies. I thought they came for the you-know-what."

"What do you mean, 'the you-know-what'? You're an adult, use your words."

"I'm talking about sex."

"I know, I'm not stupid."

They talk in his office above the cinema. It's small but bedroom-like, with a mattress on the floor, a little plastic table, stools, and a bucket to catch dripping water. The floors are concrete; a lightbulb dangles from a string. Smears of mosquito—some red, others not—mark the wall like warnings. A rat trap with peanut brittle in the corner offers a similar warning to rodents (though it means nothing to the spiders that enter the office willy-nilly). Five nights out of seven, the Projectionist stays here with Bao Mei, who is reluctant to return to a father made silent by grief. She used to rent a room owned by a woman near the market, but she gave that up—the woman had coughing fits at night, and this disturbed Bao Mei's dreams.

"I suppose they're right," Bao Mei says. "They *are* paying for a movie."

"It's the same ones, though. Day in and day out. I didn't know they cared."

"Apparently they do." She pauses. "My brother told me another story about them today."

The Projectionist nods, ready to listen. He is one of few people who believes Bao Mei when she talks about her brother, his ghost. In the beginning, he was skeptical. But with the steady approach of love came reverent belief, and this belief has become so absolute that, some days, the Projectionist thinks he hears Hen Bao's whispers himself.

"He told me about a married man who works at a construction site."

"That sounds like most of the people who come here."

"Yeah, except this man loves his wife. Really loves her. Not the touching kind of love, but a deep kind nevertheless. And she loves him back—to jealousy, to anger."

". . ."

"My brother says it's quite common, this kind of love. The wives of sissies aren't stupid. They understand their husbands and accept them."

"Would you be able to do that?" the Projectionist asks.

"Nope. Unless"—Bao Mei grins—"you're trying to tell me something."

"I'm not."

"Because I don't have the courage to love someone like that. Someone who loves other people as much as they love me." She pauses, slaps a mosquito into the wall. "Anyways, this man, the one my brother talked about, he gets into a fight with his wife. And his wife leaves, returns to the countryside. Some time passes and the man starts to miss her. He misses her so much that he goes to her village to find her. But the moment he gets there, the wife's family— her mother and her aunts—starts to beat him. Savagely, with a desire to humiliate. Fist against mouth, foot against chest, leg against thigh. The whole time the wife cries, guilty. In anger, she told her family the man doesn't touch her, that he goes after other women."

"Why didn't she tell them he was sleeping with men?"

"Because they would've killed him."

"She's a better person than me. I would've wanted the man dead."

"Yeah, well. Me, too." She swats another mosquito and misses. "My brother tells me the man is back with his boyfriend. The wife is back, too. Nobody's mad, nobody's angry . . . It's like the ending to a fairy tale, the way my brother tells it."

NINE

AN ARSONIST'S FLAME marks the beginning of the cinema's end. A weak one that causes more panic than smoke, more smoke than fire. According to Bao Mei, she is first to smell the burning. She is first to run downstairs, scrambling like a thief with a guilty conscience. There are three couples in the screening rooms that day, and the only man to experience fear is the arsonist, one hired by a government official. Look at how he graffities words onto the bathroom mirror. His writing is illegible, but hatred can be felt in the arch of his characters. The sinister colors that he uses: black mixed with a blood-like red. Afterwards, he collects a basket of paper and throws a lit match into it, burning himself. When the smoke rises, stealing what little breath he has in this windowless bathroom, the arsonist becomes paranoid. But the flames are too small, so he must light another match. Then another, and another. Hungry and desperate to receive payment for his job, the arsonist distributes the burning papers in the hallway before escaping through an emergency exit.

The flames grow larger. So do the smoke trails, which creep

under the projection room door, waking Bao Mei. She runs to warn the others. Slapstick ensues when an old man in the throes of pleasure has to leave the cinema with his lover's too-large pants. Old Second and Shun-Er are also there, and Old Second will remember how he helped the Projectionist put out the flames with a damp jacket. He doesn't see the hateful message in the bathroom's mirror, and the people outside do nothing when they see him run out with a chin darkened by soot. He's shirtless, but it's summertime and lots of Mawei City youngsters walk around without clothes on. It's perfectly normal; nobody cares.

Yet Bao Mei believes, to this day, that a link exists between the fire and the Workers' Cinema's destruction. Because the next morning, two city developers, backed by the government, visit. "To investigate the theater," they say—a short man and a tall man, both giving Bao Mei what rural people call "pervert's eyes."

"Heard there was a fire here," the tall man says.

"We put it out."

"This hallway isn't wide enough," the short man says.

"Nope." The tall man stares at Bao Mei. "It doesn't fit the proper regulations."

Bao Mei sits there, suspicious. How do they know about the fire? No firemen were called, no police. As far as she's concerned, nobody knows about it besides her, the Projectionist, and the three couples in the theater. And none of them would tell, either. The cinema's reputation prevents rational people from wanting that association. It's social suicide for people who have families or who work with the government. *No*, Bao Mei thinks, *it can't be them*. But what about that young man who scampered out of the building, the one she suspects is an arsonist? What if a nosy neighbor somehow smelled the smoke? Bao Mei's mind is a blur. She listens to the government officials—both old enough to be her father—as they drink tea, poke around the screening rooms, and examine her like a hunk of meat.

"A local woman reported a fire," the tall man says.

"She was really frightened. Said she was worried about the neighborhood burning down."

"Who's the owner of this place?"

"Talk to the man upstairs," Bao Mei says.

"You know what kind of theater this is?"

"I've heard, yes."

"Is that man your husband?" the tall man asks.

"No."

"Are you married?"

". . ."

"Are you married?"

"I heard you the first time."

The most painful words are those that reveal the two developers' intentions. This is no leisure visit, and their thin, Western-style suits should be indication enough. Their investigation, too, is a sham. They already know that the fire was malicious, man-made. Plus, who is the "local woman" they're referring to? There was no such person last night, and the fire, before it could be seen by outsiders, was contained. All this talk of the Workers' Cinema being unsafe, of it needing changes the owners can't afford, of Mawei City requiring new roads, causes Bao Mei's head to ache. Everything points to government redevelopment. To modernization and a new street for commerce, as though the ones on the main road aren't enough.

When the developers walk upstairs to talk to the Projectionist, Bao Mei leans against the wall, shaking. She doesn't know what to do. Normally, you can bribe these people, but what money does she have? What money does the Projectionist have? They could take action, but this isn't the West. Unlike in America, where cats have nine lives, in China they have but the one. A protest would be impossible, leading to nothing but broken bones. What hope is there?

"We'll fight anyway," Hen Bao says.

SIX DAYS GO BY. PEOPLE ARE BOARDING UP THEIR DOORS, frantically preparing for a typhoon to strike Mawei. Everywhere you look, there's a man holding a hammer, a paintbrush, nails. They go around in vests and coarse trousers, knock-knock-knocking on walls to search for weaknesses. Gaps that should be sealed with cement are planked over with cheap countryside wood. You see tanned legs on stepladders and wiry hairs poking out from underarms. *It'll be a rough one this year*, the men say. Their wives stock up on nonperishables, and their children, with the closing of schools, act with cautious enthusiasm, like mourners at a funeral banquet. Even government officials are wary of the storm. Trucks with loudspeakers cruise the streets of Mawei, warning citizens to seek higher ground. Businesses that have made enemies with local cadres are punished with visits from the drivers of these trucks. The Workers' Cinema is one of these businesses, and Old Second is there when the city developers visit again.

"Have you considered our offer?" the tall man asks, heading straight for Bao Mei.

"Take it," the short man says. "This cinema isn't worth the shit underneath your shoe."

"And don't forget the storm," the tall man says. "It might tear this place to shreds."

"I'm not the boss," Bao Mei says.

"You sure act like you are," the short man says.

"Go get him, then, go get the sissy-lover before he regrets it," the tall man says.

She walks past Old Second, who is hiding with Shun-Er behind a wall. Her face is one of unbridled fury. *Don't talk to me, don't even look at me.* The dragging of her left foot is a harsh reproach, one that spreads a chill through Old Second's body. He's seen these government officials before, but he doesn't know the nature of their visits. His thoughts are racing when Shun-Er puts a hand on his shoulder.

"Let's go back," he whispers, gesturing toward the screening room.

When Old Second is silent, he says: "Don't worry. This place won't close."

"..."

"And if it does, we'll find someplace else to be together."

FACTORY MANAGERS ANNOUNCE FACTORY CLOSURES, BUT fearing the loss of revenue, they change their minds. This makes no difference to the migrant workers, who receive the news with bent shoulders and chattering lips. It's true what they say about city people: Their blood is thicker than water, but thicker than both is their greed. "Might as well stay," a man whispers to his neighbor. He gestures to the factory walls, made of concrete, and the doors reinforced with metal shutters. "Yeah," the neighbor responds. His head is lowered, but we recognize his voice—playful but venomous—to be Old Second's. "And maybe when the wind picks up, the night guards can beat it back with their batons."

Hammering continues throughout the city. Successful merchants tear down their night market stands, allowing hopeless ones to take their place. New merchants see money in disaster, selling marked-up rain boots to desperate customers. Storm shutters as well, and ponchos thin as tissue paper "imported from Italy." A boy tells another boy, "My father says your home won't survive the storm." To which the other boy says, "My father says your father can't read." Rats run from sewers to roads to hills. For three days and two nights, housewives don't hear anything squeaking in their cabinets. Cats grow bored and meow more frequently; stray dogs with mangy fur disappear into the mountains. And every day, with the regularity of a bowel movement, the tall and short officials appear in the Mawei City Workers' Cinema.

They repeat the same arguments every time. *This place is not fit for business. It fails the proper safety regulations. The storm, the storm, the storm.* To deaf ears, they explain that they want Mawei to be a city on the same level as Paris; that there should be shopping malls here, and luxury homes, and, yes, a new theater with plush velvet seats. They leave notices on the cinema's walls. The Projectionist tears them down. He's too busy for the officials' nonsense and spends his days reinforcing the entrance. The sissies who visit eye him cautiously before entering with rumors in their throats. These rumors turn into whispers, then kissing, then fear. *What if the cinema closes? Where would we go?* Some sissies don't care—they'll find new places, new men—but the ones who do seek out Bao Mei.

"Hey, sister, are the rumors true?"

She knows what they're asking. "No, they're not."

"So the cinema won't close?"

"We'll fight them," Bao Mei says.

These conversations happen multiple times per day. With Old

Second, with Shun-Er, with men whose names we'll never know. We only know their stories. Their fear followed by their determination, as Bao Mei says, "We'll fight them." Every time she says those words, she feels a sensation on her shoulders, the firmness of her brother's hands. The men find confidence in Bao Mei's words, and not just confidence but friendship. Camaraderie. "We'll fight them," she says. *We, we, we.* The men who've heard the ghostly whispers attribute this phenomenon to something they call "the Spirit of the Cinema." The one they claim protects the place despite having no altar. It's this ghost that asks the men questions. It's this ghost that asks for their stories and listens to them, actually listens, while the men speak-laugh-cry about a China that refuses to love them back.

THE FACTORIES REMAIN OPEN ON THE MORNING OF THE storm. The night guard, an old man who's also the morning guard, snores with a newspaper on his lap. Workers enter with bored, sleepy expressions, cradling lunch pails while the sky transforms into steel wool.

At eleven, rain starts to fall. Reinforced buildings keep water away from windows and doorways, but Mawei City's storm drains are inadequate. At midnight, they begin to clog. Flooding follows. The factories announce emergency closures, and workers rush home with plastic bags above their heads. There are umbrellas, too—bent and twitching beside telephone poles—and women trudging along in ankle-high water. Shutters shake everywhere. The noise they make resembles teeth gnashing against bone. A startling sound, especially when accompanied with the visual: of garbage drifting, minnow-like, past trucks; of roaches wriggling their legs next to felled tree branches; of a telephone pole falling, falling, fallen against the roof of a rich man's mansion. Sparks fly, but nobody screams. Unlike in movies, where storm victims shout like soccer fans, in real life they're quiet—careful not to waste energy.

At two in the morning, a man—age sixty-two and suffering from "confusion"—is reported missing.

At four, the residents living downhill, inside and around the city's slums, climb onto their rooftops to escape the flooding. The new merchants' ponchos fall apart like moth wings as, slowly, steadily, boats arrive to take survivors to safety. A cat drowns; its owner cries. A dog clinging to the bars of a window is rescued and waits with its nose pointed eastward—past roofs that, after the storm, will have messages scribbled on them in paint ("Help us!" "No food, no water, we are a family of three." "I am alive."); past trees that will fall; past a temple that, according to local gossip, will sustain no damage from the flood; past wind, past rain, past everything, past nothing. The uncle manning the boat, sitting next to the dog, looks where the dog points his nose.

And sees a group of men trudging toward the Workers' Cinema.

THERE ARE PEOPLE HERE, ALL OF THEM WAITING IN THE CINema's second story. We see Old Second, we see Shun-Er, we see Bao Mei. The Projectionist walks around with a flashlight, flipping switches to check for lost power. He has candles prepared. Lighters, matches, boxes of cigarettes. A pile of snacks (bread, peanuts, pickles, water bottles) sits in his office, and every person who enters adds a little of what they have. There are dozens of people—many of whom are repeat customers with nowhere to go—and they all enter the cinema soaked and with exaggerated stories. Of the wind howling banshee-like across the city's upper limits; shutters snapping their teeth against metal doors; the floods sweeping away pets, mopeds, cars, and poorly built "luxury" homes. The atmosphere is anxious but easy. Everyone knows each other; they're all sissies and have seen each other's faces. Plus, there's a collective relief in knowing that the cinema, built on higher ground, is not at risk of flooding.

And so they wait, shivering, with their backs against the walls.

Sleep comes, and with it, dreams. Nightmares. What's the difference between them if you wake up screaming every time? Old Second, with his head against Shun-Er's shoulder, sees an image of his High Mountain home. There's the entryway with father and mother leaning against the door. His siblings—Big Sister, Little Sister, Old Third, and Spring Chicken—are inside, sitting at the table with a basket of water spinach. They cut away the brown, sunscorched leaves and talk to Old Second with gentle, nostalgic voices. *We haven't seen you in a while. Welcome home. Have you been to the River lately?* Old Second wants to speak, but he can't move his mouth. Only his eyes, which fill with water, and his shoulders, which tingle with the sensation of soft fingers. He turns around.

He sees Eldest standing there with a man we know to be Hen Bao.

"You have to leave," Eldest says.

The tingling on Old Second's shoulder becomes an itch. A crawling.

"You have to—and you will—leave. Not just home, but the cinema. Not just the cinema, but this country. This dream."

"Why?" Old Second croaks.

"Because they are coming."

Old Second wakes, gasping, to the sensation of pinching. It

takes a moment for his eyes to adjust, but he sees them: the dozens, hundreds, thousands of ants walking along the floor of the cinema. Like him, they are trying to escape the storm. Like him, they are wind-throttled and weakened by rain. Some die once they reach a dry strip of floor. Others struggle, moving in zigzags while a deep sense of terror overpowers Old Second. He's not afraid of ants, of insects, but there are too many of them. An army. Black ants, red ants, ants with wings, ants with five legs, four legs, three. What's worse: Nobody else seems to see them. The marching, marching, always marching insects, which crawl up the walls, fall off the ceiling, drown in puddles of water. A red ant tears the wings off a black ant's back—Old Second sees this, too. Another decapitates a winged ant with its pincers before it walks, confused, up Shun-Er's arm. He is asleep and drooling, but there are ants on him like beauty marks, like moles.

I can't move, Old Second thinks.

It doesn't occur to him that he's still dreaming, and it doesn't occur to him that he's suffering from an affliction villagers call "ghost on the chest." He continues to struggle, tries again to speak. A gurgling noise exits his mouth, barely audible. Whenever his eyes close and open, more ants appear. They double in number, and are sometimes accompanied by other insects, other shapes. Roaches that fly and rattle and hiss. Mice that scurry. And up on the ceiling: a mess of lines that look like snakes. They descend, the lines begin to fall like rain, and their bodies pelt Old Second's head, arms, shoulders with the blunt force of many fists. He can't move. He shuts his eyes until the crawling, the pinching, the punching stops. Until a moment of clarity comes. A moment of clarity that forces the question into his head:

Who was that man standing next to Eldest in his dream?

TEN

HE WAS UGLY, a little. Like my wife and the men I knew before. You couldn't tell in the screening rooms. The darkness hid everything but the planes of our bodies. The clothing we wore and the brown skin like velvet underneath. We touched each other, blind, with only hope to guide us. When I reached for a man's cigarette, I brushed my fingers against his, searching. Did he have hair on his knuckles? A ring, double joints, calluses? A sweaty hand was a good hand, a dry hand was acceptable. Regardless of which, the moment someone touched me, I trembled. We all did. We wanted love so badly, so desperately, that its absence felt like heartburn. A stomachache that never went away . . . It's why we sighed with relief whenever an offered cigarette led to hand-holding, which led to kissing and body smells and, at the end of the night, surprise. *I am a man and so is he.* Our bodies knew the truth, but our brains couldn't accept it. It's why some people kept their eyes closed, and why I kept mine wide open. *They* wanted to hide from their man-love. I wanted to prove its existence.

"The man I met last year, the one named Old Second, did both.

He snuck glances at me when we kissed. I could tell because there was hotness on my face. Hotness and a sensation that resembled tickling. It was like when you're asleep and the movement of a shadow jolts you awake from strange dreams. I opened my eyes and there he was. Grimacing. He claimed, when I asked, that he always looked like that. Something something the lines on his forehead, something something since childhood. But I recognized his expression. I knew the pain and the memories behind it—and the desire. He trembled like a coasting car when I held the softness inside his pants. 'Is this okay?' I asked. He nodded. I raised his shirt, kissed him from belly to chest. 'Is this okay?' Another nod, and I began to kiss him lower. 'What about this?' He nodded again—said yes in a quiet voice. I raised my head, stared at him straight on.

"'Then why aren't you hard?'

"The fear in his eyes changed to confusion, and he opened his mouth. Closed it. Opened it again. Words came out. Afterwards his emotions, which cracked like overbaked bread. I'll be the first to admit that his candor caught me by surprise. Few people revealed themselves like that in the cinema. It was a place for lovemaking, not love. I'd been going there for a year, and usually, you found a man, kissed him, finished, and went home. But Old Second was different. He spoke about everything in his life. He was possessed. Love, anger, happiness, disappointment, freedom. I felt his memories like a series of blows. Saw them, too:

"A boy, searching in the forest for love.

"His father's fist and his mother's spit—the spit hurting more.

"The sight of an ancient security guard waiting with lowered pants in a public toilet, and how he considered it before a shiver in his spine told him to run.

"I listened to him, mesmerized. Every word he spoke was also my history, my every day. At the worksite, I had to be careful. Because sometimes an older man would offer me a cigarette or touch me in some unexpected way, and the shiver in my spine would cause my mind to spiral. I'd seen men kiss their wives, and friends touch their girlfriends. I'd wonder: Why couldn't I do that? How come my wife elicited nothing but family-love from me? Why were our kisses nothing but saliva in the mouth? The Workers' Cinema, it let *us* feel what other men felt in the daylight. Our love wasn't flowers but the sprouting of old vegetables. 'Dark love'—that's what Old Second called it. When we met that day, and he spoke endlessly about wanting what *they* had, a stone shifted in my chest. I decided I wanted him. Even though he was strange-looking. Even though the softness between his legs refused to grow.

"We met the next week. And the week after that. Then I decided once a week was too few and we saw each other every other day. We went to restaurants. When the weather was bad, we rode the city bus, gazing out of windows and going nowhere. We saw a China under construction. Gravel in every direction, and machinery, and a city that grew like a tumor. Neighborhoods vanished behind streets clouded with dust. Pastures became factories, a wet market became a bus station. Blink once to see a building go down. Blink twice to see a new one in its place. Old Second and I watched the changes like happy children. Laughing—there was so much laughter—as our shoulders knocked together at every lurch in the road. Our feet danced, tapping a beat that followed every word and sentence we spoke. Meantime, our stomachs grumbled. Eating meant we couldn't talk, and we both preferred speaking over food.

"I told him I had a wife from an arranged marriage. He told me he didn't want to get married. I said I had one remaining relative, a mother. He said he didn't have any family at all.

"'No one?'

"'No, fuck them.'

"'I see.'

"But as the days passed, he started remembering. His childhood in the mountains. The fields, the forests, the stream they called River. He had an older brother named Eldest who died in a factory accident, and whose body was returned in a nailed-shut coffin. No details were given, no real compensation for his death. Just a final paycheck and—from the factory's manager—a promise to pay for the funeral. The mourning period was long, distracting everyone from Old Second's boy-love. Instead of striking him, his parents struck the casket. His mother didn't believe Eldest was inside. She wanted to see the body for proof, so she tried to remove the lid. She hit it. Scratched it and bit the top—leaving chips in her already rotted teeth. She tried for six days and six nights. Then, on the seventh morning, she stopped. They buried Eldest in the mountain, and nobody spoke of him again.

"'Sorry,' Old Second said, laughing.

"He wiped his tears with the inside of his arms, the outside of his wrists.

"'I don't know what's going on. This never happens.'

"'You've never cried about this before?' I asked.

"He nodded with his hands clenched tight against his face.

"'Damn,' I said. 'Damn, damn, damn.'

"There was nothing else I could do. We were in public, on a bus headed to Fuzhou. I shifted my weight so our shoulders touched, our feet, too, but anything more would have earned us a beating. So we just sat there. Silent, cautious, and there for each other.

"He told me at the end of the night that I was a good person.

"He told me at the end of the night that my body was beautiful."

71

ELEVEN

THERE'S NO REASON to detail the cinema's destruction. Not when people can imagine it themselves. The fighting, the arrests, the crying, the blood. The animal resistance of thirty-seven beaten protesters as they hold each other, telling their bodies and their minds that this is a world worth saving, a world worth dying for. Perhaps you, yourself, have lived through an event like this: a secret or not-so-secret history where one group of people devours another. In Serbia, a woman with rainbow tape over her mouth stares as nationalists pelt her body with rocks. In Argentina, a boy trembles hatefully next to his brother—both of them watching the news—as he screams slurs at the passing of a gay rights bill. And, of course, in New York, not very far from where Old Second lives with Bao Mei, there's the Stonewall Inn in the West Village. It's a part of the city neither husband nor wife visit (both consider it run-down and dirty), and if either of them did, they'd go with unimpressed expressions on their faces. Disgust would hang from Bao Mei's mouth, limp as a fatty cut of beef, and

Old Second would stand with his hands in his pockets. Bored, impatient, hungry, or all three.

They wouldn't care about the history of the landmark. They wouldn't care that the violence that once uprooted *them* also existed in the bodies of others. And because they are old and stubborn, they guard their hurt like dogs over a chewed bone. The cinema's destruction is theirs. To hear that something similar had happened (or *was* happening) would be sheer and utter nonsense. To use an American idiom, it'd be like talking to a brick wall, and to use a Chinese one, it'd be like playing piano to a bull.

Besides, there's only so much violence one can take. Before the eyes glaze over, before the mind begins to wander. *Why commemorate suffering*, Old Second used to think, *if we know it like the lines on our palm?* Especially if we can remember it, hear and see it on TV, read about it in the news, dream about a loved one bleating against your cheek as a policeman raises his arm, where the sun's ray reflects off a charm on his wrist (the policeman's grandmother gave it to him to ward off evil spirits), the same wrist he uses to bring his fist down like a gavel, though not before wincing, because no matter how many times he hits, it doesn't become easier to strike down a human being.

It's too much, Old Second thinks. *That day—all of it was too much.*

When people used to talk about "what happened that day, that day of the protest," Old Second would clam up. He'd climb into a part of himself that nobody had access to. Eventually, his pain became so unspeakable it became boring. Dull as the gray on a city bird's down. Now it exists in a cluttered corner of his mind, one he rarely visits. When he does, it's in a dream or during some quiet hour in the afternoon. Attempting to speak about the pain would be impossible. Inaccurate and therefore tacky. Like trying to describe a house fire. People always focus on the sensational when describing such an event. For instance: The volume of the flames. The destruction of its path. The number of dead and injured, the number left homeless. What's left out is the personal, the strange. A singed ball of fur next to a bracelet untouched by fire. The relieved sigh of a child who discovers that his report card, the one with the bad marks, has been lost forever.

Or, in the case of the cinema protest, the memory of a policeman's bracelet snapping as he brings his fist down. Not for the first time and not for the second. He's been hitting Old Second for what feels like an eternity, but the moment his bracelet snaps, releasing jade beads that strike the road like hail, a look of wonder enters his eyes. Not horror. Wonder. It's at that moment that he asks, perhaps to himself: "What the hell am I doing?"

It's at that moment that Old Second responds: "You're killing us.

"Brother, you're killing us."

But he had more to say that day. So much more. Not just to the policemen, and not just to the government officials. No. Old Second wanted to grab someone off the street—a woman, a child, anyone— and justify himself. Justify the people protesting with him, who were sacrificing blood, bones, and reputation to defend an old and falling-apart theater. One built by a miser who didn't love movies, just the money he'd make by screening them. It was his son, the Projectionist, who loved them, and who saw magic in the infinite combinations of image and sound on a flat screen.

And wasn't that worth something? A shy man's love of film? Old Second didn't know the Projectionist well, but they'd spoken one time, a short smoke-break conversation, about a war film that was playing in the second screening room. Shun-Er was with them, and all three men were pinching cigarettes. Old Second and Shun-Er stood close together; the Projectionist was meters away, loafing around and scratching at a pimple on his neck. He had no intention of speaking to Old Second, but he must've heard his remark about enjoying the movie that was playing on repeat. And that offhand remark prompted the Projectionist to speak.

Did Old Second know that this was so-and-so actor's first ever role? Or that they filmed such-and-such scene in the Wuyi Mountains, a short bus ride away from Fuzhou City?

He talked about the director's fidelity to state propaganda. About how, despite China having lost the war against Japan, the film ended on a note of victory for the Chinese soldiers. Shun-Er rolled his eyes when the Projectionist explained how certain character archetypes (laborers turned soldiers, uneducated but noble farmers) were used to boost national morale. When he said something about "unifying the proletariat by putting them on the big screen," Shun-Er asked, nudging Old Second in the ribs, "Then how come they hired big actors instead of real people?"

"An actor being a little ugly does not make him the proletariat," Old Second said.

"Perhaps if he's *very* ugly," Shun-Er said.

The jokes didn't faze the Projectionist, who continued speaking like a child at a schoolyard show-and-tell. He tripped over words and dropped his cigarette when he started explaining the film's use of color. Did Old Second and Shun-Er notice the saturated yellow hues in the backgrounds of certain scenes? What about the music? Did they realize that the soundtrack was made using handcrafted Chinese instruments—the pipa, the erhu, the suona, the xiao? The Projectionist's speech came out in half-mumbled waves. Shun-Er stomped his cigarette beneath his boot and made faces, signaling to Old Second that it was time to leave. But Old Second wanted to stay a little longer. He wanted to listen.

He was moved by the Projectionist's passion and was shocked that a country man with a country accent could know so much about movies. Yes, much of what he said was exaggerated. Half-truths, perhaps even lies. But lies were fine with Old Second because he had to live one to survive. So did Shun-Er; so did everyone who protested with them. To survive, all of them, every single one, had to lie, cheat people, borrow money, gamble, tell jokes, laugh, forget the past, cling to it.

And this was what Old Second wanted to say to the bystanders who watched the plainclothes policemen hit the protesters outside the cinema. That they weren't perfect people. That they weren't holy or saintlike (in fact, there were more than a few protesters who were thieves, and bigoted; plus, there was an insecure man—Shun-Er hated his guts—who took credit for other people's jokes), but none of them deserved this. Like the characters in the Projectionist's war film, the protesters were simply people.

Some, like the Projectionist, were stubborn and ambitious. Others, like Shun-Er, wanted nothing but a place to rest their heads. Their rheum-afflicted eyes. Because it was exhausting—was it not?—to live in a world where incorrect loving was worse than no loving at all. Where a sissy had to lie to his mother, his father, his wife, and his kids. A man could kiss a woman in broad daylight. He could coerce her into marrying him, into carrying his sons and daughters (as though they were nothing but parcels from the post office), and he could yell at her if she bore too many daughters. He could even beat her if she displeased him. As a young boy, Shun-Er had seen men spit on his mother. He'd seen them treat her like she was a mule. And all of that, though perhaps not the spitting, would've been fine to the bystanders who watched the theater men go down. Sure, they might've tsked a little, and sure, they might've sucked their teeth to show their anger at a husband mistreating his wife. *But*, Old Second thought, *let a man hold another man's hand in their presence. Let him kiss the other with the frankness of a child's gaze. Let those things happen and watch what hell breaks loose.*

All the theater men sought was the salt of another man's palms. The tickly sensation of hairy knuckles against their napes. The brush of fat fingers through the thinning crowns of their heads to their too-bony backs. Relief came in the form of desire. The knowledge that it could be fulfilled. Again, again, and again, until the theater men committed the fatal mistake of forgetting not one but two crucial facts of life. The first was that they'd had to humiliate their wives to satisfy their desires (but this was easy to forget in the throes of love). The second fact, which wasn't as easy to forget, was the world that existed outside the cinema's four walls: one in which a plainclothes cop could strike a man until he betrayed his own friends.

("Don't, not her!" Old Second remembers the Projectionist shouting. "Go after *them*! Beat those *faggots* instead, anyone but her! Oh God!")

It didn't hurt. No, really, it didn't. But the beating shocked and embarrassed Old Second to his core. It was a complex shock: one that began as joy when the cop's bracelet broke, and that ended as disbelief. Fear, too, and apprehension. Because if a grandmother's bracelet could snap from the mindless throwing of a man's fist, what would happen to the person getting beaten? She'd prayed over that bracelet, had gone to temple to bless it with money folded into animal shapes. And now it was nothing but hail pelting a road. How beautiful the hail was. How musical the sound. But the moment the bracelet snapped, the policeman smiled, his face twisted into one of childlike curiosity. And that look, finally, was what broke the camel's back. It did what the policeman's fists sought out to do but couldn't: make Old Second cry.

He is a youngster, barely a man, Old Second wanted to tell the bystanders. *They sent over a child to ruin my life.*

And he agreed to do it.

PART II

TWELVE

THE FIRST WORDS Yan Hua said to Frog were: "My husband is dead." This was after her silence at the airport. After she stepped out of the pink man's taxicab with tears in her eyes. Sleepy tears, not sad ones. She yawned when Frog took her suitcase and yawned again when he told her to walk faster. What was the rush? The immigrant motel was steps down the street, and its entrance was a broken door without numbers. Seeing that she was to live in a basement, Yan Hua laughed. Softly at first, then hard enough to knock the tears from her eyes.

"What's wrong?" Frog asked. "You're crying. Why are you crying?"

And that's when she told him.

"Your husband is what?"

"I swear I didn't kill him."

YAN HUA BITES AN APPLE AND THE FRAGRANCE TAKES HER home. To China, to her mother, to the husband she loved but barely kissed. A stone on the edge of a mountain marks his grave, over-looking a quarry where country women hammer stones. She pictures them: a crew of a dozen laborers with bent backs, tied-up hair, and their hands constantly moving. Grunting, coughing, smashing, and smashing again. Repetitive, like the snores of Yan Hua's American husband, whose green card is more important than his name. People call him Frog on account of his fleshy eyelids and throat, and he's sleeping right now, dreaming alongside all the workers who call the immigrant motel "home."

It's winter 1989. A month ago, Yan Hua—through luck, un-luck, or both—completed her journey to America as a puppet wife. This is the name given to Fuzhounese women whose families pay American Fuzhounese men for marriage papers, which later turn into immigration papers, which eventually become divorce papers. It's a booming industry, and like in any industry, there exists an il-lusion of choice. That you can choose your husbands. And that the husbands can choose you back. Looks, ambition, education level, and housekeeping ability (if you're a woman) are all important cri-teria. You don't choose a jobless green card husband. Or maybe you do, because he's cheap. But keep in mind that you must live with him to keep up appearances.

"Americans can sniff this kind of shit out," Frog once said. "They're like dogs in that way. Always looking around for shit to sniff."

So Yan Hua stayed with her discount-bin husband, a cousin of a family friend. He had no education, could barely read, and cost two years' salary to "marry." Furthermore, his green card came with the last thing Yan Hua wanted: actual marriage. Because (Frog said this in a casual voice, his mouth stuffed with noodles) "you don't have anyone and I don't have anyone and our families know each other..."

"And?" Yan Hua said.

"And you have nowhere to go."

True, but neither did he.

For the entirety of October, the entirety of November, Yan Hua has been living in motels with Frog. Not real ones, like the Holiday Inn or even the roadside bungalows with "A/C units!" or "Cable available!" signs decorating their fronts. No, these motels are cramped rooms in Chinatown apartments with bunk beds full of people. Chefs, prep cooks, deliverymen, mothers, daughters, and schoolchildren. You pay six dollars a night for a bed (four if you share with someone), use of a sticky unusable stove, and a toilet with a sink for a shower. There's no heat. Few or no windows. Bathing is done with rags and dish soap, stolen from restaurants and stored in water bottles. Blue Dawn in Poland Spring, yellow Joy in Dasani.

But Yan Hua grows used to her surroundings. She doesn't notice the sounds-smells-sights of strangers anymore. And Frog, after a while, is no longer a concern. Even when he touches her. Grabs her from behind, breathes his hot breath on her back, creating sweat that smells like soup scum. She's learned to ignore him, to reject his advances with a look. That or she stays away from the bed, sitting on the floor, biting fruit bought from immigrants near the Manhattan Bridge, and remembering.

YAN HUA REMEMBERS HOW SHUN-ER, HER FIRST HUSBAND by arrangement, used to compare her voice to a funeral. There was sadness there. A narrative, clenched tight like a fist. A battle-scarred fist: the kind eager to push people away. Which was what Yan Hua did the night after their wedding, when Shun-Er lowered his trousers to shove his cold, dead fish into her body (it would be his first and last time). She hardened her voice; struck his ear with it like a whip. And in the silence that followed, she asked if maybe they didn't have to.

"For now," she added.

Shun-Er said nothing. They were in his childhood bedroom, the moon gazing through the paper window like a pervert. His face was yellow-cast and unreadable, and the relief in it looked like pain to Yan Hua.

"I don't want to," she said. "Not yet."

"I don't want to if you don't," Shun-Er said.

He pulled his trousers up while Yan Hua remembered her mother's words. They were spoken the day the wedding cloth appeared in her house. The wedding cloth that came before the wedding announcement, the ring, the name of the groom. "Uneducated people don't have words to record their hurt. That's why they have children. Their children are their memories." She then went on a long, droning diatribe about how Yan Hua's father terrorized her, and how no cop or neighbor stopped him. The one citation he received was bribed away, then burned. And when he died—mysteriously, with his face in a plate of dumplings—the only document that remained was this conversation, between a hurt mother and her broken daughter. And this broken daughter was to pass on that document to *her* children, who one day might have the education to put all this hurt into words.

"I thought you wanted to," Shun-Er said. He was embarrassed. Relieved, mainly, but also embarrassed. "Your mother, she kept saying to me. And my mother, she also—"

"Forget about them. I don't want to."

"Not ever?"

"No. Not now."

"Not ever," Shun-Er said. For the first time that night, he smiled.

And true to their conversation, he'd never try to touch her like that again.

YAN HUA DIDN'T SEE WHAT WAS GOING ON AT THE TIME. Why her husband seemed happy not to have sex. Why he didn't try and why he never appeared before her naked. The rumors didn't reach her. When friends asked if Shun-Er was a queen, she ignored them. Ignored them, too, when they talked about their lovers. These girls painted a different picture of marriage, one with colors of bruises and names like anger, pleasure, loving, and pain.

"In my opinion," a girl named Big Sister said, "you have to take the good *and* the bad. Not just the good."

"A relationship with only the good isn't a relationship at all," a girl named Pearl said.

"It's a fairy tale."

"But, somehow, the good always outweighs the bad."

"What do you think, Yan?" Big Sister asked. "You're awfully quiet today."

"When is she not quiet?"

"Shush," Big Sister said, holding a finger over her lips—the bottom one dotted with a mole that embarrassed her. "And *you're* always loud."

"I think . . ." Yan Hua said. She narrowed her eyes, pretending to think. "I don't know if I've ever gotten any 'bad' from my husband. He's pretty mild-mannered."

Pearl and Big Sister looked at each other and laughed. They had a list of questions for Yan Hua, and she had to answer them while sewing trousers at her workbench. No, he never beat her. Yes, they shared the cleaning duties. No, he cooked, was that so surprising? The three girls worked at a pants factory in Mawei City and spoke in snatches throughout the day. It was their way of "evening out" their paychecks, the amounts too meager for words. They had enough to put rollers in their hair and see movies, but not to eat what they wanted. Big Sister resembled a vintage graduation photo, so did Pearl, and Yan Hua, the old maid, wore her hair in a farmer's plait. Just like her mother.

"What about when he wants it?" Pearl asked.

"Shush," Big Sister said.

"Wants what?" Yan Hua asked. She cocked her head, biting her lip when she realized what Pearl meant. "Oh. That. There's no problem there, either."

But the truth was, Shun-Er never wanted "it." Yan Hua was fine with that—their arrangement kept them happy—but she did feel, secretly, that their marriage was abnormal. Her mother certainly did. She prodded Yan Hua's belly frequently and looked miffed every time she felt flatness instead of a bump.

"Are you two trying?" she asked. Then, when Yan Hua said nothing: "I'm not getting any younger, and neither are you."

Sometimes people asked if there was something wrong with him. *Down there.* But Yan Hua didn't know what that meant and shook her head. It didn't matter to her anyway. She was happy with her marriage. She was happy that Shun-Er was gentle. She was happy that he left her alone. It was only when she found him with his lover in their bedroom, with that smell of sweat-piss-shit and something else in the air, that she cracked like a dropped vase. Yan Hua made a fuss then;

her tears felt like nothing on her cheeks. She quickly understood that she didn't know the kind of man her husband was, and that realization made her question the kind of woman she was. Even after he swallowed poison, and his secrets were revealed by the faggot who showed up, screaming, at the funeral. The cinema, the cruising spaces, the men. She didn't want to touch any of it.

IN AMERICA, YAN HUA WAKES WITH THE OTHER WORKERS AT six. Sometimes seven, sometimes eight. But never at nine. If you wake at nine, you might as well return to sleep because your job's gone. She works as a seamstress, like most other women in the motel. They walk to the garment factory together, a flock of pigeons holding fifty-cent buns and Ovaltine from the bakery.

Chinatown, American-looking with its perpendicular and gum-blackened roads, feels safer this way. There's less fear with company. You don't need to cross the street at the sight of a foreign face, sharp-nosed and white and always (to Yan Hua) wearing a grimace. You don't need to feel lonely, either, because there's always a morning conversation. About the weather, about home, about money. When it snows, the women emit steam from under their scarves with their constant babbling.

"What a lie, this country," a woman named Amy says.

"You'll get used to it," another woman named Amy says. She is younger and prettier, so everyone calls her Little Amy, and her sister, Big Amy.

"Luxury brands this. Luxury food that. House this. Cars that. The lies my husband told."

"At least we're making money," a woman named May says.

"I'd rather be poor!"

"Like I said, you'll get used to it. I was like you before."

There are four of them, walking. East Broadway, what the establishment Chinese call "the slums," peters out into Grand Street, then the subway station. Buses pass through streets dirty with snow and inside are students. Workers, cleaning women, sometimes a homeless man, slumped and resembling a sack. Yan Hua stares at these images with eyes that seem to recoil from the world before her. *What a strange city*, she thinks. Familiar mixed with unfamiliar, rich mixed with poor. You look down one road and everyone's wearing a suit. You look down the other and it's filled with workers like her, shivering.

"It'll get better," Little Amy says when Big Amy continues her complaining.

"At this rate, I could've stayed in China. At least I'd have a house there! A room to myself and the right to bathe. Here, I twist a faucet and the landlady's up my ass like an enema."

"You're quiet," May whispers to Yan Hua.

"Nope. My teeth are chattering. See?" Yan Hua demonstrates: *Rat-a-tat-tat, rat-a-tat-tat.*

"And my husband," Big Amy says, "what a cheapskate! You'd think a bowl of soup cost a hundred dollars if you listened to him go on." She turns to Yan Hua, says out of politeness and envy, "At least Frog's not tight with his wallet."

"Wallet? Don't make me laugh. He doesn't have one."

"He'll have one soon," Little Amy offers.

"Not at this rate. He works as a dishwasher for less than a thousand dollars a month. Like my mother used to say: 'The man has arms, the man has legs. But he has no spine . . .'"

"But he seems to love you," May says.

"I wish he didn't."

"He used to talk all day about his wife in China," May says, mischievous. "Showing us letters you'd written. 'My wife went to high school. When she comes, I'll have to move—she's used to a better life . . .' And look where that asshole is now!"

Yan Hua grimaces. She's aware of how he exaggerated their relationship to others, of how he seems to believe that the two are the immigrant Romeo and Juliet.

"It's just a green card marriage," she says to the women.

It's just a green card marriage, she tells herself.

YAN HUA WILL GIVE FROG CREDIT FOR TWO THINGS: HE'S not jealous, and he's generous about her past. "Everyone has one," he says. "You have one, I have one, that woman over there"—he points at a granny searching the trash for water bottles—"has one." They're walking, husband and wife, to a local temple for tomb-sweeping day. Yan Hua carries a bundle of afterlife money for Shun-Er, and Frog tags along for the free meal. He's a tall and barrel-chested man, very coarse and talkative, who asks, over and over, for Yan Hua to describe her late husband. Not in a rude or invasive way. He's merely curious the way children are curious about a story that hasn't ended.

"He's not what you expect," Yan Hua says. Her lips are a straight line, but her eyes betray an inward storm. "He was, first of all, a sissy."

"You told me that already."

"A real sissy. He loved a man and the man loved him back. But he loved *me* first."

"That's a funny way to describe adultery."

"I guess you could say that. But he respected me in a way that other men didn't. Growing up, I heard nothing but the cries of beaten women. My mother was beaten, my aunts were beaten. If I had a sister, I'm sure she'd have been beaten, too. It's one of those things you get used to, living in the provinces."

"I know what you mean. When my father hit my mother, she'd show our neighbors the bruises on her arms. With pride."

Yan Hua nods. "My mother did the same thing. She hated my father, he was a bastard, but she bragged that he was a man, *a real man*, with fists and a temper."

"I'd never hit you."

"My husband didn't have the desire to be a man. He was gentle, he was tender. If he touched you, the feeling was like that of eating chocolate. It sweetened you and it calmed you. It made you experience a different kind of love . . ."

Her voice trails off. They're at the entrance of the temple, the size of a small kitchen, and she walks in with six other Chinese: some carrying afterlife money, others holding joss sticks. In the backyard, beside a plot of scallions, is a metal tin with a raging fire. Here the worshippers throw their afterlife money, one bill at a time, and slowly. If you do it too fast, temple leaders warn, the smoke will billow and the neighbors will call the fire department. A reminder of America, Yan Hua thinks as she separates from Frog, who sneaks away to the basement, where volunteers are serving Buddhist meals.

Yan Hua burns her money and concentrates. Sweating from the fire, with smoke and wind blurring her vision, she recalls one of her long-forgotten hypotheses. An idle one, about Shun-Er. It starts with the time he went shopping with her, the time he made her try on a pile of clothes, one after the other, giddy as a child with a new toy, and happy—they were both so happy—even though neither he nor she could afford any of the dresses piling up in the dressing room. But the thing that strikes Yan Hua is the intensity in Shun-Er's eyes as he chooses the clothes. A fervor that becomes almost venomous when the shopkeeper makes them leave ("If you're not buying anything, then go home, you're making a mess for my customers"). A thought entered her head that day, a thought that has since dulled into an itch in her spine, but back in the day it frightened her, kept her up at night, gave her nightmares.

The thought—which she failed to verbalize, and which she sensed as a dull, occasional panic; a throbbing like an ice cube pressed against her temple—was that Shun-Er wanted to become a woman by using Yan Hua's body.

She was his way of experiencing womanhood, of *escaping* himself through a body that wasn't his. He could dress her up like a doll, and when she wasn't around, he'd wear her clothes, this she was certain of, because some days she'd pick out a dress and it'd stink of the cafeteria where he worked. That or cigarettes, plus the spicy, white pepper odor of sweat. To escape these thoughts, she'd argue with him, then with herself. She'd invent phantom women (she knew they were men) who entered their home with Shun-Er, women who'd contort their bodies like a pile of snakes in the closet.

"I hope," Yan Hua whispers, tossing her afterlife money into the fire, "I hope that you've become the person you've always wanted to be."

Suddenly, she becomes angry and bitter.

But what about me? What about my hurt? What about the person I want to become?

When she sees Frog, standing in the basement with a to-go box stuffed with Buddhist foods, her anger turns to rage.

Because she has problems with her husband. The real one, not this boisterous green card fake. The memories in Yan Hua's head are illusory and mask the nightmare images lurking beneath. They change shape if she thinks about them for too long. Become strange, painful, and confusing. Normally, when someone alters a memory, it's remade in their own favor. But Yan Hua only creates memories favorable to Shun-Er. The situation resembles something out of a fable: Shun-Er becomes himself by using Yan Hua's body; Yan Hua becomes herself by using Shun-Er's history.

She snips away, like loose threads, the parts of him she doesn't like. The constant disappearances. The way he reeked of sex and other men's bodies. The way he brought those men home and soiled her furniture with love, blood, sweat, and semen. In the face of all of this, Yan Hua forced herself to react with grace. Because Shun-Er was gentle, and therefore worth it. Because he listened, because he didn't push her onto their bed, because he didn't hit her or thrust his body against hers with a violence that would settle into boredom. Shun-Er loved her—this much was true—and he was considerate of her mind, her thoughts, even her dreams. But was he considerate of her body? Did not causing her pain make up for not giving her pleasure?

Confusing, painful, *I don't want to think about them* thoughts.

But she has to. They erupt from her body whenever Frog holds her.

That is the word she uses: "holds." Not "fucks." Not "has sex with." "Holds." The word makes the act seem casual, and less dirty. There is also the strange shock she experiences, the revelation of tenderness, when Frog stretches his fingers like spiders up her leg.

"Does it hurt?"

"No."

"Why are you shrinking back like that? I won't hurt you."

"You're cold. Warm yourself up first."

It is shocking to her, finding out that Frog, a boorish and impatient man, could be tender and attentive during sex. Every moment, he asks if she is okay. Is she hurting? Does it feel good when he touches her here? What about over there? His body against hers feels cold at first, then warm and heavy, the sensation of a weighted blanket. Safety spreads like a drug through Yan Hua's veins. Then desire mixed with loathing, and afterwards, despair, as Frog thrusts his hips and Yan Hua smells the blood-and-sweat love-stench that reminds her of her dead husband's deceit.

Frog is trembling. From excitement or fear, Yan Hua can't tell. Because all she can think about is the last time she saw her first husband.

Shun-Er in a chair, his head tilted back. Vomit on his chin, his lap, his hands, the table. A foul-smelling rag soiled a spot on the floor, but otherwise the room was spotless. He'd cleaned everything, or tried to, before Yan Hua came home. Shun-Er was considerate like that: He remembered that his wife had cleaned the floor that morning and didn't want to cause her trouble. He must have scooped the vomit off the floor and back into his mouth. That's why it was on his chin and hands and lap. Then, when he saw the residue, he used a rag soaked with vinegar to clean it up. Afterwards, he returned to his chair to rest. To tilt his head back, close his eyes, and die.

"You deserved it," Yan Hua whispers.

Frog doesn't hear her; he's too busy with his own body. His movements become fast and repetitive. He's leading up to it, that final spasm, that hideous male roar.

"You deserved everything, you son-of-a-bitch. You pretended

to care about me, but you didn't. All you cared about was yourself. Motherfucker. I hate you. You're a shit. Dog shit, pigeon shit, you're not fit for pigs to eat . . ."

"Are you all right?" Frog asks.

Yan Hua doesn't respond, so he repeats himself after cleaning off with a towel.

"Did it feel good?"

". . ."

"Did I hurt you?"

". . ."

"I didn't mean to if I did. I really didn't. You seemed like you were enjoying it. Like you were having fun. You have to tell me next time. You have to tell me, I want you to feel good."

Yan Hua is shivering.

"Did you hear me? I want you to feel good."

THIRTEEN

ONTHS GO BY, and Yan Hua is searching for a new home. An actual one, not a room furnished with sagging bunk beds. But the apartments she sees are dark, cramped, too expensive, and *filthy*. You can smell them from the street: a stench that causes rich folks to clutch their pearls and plug their noses. One such apartment has mold spreading across its walls. Another, wedged between the white and Chinese parts of town, asks for a down payment and a credit check. Neither is as bad, however, as the fifth-floor walk-up she and May move into. What a nightmare, to have two bedrooms but three times as many residents. Blankets, mattresses, and tired bodies litter the floor, and every morning, there are signs of the previous night's mahjong games. Fragrant fast-food bags (the rich folks once again clutch their pearls). Greasy bowls on top of greasier plates. Wilted lettuce fallen from a burger, water bottles stuffed with toothpicks, crumpled tissues, and cigarette butts. For weeks, Yan Hua and May try to beautify the place. They drape fabric across the tables. Hang calendars on the walls, pictures being too expensive. Flowers appear in vases, only to be replaced by their plastic counterparts: perky and alert-looking, then crooked and sad.

Needless to say, their efforts fail. As the saying goes, you can't chew gum to sweeten your breath—you have to brush your teeth, too. And neither woman, working ten-hour shifts at the garment factory, has the energy, let alone the patience, to rid the apartment of its filth. So when the year ends, they ask their husbands, coerce them, to move. Not to a better place, but a different one. Yan Hua's second apartment has more mold than the first. But it's closer to where she and May work; plus, there are fewer people sharing it. To keep costs low, they live with three others: a family with a baby taking its first steps. Trouble begins in the summer when rats appear. They drag garbage out of the trash cans and frighten the baby so badly he starts to scream in his sleep. It's around then that the rumors start. The rude looks and whispers, revealing something Yan Hua already knows. Which is that the baby's father, frustrated from being awoken at night, has begun to beat his own child. Not just with a switch, but with his belt, a clothes hanger, his fists . . .

The third apartment Yan Hua moves into has cracks in the wall and no heat.

The fourth has water leaks in every room.

The fifth is the site of a battle between rival Chinese gangs. For three days, Yan Hua's apartment appears on the news, which causes Kevin, May's undocumented husband, to become paranoid and irritable.

Yan Hua lives like this for years, each season moving from one home to the next. Her belongings expand, shrink, then shrink some more. The objects used to beautify the apartments are the first to be discarded, followed by the chairs with the foldable metal legs. Next are the clothes she brought from China: thin, slippery, polyester things that stretch like taffy in the wash. One year, while living in the apartment with the water leaks, she slept without a mattress. It was too much work to move large items up six flights of stairs, too exhausting to make the space comfortable after a ten-hour workday. So the temporary floor mat became permanent—almost lovely after the addition of pillows, throws, blankets, and Frog's body.

The one thing she won't discard is a wooden box with a lock on it. Nobody thinks to ask about its contents. But one night, the night before her sixth move, Frog picks the box up. Rotates it in his clumsy hands. "You're taking this with you?"

The box is small, fancy-looking—like something that might hold a jewel—and chipped at the corners. Streaks of oil come off its wood, staining Frog's hands. Yan Hua stares at the box blankly. She's just returned from work, and her eyes are dull and heavy. Even with a flashlight shining into them, there wouldn't be movement. Fired from one Chinatown garment factory, she now works at one farther away, and the commute is longer, often miserable, with the bus traffic.

"Are you keeping this?" Frog asks again.

"Yes," Yan Hua says, finally. "Give it to me, I'll put it in my bag."

But Frog doesn't let the box go. He continues swiveling it in his hands. "Will you ever tell me what's inside this thing?"

"Nothing. Trinkets. Give it to me."

"I'm just wondering, Yan. You throw everything away. Clothes, pants, perfectly good shoes. And yet."

"And yet what? Give the box to me. You may have the patience today, but I don't."

"Is Shun-Er inside?"

"He's not."

"We have to let the past go, Yan. We can't keep living like this. Not like this."

"Who's we?" Yan Hua asks, her voice rising. "Tell me again, Frog. Who's we?"

LUNCH AT THE GARMENT FACTORY IS A GROUP OF WOMEN at their worktables, laughing and talking. Yan Hua's comes in a takeout container with three compartments. One for rice, another for stewed pork, and a third for the greens she doesn't eat—they're too oily and bland. "My mother could've cooked better greens than this," Yan Hua says, "and she cooked in the mountains, without spices." Sitting at the next table is May, who chews hot dog buns from the bakery. Roommates for four years, the two have their own ways of communicating. A smirk and a raised eyebrow tell Yan Hua to look at what So-and-So is doing. A nudge of her elbow says the same, and a look toward the ceiling, sometimes accompanied by an eye roll, suggests that someone has made a mistake, a fool of himself, or both. All three gestures appear today during the speech of the factory manager, second son of the owner. He's a balding, big-bellied man who speaks about Chinese solidarity but refuses to increase his workers' wages. Only their hours, which are frequently miscalculated, and never to their benefit.

"We'll have a new distributor starting in August. Profits are up this month, but not by enough. Don't listen to the idiots protesting in the streets. Ignore them and you won't regret it. Please remember that it's your responsibility, not ours, to record your hours. A reminder again to ignore the idiots, and don't talk to any reporters. Sharing sensitive information about the company will result in your immediate dismissal . . ."

"We need to find a new job," May says, speaking in dialect.

There are twenty minutes left for lunch, but she is already sewing sequins onto blouses.

"McDonald's is hiring."

"I'm serious. Remember Little Amy? Her place is looking for seamstresses."

"It's in Brooklyn, no? The commute," Yan Hua says, moving in her seat, shifting her weight from one buttock to the other, "would kill us. We finally learned the bus route, now you want us to take the train?"

"She says it's easy. Besides"—May gestures for Yan Hua to come closer—"she says her boss is bending to the will of the strikers."

"The strikers? You're telling me a factory manager is sympathetic to workers' rights?"

"Not sympathetic to. Bending to the will of. They're deep in Brooklyn and can't hire people otherwise."

"How much is the pay?"

"Sufficient."

"How much is sufficient?"

"Little Amy says she's getting four dollars an hour. Cash."

"I'll think about it. Did you see her new purse? It's Coach, but I think it's fake."

May sneaks a mischievous look at Yan Hua. At thirty-four, May has broad shoulders, a belly she can't lose, and a face Frog describes, unkindly, as "wise-looking." She keeps her hair in a ponytail, and the bangs that frame her face are matted across her forehead. "Like spiders drenched in water," Yan Hua likes to say. She stares without expression at the bangs while May asks about a fight between Yan Hua and Frog.

"Let's talk about your man for a second. What was he screaming about last night?"

When Yan Hua doesn't answer, May adds, "I saw him this morning. The man was hot-hot. If I'd gotten any closer to him, my saliva would've evaporated."

"He's crazy," Yan Hua mutters.

"He said the same thing about you." A switch flips in May's voice. "Yan, why don't you let go of your ex-husband?"

"I already did," Yan Hua says. "Long ago. The only thing left of him is my memories."

"Frog said you keep his ashes in a box."

"Because he's crazy."

"He also said you won't have kids because of your ex-husband."

"*He's* the one who doesn't want kids!" Yan Hua starts to laugh. "I don't want them, either, but he wants them even less than me! He grits his teeth when he sees them, says the sight of a misbehaving child makes his blood boil!"

"All right, maybe I lied about that last one."

"You're stupid, don't talk to me anymore."

Yan Hua throws her lunch container away, then takes a sip from her water bottle. She sighs, stretches her legs, and rotates her hips. A sign that she's returning to work.

"You'll consider the new factory job?" May asks.

"Didn't I tell you not to talk to me?"

"We'll go together," May says. She reaches across the table to hold Yan Hua's hand.

TWO WEEKS LATER, THE GIRLS ARE ON A TRAIN TO BROOK-
lyn Chinatown. Frog doesn't want to come—he'd rather play mahjong with his buddies—and Kevin has appliances to fix. A month
has passed since their last move, and Yan Hua is already searching for a new home. This one, number five, has too many things
wrong with it. The problem isn't just the gang fights. The doors
don't shut all the way. The freezer doesn't freeze. The faucets drip
brown water, and the exhaust fan in the kitchen is a chained dog:
all bark and no function. For days, Frog and Kevin have been
running around the apartment with hammers glued to their hands.
But the place holds no love for them. The moment Kevin fixes a
table, a chair breaks. A mended gas leak becomes a flicker in the
kitchen lights. A nail in the wall, hammered in to hang a coat, becomes a chip off the toilet lid. Then a crack. And when Kevin fixes
the leaking faucets that kept the men up at night, a demon moves in
next door: an American woman who calls the cops on their mahjong
games.

Nope. Nuh-uh. You can call a house with a broken door your
home, but not one you can't have fun in.

Thankfully, the apartment didn't come with a lease. An old,
deaf, moody, and watchful landlady lives in the smallest bedroom:
a woman named Auntie (if you're Cantonese) and Who Does She
Think She Is? (if you're not). Eager for male attention, Auntie follows Kevin around as he fixes the apartment. Her conversation is
loud and repetitive, resembling the angry honks of a goose. Yan
Hua imitates her on the train to Brooklyn while May stares anx-
iously out the door. She's terrified of missing their stop and ending

up God knows where. It isn't like Little Amy didn't give them travel instructions that morning:

"Go four stops on the N in the Brooklyn direction. If you forget to count, then get off when you see a station with eight in its name. The first one, not the second. If you can't read, then get off at the first stop after seeing sunlight . . ."

"How many stops has it been?" May asks.

"Not even one."

They are sitting in the corner, their heads facing different directions. Yan Hua wears comfortable clothes, and May is dressed like a bride. Her hair is lifted in a tight bun, and the dress she wears is constructed from heavy fabric: armor-like and unsuitable for summer. It's her defense mechanism, something she drapes around herself to ward away the sneering eyes of strangers. A "proper" woman with a middle school education—the highest of anyone in her village—May wears fancy clothes whenever she finds herself in a difficult situation. Today's trip is dedicated to seeing Little Amy, but May feels the need to look unapproachable. Elegant, too, and possibly a little garish, as she lifts a foot to soothe the itch on her sole.

"I think you were right about this commute," May says. "It'll kill us."

"It was *your* idea to come. Plus, we've only been here five minutes."

"I'm tired of moving apartments, too."

"Tell that to Little Amy. She's the one who found the new place, not me."

After she gave Yan Hua instructions on how to reach Brooklyn, Little Amy asked if they all might move in together. "There's a suitable place," Little Amy said, "in a nice part of East Broadway. Close to the mall and the subway. The only bad part is the number of the apartment. Four. But that only matters if you're superstitious. Which I'm not."

"Did Little Amy visit the place yet?" May asks.

"Yeah, and to listen to her describe it, you'd think she'd visited Shangri-La. The bedrooms are big and so is the kitchen. The bathroom is small but—"

"But is it cheap?"

"If we're unsure, she said she can take us to the apartment. Today."

"Frog won't mind?"

"Who cares what he thinks?"

They sit in silence while the train stops at the first station in Brooklyn. Minutes later, May shuts her eyes and Yan Hua begins to dream. If all goes well today, she'll have a lead on a new job, perhaps a new home. And a new home means unpacking her box full of memories again. Despite what Frog believes, the box doesn't hold Shun-Er's ashes. It doesn't contain a picture of him, either, or Yan Hua's wedding veil. You'd know from the sound it makes when you shake it. Nothing but a rattle, a loose and hollow knocking. Like striking your foot against a path made of gravel, or dropping (as Yan Hua does now, falling asleep) a coin from your fist to the floor.

YAN HUA STANDS OUTSIDE THE WORKERS' CINEMA ON FEET that demand stillness. They're swollen, pregnant-like, and her arches, flattening the back straps of her sandals, have stiffened into straight lines.

All around her are sissies who stare with cast-iron eyes. Their expressions are defiant but fearful, and reflected off the surface of their eyes is a crooked wall of police. They wear street clothes and would've resembled thugs, if not for their handcuffs and batons. The handcuffs dangle, knocking against each other, but the batons, clenched inside sweaty palms, are still. *Salivating*, Yan Hua thinks as their sweat drips from their wrists to their batons, from their batons to the floor. She is also sweating and holds a coin in her fist. It feels strange there, pressed like a jewel inside her palm, and dangerous. Like a secret whispered at the wrong time. The cops will rush forward the moment she throws the coin. That's what Yan Hua believes. They are waiting for her, waiting for a sign. Then they'll crash forward like a wave.

She lifts her arm, trembling like a child before her father's belt. Are these tears streaming down her face, or is it perspiration? She licks them, the salty-sweat tears, and then she remembers that Shun-Er is here. He's only a few meters away from her, shouting something Yan Hua can't make out, but the man beside him, the one Shun-Er's eyes call "lover," makes him feel as distant as the moon. Right then, staring at her husband holding another man, a feeling like excitement rises in Yan Hua's chest. After that, the warmth of a blanket in wintertime. Happiness descends upon her, followed by stillness, followed by panic.

The coin in her fist is gone.

She wakes up hot, sweaty, and with too many things on top of her. The blanket she bought from Canal Street. The pillow with the too-large pillowcase. Frog's leg and, under her neck, the fish-white length of his arm. He sleeps, as he always does, with his head facing her and his mouth wide open, emitting air that reminds Yan Hua of a toilet. She wrinkles her nose and shakes him off her. Then she sits up and wipes the gunk from her eyes. It's three in the morning, and the only sounds are the desk fan and Frog's snoring. He groans when Yan Hua lifts her body from their mattress. When she confirms that he's still asleep, she breathes a sigh of relief. Then decides, with the clock hands ticking in her ear, that maybe she should wake him after all.

Because then she wouldn't have to consider the dream she'd had. Nor the startling realism of its lies. That is what scares her the most. The way Yan Hua's dream tricked her, if only for a moment, into believing that she'd sabotaged the protest at the Workers' Cinema. In her room's darkness, which feels like a gift one minute and a curse the next, Yan Hua examines the soles of her feet. Satisfied by their appearance, she moves her gaze upward, stopping at her dominant hand. She clenches it into a fist. Afterwards, she holds it above a shaft of window light, trembling like a leaf in strong winds. Yan Hua has rough hands, laborer's hands, that look older than her face. But they never threw a coin at a protest. They have never, until now, wanted to break something with the deadly force of a sledgehammer.

All I did was have a conversation, Yan Hua reasons. A conversation in an air-conditioned office with carpet under her feet. To this day, she is embarrassed to walk on carpet with muddy and laceless shoes. And yet the government officials were kind to her that day. They cracked jokes, offered her tea, and listened with the smiling faces of wolves. Not once did they let their guards down. The coin tricks they played with their words masked the greed hiding behind their eyes. Not just the greed, but the haughtiness. The *do you see what she's wearing?* expressions dancing on the tips of their tongues. Of course, Yan Hua didn't notice any of this. She was blinded by her pain, the complaints she had to dislodge like fish bones from her throat. It wasn't until a Bible-sized box was handed to her, one with a solid gold coin inside, that she realized what she'd done.

"This is only a conversation," she remembers saying.

"Of course," one of the officials says. "And this is only a gift."

A gift that she now, in the darkness of her Chinatown apartment, is frantically trying to find. It isn't in the top drawer of her dresser. Nor is it in the second. When she finds it in the third drawer, she's convinced she has to throw the box away. It's haunting her. Her dream is solid proof of that.

"What are you doing?" Frog asks.

He sits on the mattress with the blanket over his legs, yawning and searching the floor for a cigarette. Finding none, he reaches for a bottle of water.

"Nothing, go back to sleep."

"You were muttering something."

". . ."

"What's that in your hand?"

"In your own words, my dead husband."

"C'mon, get back to bed, you know I didn't mean that."

"I'm going to throw it away."

"I was joking, I don't believe you keep him in there. Honest."

"It's giving me bad dreams."

"Like?"

"I don't remember."

Yan Hua turns around, stares at her husband. Her eyes are moist, but she's no longer crying. Her rage, her sorrow, her loneliness—all are blunted by the comical sight of Frog's body. Unlike Shun-Er's, Frog's body is firm. Muscular, even, in the shoulders, the arms, the legs, the chest. But his soft belly protruding from the blanket, and the dried spit like chalk dust frosting his lips—something about it makes Yan Hua laugh. They have been married five years, but Yan Hua feels nothing for her husband. Yes, he is kind at times, and yes, he is patient. But the love she feels for him isn't spouse-love, or friend-love, or even sibling-love. It's more like a tolerance that sometimes creeps toward friendship. Except when he presses his body against hers, and she has to smell the love-stench coming off his skin. Afraid he would do that now (in the state she's in, she'd start crying), Yan Hua remains standing with the box in her hands.

"You won't come back to bed?"

"I'm serious about throwing the box away. I want to do it now."

Frog's face changes, and his voice becomes moody. "You're doing this to spite me."

"It has nothing to do with you."

"Whatever. Do whatever you want."

She turns around and opens the door.

FOURTEEN

FROG COULD NOT take his eyes off his wife. Even before they met, he was loving her. Kissing, holding, and desiring her through the half-moon gaze of his vision. Back then, when he was young and new to America, the only thing he knew was her name. Then, when her passport photo arrived, he discovered that she'd lied about her age. Not by a lot, but he saw the signs, and none of them pointed to twenty. The creases like pine needles beside her mouth, open and revealing yellow teeth, made Frog suck in his breath. The brittleness of the fringe sweeping past her forehead made him blow it back out. Afterwards, when he caught the silent but tearful look in her eyes, he laughed. A low, mirthless, unhappy laugh that asked the Snakehead woman (she was arranging Frog's green card marriage) if she was joking.

"This girl?" Frog asked. This girl, with her neck thin as a cane stalk? Whose lips have never tasted, let alone spoken, a hint of sugar?

"It's not a real marriage," the Snakehead woman said. "After you get your money, you can divorce her."

Frog puffed on his cigarette and spat its brown taste out of his mouth. He was acting like a picky bachelor, but his heart had begun to ramble like a buffoon. That's the phrase his grandmother used to describe spouse-love. She was the only person in his family who'd married for it, and she told Frog that it was the only feeling worth living for. Nothing compared to it. Not the glorious smell of eggs and fish in the morning, not the sound of money in your pocket, not even the first drink of water after a long day in the fields. She was a lonely woman, Grandmother Frog, and an early widow, but her memory of the heart-rambling kept her alive for a long time. It kept Frog alive, too, even though his face told a lie and his mouth repeated it.

"She looks like she's never eaten a meal," Frog said.

"Like I said, it's easy to divorce in America. I've done it before. Many times."

The Snakehead woman laughed while Frog stared at the photo in his hands. Hungry and lonely, he evaluated the planes of his bride's face. Transformed its flaws into kindness. He wondered what Yan Hua's story was. Because everyone who came to America had one. What made her want to immigrate? Did she know anyone, or was she alone? With his oily and dirt-filled fingernails, Frog traced lines around the photograph, creasing it everywhere except for on her face. There were already plenty of lines there. Lines he wanted to touch, brush with his hands, and, someday, ask about. The way his grandmother used to, may her spirit rest in peace.

That crease around your lips—you must've had a hard life.

Tell me the story of the gray hairs in your head.

The look in your eyes, the tears behind them. What happened there?

YAN HUA WAS SILENT WHEN FROG MET HER AT THE AIRPORT. Aside from a nod and a distant smile, she didn't acknowledge the man who called himself her husband. Not with her mouth and not with her eyes. They looked elsewhere. At the smooth stems of potted plants, the rolling wheels of nearby suitcases, the drawn-in faces of Chinese travelers. Blaming shyness, then jet lag, then homesickness, Frog took it upon himself to knock his wife out of her stupor. He told stories about himself. Exhausting those, he spoke about the country they lived in. He mixed lies with truth and told jokes that were so bad, even the cabdriver was sucking his teeth. The whole time, Yan Hua sat in a corner of the car, her neck bent and her eyes half open. She looked tired. When Frog asked if she was sleepy, she shook her head. And once, when she opened her mouth to answer a question, a spit bubble came out instead of words.

"Do you remember when we first met?" Frog asked, a year later. "You barely spoke."

They were living in their first apartment then. Clutching a mop in one hand and hope in the other, Yan Hua cleaned the bedroom with music stuck between her teeth. She hummed melodies while Frog talked about the past. Poorly, because he didn't (and refused to) bring up the first vicious words Yan Hua said to him: "My husband is dead. I swear I didn't kill him."

"For two days you were ill. You just laid there"—Frog pointed at their bed—"and looked. Sometimes with sadness in your eyes, sometimes with laughter. And the whole time I wondered what your deal was. Whether or not you'd last."

"Move your legs," Yan Hua said. When Frog did, she swept the mop under his chair.

"Most folks would've left you for dead," Frog said. "But I didn't. I knew that a story hid behind your quiet. My grandmother on my father's side was a fortune teller, the kind that could read faces and palms. And I have the tiniest bit of her power."

"What's the story behind my face then?"

"It doesn't work like that. You can't read the whole face. Different features tell different stories. Like your hair. It tells the story of your ex-husband, his funeral."

"Seeing the connection between gray hairs and grief isn't a superpower," Yan Hua said. "What are you gonna say next? That my nose tells the story of my allergies? Or that my tongue is a novel about thirst?"

"No, but a mouth like yours tells me that you've got bad love luck."

"Tell me about it," Yan Hua muttered.

"And your high forehead, the creases on it. They say you've had a tough childhood. And maybe a tough adulthood, too. But life will be good when you're an old woman."

Yan Hua snickered while she wrung her mop out.

"The feature that caught my attention the most, though, the feature whose story I could never read, was your eyes. Especially in your passport photo."

"What're you talking about?"

"You were crying in that picture. The tears were hidden, but I could see them."

". . ."

"And I could tell it wasn't grief for Shun-Er. There was

something else there. Hatred, maybe? An anger you've buried in your chest like a seed."

"I don't know if that's something I can talk about, Frog."

"You don't have to if you don't want. I'm only speculating."

Yan Hua stood her mop at an angle and leaned against it. Feeling weak, then strong, then weak again, she closed her eyes. Walked to her bed and sat down. Meanwhile, the past, like tendrils wrapping around a beanpole, crept up her spine and into her neck. Its meanness dulled her skin and she had to blink until the lump in her throat became a breath. Then the breath turned into nervous laughter, before she said, "His lover came to his funeral." She spoke in dialect, and the harshness of her words made Frog's skin prickle with gooseflesh. "He heard about it somehow and came."

Her words stopped and, in their place, came memory.

She remembered the bored faces streaked with sweat. The joss stick ash that clung like flies to wet skin. Yan Hua's mother appeared in her memory first. Afterwards, her four bickering aunts. All six women performed their grief while standing before Shun-Er's coffin. One so poorly made, it became the subject of local gossip. Funeral guests whispered to each other about the crooked nails they saw in the wood. Then, reacting to the smell of sawdust, they remarked that the room was more like a woodshop. "I wouldn't want to be sent off like that," one of Yan Hua's aunts said. Another aunt, who refused to wear her mourning robes, nodded her affirmation with sinister glee. A third aunt said *"Phew!"* (which meant everything and nothing at once), while a fourth said, replying to the first: "I'll come back to haunt you if you bury me like that."

"I was on edge when he entered the room," Yan Hua said. "First, there was calmness on his face. A serene expression like that of the goddess Guanyin. But then, seeing the coffin, he began to moan. All his features scrunched up"—Yan Hua demonstrated with her eyes, nose, and mouth—"until his face resembled a dirty rag."

"My God."

"It would've been fine if he'd wept like the rest of us. But he had to scream, too. He had to beat his chest like an idiot and call my husband, yes, *my* husband, the word 'lover.' In front of everyone and in that sick faggot voice of his. And then he saw me."

Yan Hua remembered how he screamed at her. How he raised his dirty, knife-thin finger and shouted, for everyone to hear, that *she'd* done this. That *she'd* killed Shun-Er, may God strike her down. But instead of mentioning his outburst to Frog, she decided to lie.

"You have to understand, I wasn't jealous before," Yan Hua said. Her lie emboldened her. Courage shot through her body like a bullet. "I was aware of their relationship," she said, bristling like a cat. "I saw them together."

"You saw?"

"With these same two eyes."

"And you were okay with it?"

"I was okay until I saw my aunts' faces. Judging him, then me, then the body not even cold in its coffin. With that I became jealous. Hateful. The people around me, the situation, both taught me to feel envy toward the man sobbing like a mad person in love. And if I didn't, then I wasn't a woman, let alone a wife."

"You've told me this next part. Your cousins beat him, then kicked him out."

Yan Hua shook her head.

"They didn't?"

"No, they did. But at the time that didn't feel like sufficient punishment."

"You wanted them to kill him."

With a catch in her breath that said she didn't want to speak anymore, Yan Hua sat down.

"So that's what the tears were for," Frog said. He sat beside his wife, took both of her hands, and massaged them. "They weren't grief tears or anger tears."

No, Yan Hua thought. Dazed by her outburst, she couldn't tell which part of her story was a lie and which part was the truth. Yan Hua had long accepted Shun-Er's infidelity—this part was factual. But her words about not being jealous until the funeral—that was a lie. But that lie wasn't half as evil as the falsehood she'd managed to transform into a truth, *her* truth, when telling it to Frog. The kicking out of Shun-Er's lover from the funeral, which Yan Hua said was facilitated by her cousins, was an action she'd performed herself. She beat him to a pulp for daring to accuse her of murder. And he, the poor man, did nothing to fight back. Frog was correct in saying that they weren't grief tears or anger tears in her passport photo.

Because they were shame tears, Yan Hua thought. *Regret tears. Not because I didn't kill the man but because the thought crossed my mind in the first place. God knows I would've done it if someone had handed me a knife. Any kind: steak, bread, butter, fruit. I would've plunged the blade deep into that nasty bird chest of his, deep into that body wracked with my own pain. Why did I punch him, and so fiercely? Was it because of the people in the crowd; the people who, seeing this man with hickeys on his neck and "lover" on his lips, did the math and saw it add up? There was no denying the truth of my husband any longer. The truth I hid from my relatives and transformed into blood as I punched. Palms struck cheekbones and their skin-feeling made my hurt bloom like flowers. But when I saw my relatives rush forward, when I felt their body heat and their hands grab my own, I saw it again. The red-hot rage that made me want*

Shun-Er to suffer and die. I remember cursing at his lover. "Faggot" came first. Afterwards came "sissy," then "bitch," then "son of one." Words I don't—to this day—believe in. But he (no, they) deserved them. And my mother and her sisters expected them from me. They held me back while their eyes goaded me. They even chanted my name like gamblers at a dog fight. Not Yan Hua but the childhood nickname I loathed.

"My Heart!" they yelled, a chorus of sneering female voices. "My Heart, My Liver, My Precious Baby Love . . ."

FROG WATCHED WHILE YAN HUA TWITCHED IN HER SLEEP. Like a child trapped in a nightmare, she moaned, whimpered, shuddered, and thrashed. Sometimes her eyes fluttered open, and sometimes they roamed under their lids. To Frog, her movements resembled those of a fetus kicking its mother's belly. He was sitting in his chair with a match in one hand, a cigarette in the other. The water bottle he used as an ashtray stood beside him on a table covered with flowers. Printed ones, not real. The large, cheap, waxy-looking tablecloth with roses on it was bought in bulk from the dollar store. Yan Hua draped it over everything. Over the tops of tables, over the lid of the toilet tank—she even glued some over the mold spots marking the bedroom walls. Their home resembled a beggar in cheap lace—one who hadn't showered, brushed his hair, or chewed mint leaves to sweeten his breath. In short, the place was falling apart. The floors shuddered when you walked on them, and Yan Hua's tablecloth had begun to peel off the walls, revealing holes, scratches, cigarette stains, and twice as much mold as before.

Maybe we should move, Frog thought. He didn't care about mold or dirtiness, but Yan Hua did. She kept Raid beside the mattress.

Next to the spray was a box crammed with cleaning products. Vinegar, air freshener, baking soda, Tide powder, Fabuloso, window spray, grout cleaner. None of which, aside from the vinegar, Frog used. He wasn't thoughtful in that way. If Yan Hua asked him to defrost a chicken, he'd forget, then snap at her for reminding him. He knew her favorite fruit (pears) but never bought them. And this selfishness of his allowed Frog to light a cigarette in his home jaundiced by smoke. The same one his wife had failed to beautify, and which Frog hoped leaving would help to end her nightmares.

Never mind that the nightmares had a different source.

She was obsessed with Shun-Er's death. After exiting the taxi, Yan Hua spent an hour desperately telling Frog that she didn't kill him. She'd done nothing but speak to a pair of government officials in Mawei City, was guilty of nothing but being in the wrong place at the wrong time. Nevertheless, her obsession sank her. Threw her, the moment she arrived at the immigrant motel, into a deep and sleepless fever. Too weak to bathe, sit up, talk, or chew, she directed Frog to bring her water and nothing but. At first, it was cold and bottled. Afterwards, when she asked for more, he gave her a bowl filled with tap. Yan Hua drank it all with a greedy expression. It was as though she'd never had a sip of anything in her life. So deep was her thirst, she failed to notice the women seated around her, murmuring and caring. Women who worked as laborers, who couldn't afford to live anywhere but the immigrant motel, and who—with laughter or stories, or just by listening—would help Yan Hua to stand on her own two feet. In that moment, however, Yan Hua was content with the water that touched her lips. She didn't care that the women told her their names (May, Big Amy, and Little Amy), and she didn't care that they scolded Frog for giving a sick woman sink water.

"What's the matter with you? Your mother didn't teach you to turn on a stove?"

"To get water from the sink, too . . . I don't know what's in there, but I wouldn't drink it."

"He just met his bride and already he's trying to kill her."

Tossing Frog aside, the women took care of Yan Hua. They held her hands, they spoke to her, they listened. Even when nothing Yan Hua said was intelligible, they tried to (and miraculously did) understand her. A grunt to Frog was, to the women, a story about love. A groan was a poem about betrayal. And a movement of the legs caused the women to say "There, there" in maternal tones. Like a chorus, they moaned when Yan Hua had to moan, cried out when Yan Hua had to cry out. Then, when Yan Hua started having nightmares, they closed their eyes and prayed. Not American-prayed. No, this was folk-Chinese praying, the kind the women learned by watching their mothers and grandmothers. Prayers were accompanied by mule-strong massages of the feet. Of the shoulders and the back, until the women's fierce, strong, ugly, kneading fingers made Yan Hua's sickness go away. It took two days and two nights. The whole time, Frog watched from a corner of the room. He sat away from the commotion, feeling excluded, then angry that he was. *What the hell*, he thought, *is all this mumbo-jumbo?* Why did the Snakehead woman tell him his wife had been single? And why did she say Yan Hua was young, normal, and educated? For a second, he considered leaving his wife. Thought about taking her green card money and running far, far away.

But because his heart had already started rambling, he decided to stay.

FIFTEEN

A BOAT APPROACHES THE Rockaway shore. At three in the morning, it's a stain on the horizon, a mark left after slapping a mosquito. But steadily, as the boat jerks forward, the stain grows bigger. Develops shape and color and texture. Squinting through the darkness, a Snakehead gangster sees what the Coast Guard does not. He sees rust staining the outside of the boat. Then barnacles, like pigeon shit, frosting the stern. Afterwards, he sees immigrants, the ones called "cargo" by American journalists, crowding the deck in black coats and black hats. They tremble as the coastline expands, a blurred shape in the night. Laughing before cursing and cursing before praying. The immigrants have been waiting, dreaming of this moment for months. Some of them for years. But suddenly, *finally*, they're here. Thank God they're here. This last prayer is whispered by the Snakehead gangster, who, feeling the relief of a successful business venture, starts dialing a number on his phone. He barks orders into it.

"Come now," he says. "They're here."

The immigrants have begun to disembark. Slowly, cautiously, and one by one, like astronauts on the moon. Used to the jerking movements of the ocean, they find the soft and level beach difficult to walk on. It slants beneath their feet. Sinks them into damp and foreign earth. They discover, quickly, that America is a cold place. That their jackets are inadequate, and that the wind, in October, is relentless. It pierces through the skin to cause pain in the bones. A pain that feels, strangely enough, like burning. But the immigrants don't have to suffer long, because their smugglers—the ones who helped them to steal across the ocean—are pointing to the road above the beach. There are lights there, running faintly, from yellow to dull white. Panic moves through the crowd and the immigrants dart for the bushes.

But it's not the police.

It's the vans, buses, and cars the Snakehead gangster has chartered.

He herds the immigrants, directs them into dirty seats, and pays the smugglers their smuggling fee. The captain of the boat will get his share, as will other members of the crew. The immigrants watch the transactions through the windows. A few joke about the amount of money passing from hand to hand, but most remain silent. Stern-looking and afraid, they complete the final leg of their journey without once letting their guards down. *You'll be ruined if you're not careful*, one immigrant thinks. He has a round and shaved head, square albeit feminine features, and, to the amusement of his companions, a numerical name. Old Second. Beside him is his wife, Bao Mei, asleep or pretending to be, her head knocking against the window. She mutters words in the crooked darkness of the car as the driver takes them to Chinatown.

To East Broadway, to home.

THE ELDRIDGE STREET HOTEL IS A RESTAURANT AND A SA-
lon, a gambling parlor and a church. It's everything but a home, and
the new immigrants who stay there, paying six dollars a night for
mattress space, are eager to line their pockets with money. It's what
they've come to America for. Not just a little money, but lots of
it, the easy kind, too. Tired of wielding shovels and sledgehammers,
the immigrants search for jobs where the heaviest tool is a wok.
They long to feel sneakers instead of work boots on their feet.
Breathe fan-cooled air instead of dust under a white-hot summer
sun. To that end, they've been pestering the clerks at the Chinatown
job agencies. There are two on Eldridge Street: one with a sign full
of Chinese characters, the other with barely anything to announce
its presence. Just steps and the men waiting on it.

One of whom is Old Second.

He's been in New York three days, and the shock of the city's
filth has fallen like a stone into his mind's heart. He can't believe that
people call the Eldridge Street Hotel home. A building without
numbers or a mailbox. Inside, there are rooms of men whispering
about jobs, and children lonely for their garment factory mothers.
Rats rummage through the trash, chewing on bones and used nap-
kins, while mice drown noiselessly in the sinks. The bathroom—
airless and unwashed—is infested with ants. Roaches, too. The
too-large kind with veiny wings and a clicking sound when you
chase them. The only decent room is the one the managers call the
"parlor." Set up like a place of worship, with statues of gods staring
down from wooden mantels, the parlor has become, over the years,
a banquet hall for weddings and birthday parties. Which explains

the noise, and sometimes the smell. Of Marlboro smoke and ladies' perfume, alcohol and—

"Lobster," Bao Mei whispers to Old Second. "I smell lobster in the parlor room."

"Lobster? Who the hell's eating lobster?"

"Keep your voice down," Bao Mei says.

The excitement in her eyes contradicts the volume of her voice: quiet as a tiptoeing child. It's their third evening in America, and Bao Mei sits with her husband in a shared bunk bed. The room they sleep in is used by a dozen others in their situation. Luckless and work-hungry immigrants who visit the job agencies every morning and return in the afternoons with false optimism. With jokes and downcast eyes, they ask the hotel managers for one day, just one more, to find work. After which they'll disappear like the lucky others: with plaid duffel bags, a spring in their step, and the entire world dripping from their lips. *Come find me in Philadelphia*, they'll say. Or, *If you ever need a bed, come to Syracuse*. Place names get jumbled in village accents. And yet the breath behind them is sweet. "I'll be a dishwasher in Cherry Hill," one immigrant says, causing the others to go mad with envy. "I'm going to Boston," another immigrant adds, and the room dampens with the love-sweat of a groom dancing on his wedding night.

It's in this atmosphere, of people coming and going, of jealousy, envy, and love, that Bao Mei tells Old Second about the lobster stench. They've moved downstairs and are watching the festivities from beyond the parlor's door. Inside, there's music and the oily laughter of city folks—their bodies draped in luxury. The kind that's known and revered by the hotel's new immigrants, who think nothing of wearing a T-shirt to a wedding. Or jeans, for that matter. "Because it's Armani," they say, paying dust to the Exchange.

Because it's Tommy Hilfiger, Banana Republic, or Abercrombie. Sandals become wedding attire when they're paired with polo riders. As do baseball caps with grease stains on the brim. Torn jeans look brand-new when tucked under Gucci belts, and the ugliest arms in the room are seductive when Coach bags dangle from their shoulders. They don't dangle for long, though, because this isn't a walking-and-talking event. No, it's a wedding banquet, and an announcement from the emcee informs everyone that they should—must—sit down.

Because nobody wants to miss the food, do they? Cold-plate beef followed by lobster salad followed by ten-dollars-a-pound abalone. Everything's served family-style, and the *don't talk to me* waiters pay zero attention to the sneaky guests. Some of whom take, along with seconds, the tenderest parts of the fish. The meatiest cuts of the "filet mignon" (which, because this is a Fuzhounese wedding, is neither fileted nor mignoned). Meanwhile, because the groom has tacky tastes, a magician performs cheap tricks on a tiny stage. Mid-priced wines disappear into brown paper bags before reappearing on the tables of clapping guests. They ignore the amateur singers who perform next, and snicker with quiet enthusiasm when the bride enters the room. At which point the gossip begins.

"Isn't that So-and-So's daughter?"

"You mean Little Amy? Because it's not. This girl's thinner."

"I hear the bride has a husband back home. In Tingjiang . . ."

"You call that useless drunk of hers a husband?"

"Look, look! You can see the tags on her jewelry."

"Or maybe that *is* Little Amy . . ."

"It's a shame when folks pretend to live beyond their means."

"Oh, look, an Armani suit!"

"You know, I'd rent jewelry for my wedding, too. What can owning a gold bracelet do? Clothe my kids? Put food on my table?"

The groom asks the bride to dance. They do so poorly, laughing the entire time, stepping on each other's feet (but not caring about it), while camera flashes illuminate their sweaty, made-up faces. They change costumes and share vows with each other. The groom reading off a piece of paper; the bride, having no education, speaking from the heart. Tearfully. Then giggling, while Old Second and Bao Mei listen from right outside the door. It's their first time witnessing luxury in America, and they are stunned by the richness of the food, the guests, the room itself. All of it is Fuzhounese, like them. The event's excess annoys Bao Mei (who leaves, huffing and puffing), but Old Second is left slack-jawed with awe. Even though he's forbidden to enter the parlor, it allows him to imagine a light for his future. One similar in its tacky, god-defying opulence. Because who wouldn't want a celebration where your friends are, afterwards, puking in the streets? Not only from drinking, but from their ability to lose themselves in the luxury? The fun?

The selves they lose aren't nothing, either.

These are selves that used to work as laborers in China. Selves that crushed stones for pocket change that, back then, wasn't called pocket change. It was food on the table and clothes for small children. A roof over their heads and formula for new mothers. More colloquially, it was called life. But when life in the village wasn't enough, the laborers had to leave for America. Some on boats, others on planes, all with fake documents and new names. Some folks died while others were jailed or sent back to China. The ones who survived are here now: laughing, joking, and taking bites out of the food Old Second will later steal from the waiters.

Old Second, who hopes to sit at his own banquet table one day.

But before that happens, he has to visit the job agencies. Before that happens, he has to count the final dollars in his pockets, eat leftover noodles out of plastic bags, and learn to pronounce the names of impossibly distant American cities. Like Philadelphia. Like Syracuse. Like, when Old Second gets his job placement, Parsippany.

HE WAS OFFERED THE POSITION TWO DAYS AFTER THE BANquet. Nothing special: He'll be a prep cook in a Chinese restaurant in New Jersey. And while he waits for the bus that'll whisk him away, he recalls, with the sudden shock of a nightmare, the woman he saw in the parlor room. He thinks about her familiar and quietly simmering face. Like a temple goddess staring down at her worshippers, her gentle, faraway expressions seemed to mask a thousand meanings. Secrets and perhaps hideous intentions. Old Second wonders if it's possible that this woman, whose face was somehow always turned away or slanted in profile, is the person he's thinking of. He would've followed her, but when he took a step forward, a man named Kevin stopped him.

And asked if he could spare a cigarette.

SIXTEEN

YAN HUA'S SEVENTH home, Apartment 4A, was haunted. Women walked in and felt shivers, like insects, crawling up and down their arms. They scratched without knowing why, bled from sores that opened, then closed, with scabs darker than coal. Children refused to enter without holding the comforting hand of a mother. Babies cried; fetuses kicked. And one day, when a frightened yellow cat entered the building—nobody knew how— walking up the four flights of stairs to reach 4A, it yowled: a sound like metal scraping against metal. A minute later, the cat was dead.

There was a wound on its belly. A large gash that was festering when Yan Hua, in her pea jacket and scarf, opened the door with Little Amy. They moved into Apartment 4A with May and their respective husbands, sharing a bathroom and a kitchen, and worked in Brooklyn Chinatown at a garment factory. Late for work, the two women stared at the cat bleeding on their doorstep before shouting curses at Frog.

"My God," Little Amy said, "what's wrong with this place?"

Yan Hua returned with Frog, a garbage bag, and plastic gloves. He removed the cat with his face scrunched like tissue paper while Yan Hua considered the events of the past year. Two days after she lied about beating Old Second, she started to have strange dreams. She forgot them when she woke up, but their textures returned over the course of several days. Three weeks ago, she walked past May's room and heard arguing. Yan Hua couldn't make out the words (May and Kevin were whispering), but the whispers were like hushed screaming. The next morning, when she saw May leaving the house in a parka and a scarf, she remembered the dream she'd had: of herself raising a hand to strike someone.

"What are you doing?" Little Amy asked. "It's sixty-five degrees. You'll sweat to death."

"I'm fine," May said. She didn't take her scarf off, and her voice sounded like a stuffed pipe. "I'm sensitive to the cold."

This morning, staring at the cat, at Frog disposing of the thing in his sweatpants and house shoes, Yan Hua recalled a more familiar dream. She experienced it like a patron at a movie theater because the dream featured, instead of her, Shun-Er and the man he loved. They were standing outside an old cinema while a crowd of police arrived, brandishing batons, iron poles, knives, and sharp teeth. An itching sensation appeared on Yan Hua's wrist, and she scratched it. Hard and then harder, while Little Amy spoke.

"We have to leave this place. Forget the cheap rent. It's *dirty*." She said this last word in dialect, and meant dirty as in tainted with spirits, not dirty as in filthy.

"We signed a lease," Yan Hua said. "Is May staying in again?"

"Kevin says she's tired."

They waved goodbye to Frog, walked down the stairs, and shivered.

"I think her husband hits her," Yan Hua said.

"I *know* he hits her. That fucker." Little Amy leapt across a puddle. "I'll confront him tonight. I've had several bones to pick for a while. The man never washes his dishes, he never puts the toilet seat up, he never . . ."

She continued complaining on the subway platform, on the train, and upon entering the garment factory. It was a large and dark place with opaque windows, many rooms, and tables illuminated by weak overhead lights. The women sat on cushioned stools, squinting their eyes as they sewed. Some brought along their children, who slept for hours on the floor, or who woke up and played tic-tac-toe. Yan Hua and Little Amy worked in a different room, better lit, and they stood on their feet all day, folding nurses' scrubs, then packaging them in plastic. Like everyone else, they were paid at a piece rate. And, like everyone else, they spent the bulk of their work hours gossiping. No topic was forbidden except that of unionizing, or of the strikers who continued to show up with signs and loudspeakers.

"I wouldn't allow a man to put his hands on me," Little Amy said. "I'd kill the bastard."

"Calm down, you've been going on about this for hours."

"Easy for you to say. Your husband's not a son-of-a-bitch."

"You don't know him," Yan Hua said. "And it doesn't seem like yours is one, either."

"That's because you don't see him that often."

Little Amy married her husband in September, against Big Amy's wishes. Like many Fuzhounese men, he worked somewhere outside the city, at a takeout restaurant in Connecticut. He lived with his boss in an apartment crammed with all the other workers and took, for his room, a fifty-dollar cut in pay. His name was Lu something—Yan Hua couldn't remember—and he came home once every two months to give Little Amy his earnings.

"You don't see him," Little Amy continued, "but every time he comes home, there's evil in his mouth. Says I'm cheating on him, that there's two dogs in this apartment, two dogs ready to fight over a bone."

"Two dogs?" Yan Hua was amused. "You mean Frog? And Kevin?"

"Yeah. I told him to talk to you if he's so concerned. And don't get me started on that bone comment." She grabbed her belly, jiggled it. "I'm telling you. It's our apartment. There's evil there."

"Not more than anywhere else. I think it's because of the men."

"He didn't used to be jealous like that. After we first met, when we lived in the motel, he'd let me run around like a madwoman, no questions asked. Now I miss *one* phone call and he threatens to come home with raised fists. Not to hit me, though. He wouldn't dare."

"That's what happens after marriage," Yan Hua said.

They worked for a while in silence, and then their voices returned. Life was like that in the factories. People spoke, then worked, spoke, then worked. Eventually, Little Amy brought up Big Amy, who had suffered a nervous breakdown and moved to Chicago. She managed a restaurant with her husband now and was the mother of two kids. Afterwards, when the ground began to shift, rumbling with laughter and the lunch-hour foot traffic, both women stayed to fold one more garment—just one more—and talk. It was comforting to hear themselves in the packaging room, full of plastic and chemical smells, comforting to know they'd earn an extra dollar by ignoring their urges. The smells, too, reminded them of childhood. Of the factories in Fuzhou, where similar work was done by girls scrawnier than twigs. For a moment, the past returned: Yan Hua told Little Amy she used to work at a pants factory in Mawei, and that she'd quit school to sew buttons onto jeans.

"I was fifteen when they hired me. Back then, the managers took anyone with hands."

"May told me the same thing. Except she, I believe, was hired at twelve."

"We weren't women yet, but we were treated like women. My mother married me off to my first husband at nineteen."

"My mother tried to do the same. It was either a husband or America."

"You chose America? How old were you?"

"No, I was stupid and chose the husband. But he was a shit and I ended up here anyway."

They laughed.

Yan Hua started talking about Shun-Er. She described him with imprecise words, imprecise motions, and hid the fear (or was it hope?) that his spirit was connected to her recent dreams. Sometimes she saw images of him in Apartment 4A. In the mirror at night when the lights flickered, in the distorted reflection of a tea kettle, in Kevin's face when he kissed May. *Maybe the apartment is haunted*, Yan Hua thought. Yet it was also cheap. At $200 a month per couple, the apartment was the only thing Yan Hua could afford. Besides: She'd already moved six times, and there was the lease to consider—the lease with six months left on it, and thirteen days after that.

"Let's go to lunch," Little Amy said. "I'm getting a headache. The smells," she said, gesturing toward the packages on her table. "One can only take so much at a time."

"You go on ahead. I'll work on a few more."

"Oh?" Little Amy leaned forward with a mischievous smile.

"What are you saving up for, Yan? A scarf, a handbag, a new jacket?"

"Just in case May needs it. I'm worried for her." Yan Hua paused. "I'm worried she won't make this month's rent."

WHEN THEY RETURNED, APARTMENT 4A WAS GLOWING WITH a dim and malevolent light. The door was open, and traces of the morning's cat remained. A streak of blood lay like marbling on the floor, leading to a clump of matted fur. And inside the fur, when Yan Hua stooped to pick it up, was the sound of yowling. Painful, deep-from-the-heart *how can I go on like this?* yowling. She'd learn later that it was May, sobbing in their kitchen. The lights were off except the one attached to the stove, and her skin, under the glow, resembled that of a tree. Honey-colored and lined with misery. Deep, uncontrolled misery. It took a while for Yan Hua to understand what May was saying. She listened while Little Amy moved around, frightened and shouting.

Something had happened. The apartment was charged with an odd energy, and every glance around its rooms revealed a new and malicious detail. Dead roaches in the corners. Infestations of wing-less black ants. A stain caused by water thrown against a wall, its shape like that of a malnourished body.

"Get out!" Little Amy cried. "Go fuck around somewhere else, whatever you are!"

Yan Hua closed the door, frightened that the neighbors could hear. She checked her bedroom, but nobody was inside—Frog was working late at his cousin's noodle shop.

"Get out!" Little Amy cried again. "Go haunt someplace else!"

"Stop it," May cried, "stop it, come back, stop it!"

"What are you talking about?" Yan Hua asked. "May, calm down. What happened?"

Kevin was gone. That was what happened. Fled, this afternoon, because the reality of his life was leaking like water from a cracked jug. Yan Hua listened to May while Little Amy straightened up the apartment. She wasn't anxious about the apartment's energy anymore, but the idea of there being a presence in 4A settled like heavy food in her stomach. Yan Hua distracted herself from this feeling by searching May's body for answers. To her surprise, there were no signs of fighting. There weren't marks on her arms, her neck, her face, or even her legs.

"He didn't hit you, did he?"

"No," May moaned. "He didn't hit me."

But he had hurt her in a deeper way. Three weeks ago, the same night Yan Hua dreamed of her hand raised to strike someone, May discovered a man's underwear (not Kevin's) stuffed between her mattress and the crates she called a box spring. The briefs were small, yellow, dusty, and soiled. Kevin said he had no idea who the underwear belonged to and tried, instead, to pin it on May. He punched her: a light punch, tinged with a smile that betrayed the secret in his eyes. May forgot the punch but remembered the smile, because it dared her to seek its hidden source. The next day, she snuck home from the factory when 4A should've been empty. Before entering, she heard two voices on the landing. She smelled the stench of grease soaked on a napkin, and something else. Something she recognized but didn't receive from her husband.

Desire.

Desire, certain as the key she pushed into the lock. When the door opened, and she realized that the two voices belonged to one person, that it was her husband speaking in two tones and for two people—the other a thin man pinned under his weight—she laughed. Cackled with hot tears rolling down her tight, red cheeks. The sight was comical. Her husband's muscular body atop his lover's slender one, resembling an ant lifting a crumb, and the whole time he chanted, breathed out a performance meant for two. And when the sight stopped being funny, when it transformed itself into the horror that'd chain May in her bed for twenty days, she screamed. Became a person other than herself. May, who was usually quiet, who put CDs into a Discman and sang to herself, who learned how to read by connecting pictures to words in newspapers, who missed her siblings more than her parents, and who was too ashamed of her penmanship to write letters to China—she'd only reached junior high—she saw her husband fucking another man and became possessed. She discovered her ability to be jealous. Although she didn't love Kevin, she didn't want him loving anyone else, and she didn't want anyone loving him, either. She chased her husband's lover out, cursing. And she vowed never to leave the apartment, to never let this (whatever this was) happen again.

"Calm down," Kevin said. "I can explain."

"So do it! Explain."

But he didn't. In fact, he acted as though nothing had happened, as though what May saw was only a dream. For twenty days, he played along with her, gave into her jealousies, and came home straight, sometimes early, from work. He gave her his phone. He let her smell his body; he kissed her, held her, made love to her, argued with her. But none of it was enough. May knew the truth now. She watched the darkness under his eyes spread like mold. And then came the dreams: of men kissing in a dark theater, of police beating them, of storm clouds thick as toast. Descending, descending, descending.

Yan Hua felt a shock when she heard this part of May's story. What May described were her dreams—the ones Yan Hua attributed to Shun-Er—and not only were they her dreams; they were her history. Yan Hua tried to get May to return to this part of her story; she tried to get May to elaborate. But May had already moved on and was speaking in quiet, furious tones.

"He left today, in the afternoon," she said. Tears rolled down her cheeks, but she was no longer sobbing. "He packed his suitcase while I watched. I was too tired to do anything."

"Fuck him," Little Amy said. "A man's just a man."

"I watched him pack and listened as he opened the door. I listened as he thumped down the stairs. I listened as the apartment wept."

"He's just a man," Little Amy repeated.

"He's not a man, he's a shit. Nothing but a shit. Dog shit, baby shit, he's worse than shit, he's a fag. Can you believe it?" May started laughing. "Me, marrying a fag. Can you believe it?"

"It's this apartment," Little Amy said. "The place is filthy. I've been telling Yan Hua all day. We have to get out of here."

"You say that like it's easy," Yan Hua said, her anger rising. "You say 'leave' like we didn't sign a lease. You say 'leave' like there's another apartment—large as this, *cheap* as this. What about our security deposit? Our rent? We can barely afford one rent, you want us to pay another?"

"Can you believe it?" May said again.

The light above the stove began to flicker. From the window, Yan Hua heard the noise of wind and heavy traffic. She looked around at their apartment, at the cheap, ordinary, overused, and fallen-apart furniture. Little Amy didn't say anything, so Yan Hua put a hand on her shoulder. Maybe she'd been mean in her outburst. Yet she'd spoken the truth. Apartment 4A, haunted or not, evil or not, was theirs for the remainder of the year. Afterwards, they'd reevaluate. Afterwards, they'd see if some other cheap and un-haunted place would take them: three women who refused to love their husbands, and who instead chose to love each other.

"What are you going to do now?" Little Amy asked. She said "you," but from the tone of her voice, Yan Hua knew she meant "we."

"I want to hurt him," May said. "I want to hurt him really bad."

"You should come back to work," Yan Hua said.

"I'll go to his restaurant and tell everyone about the kind of person he is. The kind of person he fucks."

"Come back to work," Yan Hua said. She thought about Shun-Er, about her past, about how that past seemed to be pressing against May's present. "It'll pass. Everything will pass."

MAY NEVER SPOKE OF HER HUSBAND'S DEPARTURE AGAIN. After he left, she worked hard to forget her outbursts in Apartment 4A. Any references to them were met with silence and a look as vicious as animal teeth. Yan Hua, wanting to learn more about May's dreams, was rebuffed and yelled at, even threatened. All she wanted was confirmation of their shared dream. To calm the itch in her heart, which grew into fear about May experiencing the same things she did and therefore discovering her secret. In the end, Yan Hua decided to give up. Her fourth attempt at asking caused May to break down into angry tears.

"You can't keep bothering her about this," Little Amy told Yan Hua. "It's not right. Her wounds are fresh and you're sprinkling salt on them."

"But I need to talk about her dreams," Yan Hua said.

"Why do you care? Are you . . . ?" Little Amy put her palm on Yan Hua's forehead. "Don't tell me you're having one of those spiritual awakenings!"

"No! Not in a hundred years. It's just weird that her dreams and mine are the same."

"Is it? As children, my sisters and I often shared the same dreams. Butterflies turning into spiders, butterflies turning into blood. One morning, all three of us ran for the mirror because we had a nightmare about our teeth falling out. It's inevitable when girls live together."

"You didn't dream our dreams, though? Of men kissing in a theater, and police coming to beat them?"

"Not that I recall."

Frog shared Little Amy's sentiments. At thirty-eight, he was a tired-looking man with wrinkled skin from the neck up, smooth skin from the neck down. His biceps were the shape of beer mugs, like Popeye's, and his joints suffered from flares of arthritis. One night, while he slapped Tiger Balm into his left arm with a rolling pin (people from his village said this relieved muscle pain), Yan Hua told him her theory about her and May's dreams. She said that they were a product of their shared experiences. They'd both married men who loved men and were haunted by the feelings those men had.

"Something about this apartment brings out those feelings," Yan Hua said. "It's why the atmosphere is sad here all the time. Not just sad—lonely. A loneliness thicker than grief."

Frog listened with skepticism. He winced every time he brought the rolling pin down on his arm. Despite his long shower, he smelled of the noodle shop. A stench of onions, cabbages, ground meat, and grease.

"You've been talking to Little Amy too much," Frog said.

"I'm not saying we move from here. The haunting doesn't bother me that much."

"And I'm saying this place isn't haunted. Who's haunting it? Last I checked, May's husband is still alive."

"My husband isn't."

"Ex-husband. And he died in China. Ghosts don't immigrate like people do."

But the past does, Yan Hua thought. It's followed her. To America, to Chinatown, to Apartment 4A. The dreams were proof of that. She launched into a long story that Frog had heard many times already: about Shun-Er, the protest, his homosexuality, and the cinema where gay men cruised.

"My theory is that my dreams aren't dreams at all. They're a window into the past. Not my past, but my husband's. My ex-husband's, sorry."

"So why's May having these dreams? 'Cause Kevin's gay?"

"I don't know," Yan Hua said, softly. "That's the one thing I can't figure out. Every time I try to ask her about it, she gets mad."

"Give it up," Frog said. "They're dreams. That's what I think. Dreams are just that. Dreams."

"I could ask Kevin."

"Don't even think about it. I don't want to deal with the drama, and I guarantee that you don't, either."

"Just a thought."

"You've been having too many of those lately. Come on, I'm tired. Let's go to bed."

But Frog was lying. He wasn't tired. The moment the lights turned off, he started pressing his sex against Yan Hua's legs. It was solid and nasty-feeling, and Yan Hua didn't react when she felt his mouth against her neck and shoulders. Her mind was elsewhere. She pictured the dead yellow cat in front of her apartment. It wasn't a random cat. Earlier that week, she'd learned from Little Amy that it was a cat May's husband had befriended. He fed it when he came home from work. Little Amy saw him once: how he made kissing noises at the cat, and how he rubbed its head with his hands, which were whiter than bar soap.

"I should've known he was a fag right then and there," Little Amy said. "The sounds he was making. And his hands. Whoever saw a man with hands like that?"

SEVENTEEN

FOR MAY, THE humiliation sat between the pages of the newspaper she clenched. Her sweat-soaked fingers dampened the paper until the ink blurred and the pictures (of men in suits, men in handcuffs, men on smuggling boats) leaked beyond the edges. The words ran together, becoming smudged and even beautiful when they transferred their blackness onto her hands. Which, because of her years of touching fabric, of threads chafing against baby-soft palms, were covered in cuts. A slice here and a slice there, each one smeared with winter cream. She used to love them, her hands. Aside from the cuts, they looked nothing like the rough, callused, and mean things factory workers hid beneath their gloves. May especially liked the slender nails that sat on the tips of her fingers. Called "piano fingers" by city folks, she used them to trace lines over the pictures in newspapers. Over the headlines, too, and the stories underneath, as May's mouth slowly twisted into a smile.

Why? Because the world was a filthy, frightening, and dangerous place. And she, despite the cards that were dealt her, had managed to avoid it. All of it: the burglars, the adulterers, the drug abusers, even the scheming politicians.

"Look," she used to say. She'd point at a picture of a child-killer and tsk through smiling lips. "Isn't it sad how violent the world is? How dark and evil?"

What at first sounded like a lament was, if you listened closely, a chilling and childlike enjoyment of the world's myriad misfortunes. May marveled at them. She read newspapers and was thankful that her life wasn't mean enough to appear in print. Believing that politics was for men, and therefore boring, she didn't care that cops were firing at civilians in such-and-such part of China. She fluttered her eyes at the burning theater in Karamay, then scratched her nose at the mothers who vanished for protesting the one-child policy. Rural women were sterilized for daring to want boys, and May did nothing but tsk and thank God. Every morning with a bite of her pork sung bun, a sip of her too-hot tea. Hers was a hard-knock life, and $6.50 an hour was nothing to write home about. But it was enough: enough for her to find pleasure in the evil she didn't have to witness.

For instance: the running aground of a fishing boat that smuggled Chinese laborers to America. There were stories about it in every newspaper in Chinatown, and for seven straight mornings, May bought one to search for misfortune. Day after day, the number of drowned laborers increased. The first morning it was one. The second, three. By the third, it was ten. The news that knocked others off their feet did nothing but bring a smile to May's lips. One she had to hide by clapping a hand against her mouth, muffling the pigeon-coo sympathy in her words.

One time, while May was eating lunch at the garment factory, she'd said that she didn't understand why the laborers had to come to America, "especially in that foolish, dangerous way."

"Why risk your life for some coins in your pocket?" she added. "A green card and a bundle of cash?"

Yan Hua bristled while Little Amy asked: "Didn't you get here the same way?"

"No, I came on a plane. The Snakehead arranged my passage."

"Were you jailed?"

"For a week and they released me. But that's neither here nor there."

"*That's neither here nor there*," Yan Hua said.

Not knowing how to react to her friend's words, Yan Hua mimicked her. May's ignorance was the worst kind possible: that which belonged to the lucky. The god-chosen and the few. Respectable now, and earning enough to feed herself, May had forgotten that she'd ever suffered, that her first days in America were spent pacing a room too small to contain her mind. She sang—did anybody know that? Back in China, back in that sprawling, seaside village called Stone. And the elders who lived there could no doubt remember— when they closed their gummy, narrowed-to-slits eyes—the young girl with the sweeter-than-syrup voice. Who wore dresses (how did her parents get the money?) with holes in them, and threads hanging off the sleeves (oh, that's how), and whose skin was pitted by genetics and too-harsh soap. She sang at schools and in the park, and once, on National Day, she was invited to perform with nineteen others at a gala her family was too poor to attend. They stood on the margins of the event, struggling to hear her voice.

"Seven days in jail versus seventy on a boat," May said. "An airless, rocking one. Which would you choose?"

Yan Hua stuck her lower lip out. "That's not the point, May. Some folks don't have the luxury of choosing. Frog didn't and neither did Little Amy. You think they wanted to come to America on a boat?"

"All right, all right, let's get back to work," Little Amy said.

"I'm just talking. I don't know why she's mad," May said.

"I'm not mad. I just don't like the shit that comes out of your mouth."

"What shit?"

"Ten people drowned. And two hundred more are in jail. They're scared to death, probably, with all those cameras in their faces. All those journalists speaking English, hungry to capture their shame. But instead of keeping your mouth shut, you start running it. 'Oh, I'd never come here on a boat. Oh, if it were me, I'd take a plane!'"

May opened her mouth, then closed it. When she opened it a second time, the shadow of a giggle appeared: catlike and ready to scratch the women around her. But she bit it. Once again, May had to clap a hand against her mouth. And once again, she had to cough to hide the laughter bubbling like soda gas in her throat. Why fight? Why die on a hill she didn't care about? Unlike the people in the newspapers, May was a respectable woman. A self-made one who was prideful enough to start a fight, but not stubborn enough to win it. So, she apologized. But the sneaky expression on her face suggested that she wouldn't forget this. Not for a long, long, long time.

She picked up yesterday's newspaper, opened it to a random page. And thought, to comfort herself: *At least my life isn't like that of the low-down people on these pages.*

Until, of course, it was.

MAN POISONS WIFE. WIFE STRANGLES HUSBAND. BOY MUR-
dered while grandmother sleeps. Actor loses fight to cancer. Con-
gressman embezzles money. Tennis player fined for doping. To
these, May added her own tragedy: Local woman marries faggot.
When her mind was clear, and she was able to leave her room, her
breakup turned into a source of humor. She imagined headlines for
herself, pictured her face in the pages of *The Daily*. A walnut-
colored woman with coal-black eyes and a nose shaped like a fist.
One that May, since childhood, was instructed to pinch so that it
might look smaller, more elegant. She did so now, muttering in a
slanted voice that people mistook for a warning. In reality, she was
repeating the headlines she'd created for herself: "Sissy cheats on
wife. Annoying roommates worry. Woman locks self in room." On
and on, an endless stream of jokes that May laughed at. Inwardly. A
thin, nasal, and dry-as-bones laughter that reminded her of Yan
Hua's initial misery in America.

May didn't want to be like that. No, never like that. She was a
proper and respectable woman, and even after losing her job, even
after her outburst at the discovery of Kevin's betrayal, she was
working to retrieve the broken pieces of herself. Some manifested as
crumbs on the floor. Others were hidden in the box of Argo she kept
in her desk drawer. May called the cornstarch, along with the floor
crumbs, her dinner. Too depressed to cook, she mixed chicken powder into the starch and ate it by the spoonful. Ravenously and in
secret. The mixture was delicious, but she considered the act shame-
ful, even if it was keeping her alive. Comforting her (she liked how
the starch dissolved into goo on her tongue) and filling her belly.

She understood, now, the cravings the women in her family developed whenever they grieved. May's mother, the moment somebody died, would run to the river to eat clay. May's grandmother ate charcoal, and her great-grandmother, also named May, liked to lick the burnt edges of charred rice. Decades later, May repeated their actions in her bedroom, thinking and trying to collect herself.

She wondered if this was how Kevin felt when he forced himself to hide his man-love. Did he neglect to brush his teeth like May did? And did he skip meals out of laziness, shaking like a dog the entire time, a baby's rattle, while his mind forgot respectability and (yes) starvation, too? May walked to her window, opened it. The broken screen was patched with masking tape. Dried-out husks of fruit flies clung to the sticky side. Beyond the window was Chinatown. East Broadway with its lackluster reproductions of the country May left behind. There was a market street packed with fish- and fruit-mongers. Behind them hid a group of stores so secretive, they lacked names. Not that they needed them. Locals could identify each by sight and gossip. Someone might ask, "I have a toothache, can you recommend a dentist to me?" and nine times out of ten, they'd be directed to the secret clinic on Eldridge Street. The one that operated out of a holy woman's kitchen, and which, when night fell, transformed into a gambling parlor where immigrants played cards.

May hated those places. She also hated the motels and the job agencies, the churches where folks did everything but pray. But worst of all were the nail salons where unspeakable women did unspeakable things. Like swinging their hips too fast to pop music. Or wearing shirts that revealed a thimble's length of cleavage (which was too much for May, far too much). The sight of these women used to make May sneer. But the memory of them, and the intrusive thought that she was the same, sent shivers down her spine. Shivers that made her cry out and wonder who she was. Because the evil of their appearance no longer bothered her. People had warned her about America. They had warned her about the drugs, the pickpockets, the loose women, the police. But they failed to warn May about the way she'd lose her sense of identity. They failed to tell her that, one day, when her feet touched the pavement, and music was blaring out of lowered car windows, she'd skip instead of walk. Kick her legs to the beat that told her to forget the May who once watched her scorned family waiting outside a festival's gates.

"No, you must be mistaken," she said to people who claimed to know her. People whose names she remembered, whose parents she'd said hello to as a girl walking home from the fields.

"Aren't you Fishball's daughter? Fishball from Stone Village?"

"No," May lied. "I grew up in Fuzhou."

"You look just like her. Like Fishball's daughter."

"Well, I'm not." And she'd have to bite down hard on her tongue to keep from uttering, like it was her last salvation, the name of the person she knew. Whose body she remembered and longed for. Not for the purpose of sentiment, since she hated any association with her hard-knock past. No. May simply wanted to savor the act of remembering itself.

Who am I? May wondered. *Am I this May, or am I that one?*

She held her hands out. They were pretty despite the cuts on them, the ruined nail beds, and the faint blotch of Argo dusting the knuckle of her left pinky. Licking it, she saw that more had spilled onto the clothes that she now used as rags on the floor. Around her were signs of the diligent and proud May she used to be. One who bought picture frames for the stock photos within them (from a dog in a field to a black-and-white lily of the valley), and who hung them on her spotless, nail-filled walls. When *that* May first moved into Apartment 4A, the walls looked like a chain-smoker's teeth. But she washed them, erasing the stains with soap and rough rags. Afterwards she ordered Kevin to hammer nails into the clean walls while she prettied up the dresser, the end tables, the chairs, the mattress. With fabric stolen from the garment factory, she fashioned a bed skirt, then hung it around the crates she had pushed together as a frame. She went to the dollar store with Yan Hua to purchase tablecloths to drape over the plastic furniture. The result was a clean room: the kind strangers could feel comfortable in, despite the lack of amenities. There were no signs, even now, of the gross secret her husband tried to hide. But when May (which one?) started to hear footsteps in the foyer, she panicked. Moved quickly to hide the one thing she no longer could.

The truth.

"May," Yan Hua said, from the other side of the door. "May, have you eaten yet?"

Little Amy was there, too. May could hear her whispering and feeding Yan Hua questions. Then Little Amy jumped in. In a steady voice, she chatted about the weather (bad), work at the factory (worse), and current events (catastrophic). Did May know that the police were targeting Fuzhounese immigrants? And that the laborers who came on "that boat" last year, the one that ran aground in June, remained in prison, after all this time? Next week it would be a year and twenty-six days, and news about the disaster still came to the people of East Broadway in flashes. With the frequency of lightning during a storm, they'd hear about deportations. Arrests and stalled court cases. This Snakehead gang member was still at large, that Snakehead gang member was going to trial. Bits and pieces of Chinatown news that Little Amy was obsessed with, her voice a never-ending stream of words. Until, that is, Yan Hua interrupted her.

"C'mon, Amy, she doesn't want to hear that. Not right now."

Yan Hua was right. May didn't. But something about the tone of Yan Hua's voice—something that lurked, playing hide-and-seek behind her teeth—made the down on May's arms bristle. Afterwards the bristle traveled to her shoulders and up her neck, until it parked, finally, in the howling space between her ears. She heard, then, the words that would infuriate her: "Let's leave May alone, she's clearly sick."

"How dare she!" May spat out like venom sucked from an open wound. Weeks later, when her mind was less cloudy, she would realize that the words Yan Hua had spoken weren't so bad. That there was no sting beneath her breath. But now, with the cornstarch frosting her clothes on the floor, and the hunger aches poised to erupt from her body, May could dwell on only one thing. And that one thing was her memory of Yan Hua when she first came to America.

Didn't Yan Hua remember? How she fell into a fever and wouldn't speak for days? How afterwards she trembled and moaned in the motel while May, Little Amy, and Big Amy prayed her back to health? Yan Hua arrived in America a broken woman, and now she acted as though her flaws weren't visible. That she didn't have them at all. But May saw how—when Yan Hua thought people weren't looking—she used to mutter and shake and act a whole goddamned fool.

May shook the lock loose and opened the door. In front of her were her roommates, who were surprised to see her. Little Amy in a shirt too small to hide her belly, Yan Hua in a sweater she'd found on the subway. The latter held an oily brown bag between her hands, one that reeked of chicken, oil, and onion.

"We bought noodles for you."

"From the new place," Little Amy said quickly, "near the mall. They're good."

"I ate already," May said.

"Then save them for later."

"Yan Hua bought them," Little Amy said. "She's rolling in dough these days. The boss man gave her a raise."

"For what?"

"It's not a raise. He doesn't give raises. Even if we work the skin off our bones."

Maybe not to someone like you, May thought.

"Truth is, she's been working during her lunch break. She holds a needle in one hand, a bun in the other. It's really impressive, you should come around to see it."

"So you're working extra hours, then," May said.

"For you," Little Amy said, in a half-joking, half-accusatory voice. "It's all so you can make next month's rent."

"Why don't you come back to work, May?" Yan Hua asked.

May opened her mouth and smelled a dark and cavernous odor, like spoiled milk. She knew the stench well, from childhood. It was that of hunger, of stomach gases rising to the throat. Ashamed, she clamped a hand over her face, and uttered a lie about how she was too busy looking for another job. But the hideous truth that bobbed in May's throat, almost emerging but refusing to come out, was that she'd been fired. That one night, while May was laying out the next day's clothes, she'd gotten a phone call from the factory boss, who said that May wasn't expected to come in anymore. She'd been grieving her divorce for too long and her spot had been filled.

In the howling darkness of her mind, May was able to imagine herself. Her true self: a sick and defiant woman wearing a loose

T-shirt with nothing to support her body. The proud, giggling May she constructed, whom she wore like armor, was no longer visible. And even if she was, all it'd take to banish her was a look from Yan Hua. A flitting, sideways glance at the clothes piled on the floor and the boxes of Argo sitting by the bed. Yes, the illusion that May believed in—that she was somehow different from Yan Hua, different from the people in the newspapers—that illusion would be lost. Today and perhaps forever. But May didn't want to accept that. No, not yet. She closed her eyes, clenched them tight so her tears wouldn't spill out.

They didn't.

EIGHTEEN

LITTLE AMY LEFT May's room without noticing the extent of her friend's hurt. She knew that she was angry, and she could hear pain howling in her sharp and tinny voice. But vengefulness? Wrath? These feelings flew over Little Amy's head like geese migrating south. Or arrows, since they struck the nervous and suddenly tight-chested Yan Hua. It wasn't that Yan Hua was more perceptive, and it wasn't that she could see, in the clutter of May's bedroom, the butcher knife disguising itself as sadness. No, it was more like she remembered the hatred that once struck her, making her dizzy and dangerous and, yes, split down the middle. Like a fallen plate that had to be pieced together. But some days, the glue wouldn't hold. Some days, Yan Hua would look down a staircase and think, sometimes even say out loud, the word "jump." It happened once in the presence of Frog, who heard his wife but pretended not to. The second time it happened, in front of May, both women stopped and stared at each other.

May asked, quietly, "Are you thinking of doing it?"

Then, when Yan Hua didn't respond: "Don't. Not here. You won't die and you'll drown yourself in medical bills."

"I didn't say anything," Yan Hua said.

"Good. Then I didn't hear anything."

A ten-second conversation that Yan Hua forgot, until the next time she fell into her own rifts. This was the phrase she used. She'd gotten it from her father, who believed that all people had tiny holes in them, and shadows beneath the holes. As you got older, the holes lengthened into rifts, and some of them were large enough for you to fall into. At which point you'd say a strange or dangerous word, perform a silly or mysterious action. Yan Hua saying "jump" was a result of her falling into one of these rifts. A small one, insignificant compared to the rift that swallowed her when her husband died. That rift lasted until she came to America, until her friends cured her with contradictory hands: firm yet soft, secular yet holy.

Because she'd experienced a rift herself, Yan Hua was alert to it in others. Like May. Whose cavernous breath made every eye in the room water, and whose hands resembled the cranes of claw machines. There was a jagged break in the nail of her pointer finger, as though someone had taken a bite out of it. There was also a powdery substance that Yan Hua couldn't identify, clumped on the piles of clothes sitting on May's floor. Worried, she decided to ask Little Amy about it; Little Amy, who said:

"Maybe she's snorting cocaine."

"I'm serious," Yan Hua said. "And keep your voice down."

"You're the one shouting."

"Do you think she'll be all right?"

Little Amy was thoughtful for a minute. The two friends were eating dinner in the kitchen of Apartment 4A: a small and messy place that showed signs of a country woman's shrewdness. Tinfoil was wrapped around the gas cookers as well as the stove's control panel. The fridge had no magnets or pictures on it, but the walls were decorated with all sorts of calendars, some of them outdated. The dining table was covered with plastic for easy cleaning, and bamboo coasters held the McDonald's meal that Little Amy shared with Yan Hua. Four McChickens sat between the two women: Yan Hua's without the mayo, Little Amy's with ketchup.

"No. In all honesty, I don't. But we can't help her. The kind of grief she's experiencing—it's stubborn. Not to mention private. Better for us not to interfere. Besides—"

"You have ketchup on your chin."

"Besides, she's paying her rent."

"But she's not eating."

"She might be eating when we're not here."

"The food quantities in the fridge. They're not decreasing."

"Maybe she keeps a stash in her room. We used to do that at the motel, remember?"

Unlike Yan Hua and May, Little Amy was what Fuzhounese people would call a "too-straight" woman. Not too-straight as in heterosexual. She was just direct. Blunt and perhaps a little simple. She saw things as they were and developed a no-nonsense attitude about the drollness of American life. She took it as a given that illegal immigrants would be captured by police and shrugged when hearing about factory workers being mistreated. People who didn't know her said that she had a conservative streak, a meanness that allowed her to ignore the suffering of others. Another strike against her, and this one more serious, was her nonchalant attitude toward religion. Put simply: Little Amy didn't believe in any gods, but she practiced whatever faith was placed before her, the way a child might eat whatever was on their plate. She did it for the convenience and because her husband was a believer. Her family, too, and her friends. And though Yan Hua normally found Little Amy's "rationality" (which seemed more like stubbornness to her) to be irritating, today she was thankful for it. So what if May was a little depressed? They couldn't do anything about it, so why bother worrying?

"Are you asking all these questions," Little Amy asked, "because you're afraid she'll hurt herself?"

"No," Yan Hua lied. Or half lied. In truth, she was afraid that May would end up hurting the people around her. Kevin came to mind, as did his lover, but what if she decided to point her knife's blade at Yan Hua herself? At Frog and Little Amy? May was erratic enough—Yan Hua had known her the longest out of everyone. This was a woman who opened newspapers just to laugh at the misfortune in them. At the evil, too: hard and blunt as a hammer's strike. She sneered at women in hair salons, calling them whores. Yan Hua took a final bite of her McChicken, thought hard for a moment. Chewed and belched while the food settled.

"I don't know what I'm worried about," Yan Hua said. "I have this feeling in my belly. I've had it for days."

"Maybe it's indigestion. Or a stomach bug. Something's been going around the apartment."

"You're feeling sick, too?"

"Sure. But it's nothing serious. I've been taking pills for it, after every meal."

"And that makes you feel better?"

"No. But what else can I do?"

YAN HUA'S FIRST RIFT APPEARED LONG BEFORE SHE SPLIT into two. She'd always been a clever girl, the kind who stuck her nose into gossip without revealing herself. Nonchalance was key. When Shun-Er first disappeared from their apartment, she'd sensed that something was off. A feeling spread from her belly to her chest, which prompted her to follow him. Looking back, she wonders why she did such a silly thing. It wasn't like she was jealous. And she didn't crave, the way a young bride would, the taste of Shun-Er's body. In fact, she treated his body the way she treated any other body she saw on the street: as something to be wary of—until he touched her. Not in a sexual way, but there was tenderness there, and communication: the silent kind that belonged to elderly couples. Perhaps that was what Yan Hua yearned for, and that's why she disguised herself and followed her husband.

No. That wasn't it. Lying in the darkness of Apartment 4A, with Frog snoring beside her and May pacing in another room (Yan Hua could hear the slide-slap of her slippers), she wondered if her trailing was an early sign of the rifts in her. Because why, otherwise, had she disguised herself those nights? She wore Shun-Er's trousers, a loose and shapeless raincoat, and his galoshes. She slicked her hair back and tied it in a ponytail that made her look bald. She took ash from the coal stove, added water, and mixed it into a gray liquid. Then she smeared it on her cheeks in front of the window she used as a mirror. Was this all so she could go unrecognized? Or was it simply to enhance her sense of adventure, the dangerous, deep-down feeling that she was brushing up against something she wasn't meant to witness?

The truth, as they say, was probably somewhere in between. Regardless, the fact remained that Yan Hua was following her husband. Eight meters behind and in disguise, she saw the places he hid from her. The Mawei City Workers' Cinema was one of these places. The night was pitch-black and cloudless the first time she trailed Shun-Er, and she did a double take when he stopped before a building that barely announced its presence. Just some metal shutters blocking a length of what she guessed were windows, a dimly lit doorway, and a sign that was unreadable in the darkness. In front was a dirty alleyway with garbage bags sitting next to electric poles and abandoned chairs on street corners. It was a place people warned you about in low whispers. And Yan Hua, staring at the chairs—she imagined people sitting on them to gamble in the daylight—wondered why her husband had been drawn to a place like this.

The first word that flitted through her mind was "prostitute." Afterwards, "loan shark." Both possibilities were terrible, but their realities made sense to Yan Hua. But when Yan Hua stepped closer, when she walked into the jaundiced light of the building's open door, a feeling took hold of her, a clarity like nothing she'd ever felt. It paralyzed her. Made her wonder why she was here, and what she was searching for. Did she know what she wanted? And was she okay, truly okay, with the consequences of getting it? What if the answer wasn't to her liking? A presence materialized in her mind. A calming, soft-spoken presence that raised the hairs on her back and urged her to turn around. But curiosity enveloped Yan Hua and she walked into the building. Past the hallway with its carpet full of madams' cards, past the office with the shocked woman staring at her from a folding chair. When she got to the entrance of the first screening room, she heard a noise that made her stop and face the woman who was now limping behind her, asking who the hell Yan Hua thought she was.

AWAKE NOW, WIDE AWAKE, SHE SAT UPRIGHT IN BED AND wondered about the sudden noise. Frog was awake, too, and the tenseness of his body, the signal that preceded the love-hungry strokes of his hands, made her feign sleep. She wanted to be alone, to remain with her thoughts for a while longer.

Perhaps it was a rat? The loud, squeaking scurry of one running across the theater's lobby certainly would've raised the gooseflesh on Yan Hua's neck. But no, that couldn't be it. Back then, she wasn't afraid of rats. She had honed that fear in America when she saw a severed, cream-colored tail under a roommate's work boot. A roach was lying next to it, overturned but alive (lazily so—its legs moving in slow circles), and Yan Hua had to remove both with a tissue. One thin enough for her to feel the texture and the twitch of the rat tail in her hand.

"Yan," Frog asked cautiously in the dark. "Yan, are you awake?"

Maybe it was a voice she'd heard. Maybe the woman who worked in the cinema—the one we know to be Bao Mei—maybe she'd said something that wasn't meant to be uttered. Yan Hua felt sick to her stomach. Anxious, too: as anxious as a woman awaiting her pregnancy results. Yan Hua turned away from Frog and released a sigh that made him think she was dreaming. She remembered saying nothing to the woman in her excited state. But the woman had given her an earful, first in an angry register, then in a softer tone. The memory of her gentleness was what made Yan Hua shiver. Because despite the relative innocence of her words—"You shouldn't be here. This place isn't meant for you."—the cadence of her speech made Yan Hua understand that something terrible had happened. Had and *would be* happening. It was the kind of voice you'd use when speaking to someone standing on a ledge. The kind of voice you'd use when a gun was pointed at you, and you had to plead your case. A voice that communicated to Yan Hua that she'd been betrayed by her husband.

It was then that Yan Hua began to lose the meaning of her words. It was then that the rifts in her psyche expanded to the size of potholes. She detached from herself, became a ghost. In the days that followed, when Yan Hua dropped the scissors she was using at work, she reacted as though it was a different Yan Hua who dropped them. Same as when she was talking to her girlfriends, who all spoke about the superficial things twenty-somethings were supposed to. Once, after getting her hair done, she went home and stared in the mirror. Shocked and sobbing, because who—oh God, who?—put these curls on her head? These colors like dead and trampled leaves? Another time, she watched herself enter the office of two city developers in Mawei. These were government men, important and powerful ones, and she watched as she said hello to them. Listened as she explained why she was visiting, busy as the men were: "Hi, my name is . . . I'm here to talk about . . . There's a theater in the old part of town . . ." A nothing-conversation that might not have amounted to anything, had the shorter of the two men, who looked like a jolly Buddha, asked: "Are you talking about the Workers' Cinema?"

"I can't sleep," Frog said. He was speaking louder, trying to wake his wife up. But all he did was interrupt the steady stream of her thoughts, bringing her, with a jerk of the legs, back into the present.

In response, Yan Hua formed a spit bubble with her lips.

"It's May. She keeps pacing in her room. I wish she'd stop."

Frog was lying. The pacing had ended earlier. Right now, at four in the morning, May was quiet. Perhaps a little too quiet. Yan Hua twisted her body to lie on her flank, positioning her neck so that she faced the wall. Her stillness was focused as she listened for movement in May's room. But the only sounds in the apartment were that of her own bedsheets rustling. That and the mutters of her husband. Perhaps the distant buzz of the fridge. Seconds later, she heard a thump. Followed by footsteps and the frantic opening of a door. Frog was sitting up now, and excitement coursed through Yan Hua.

"What's going on?" Frog asked.

He received his answer in the form of Little Amy's voice. Little Amy, who knocked on May's door and asked, practically screaming, if everything was all right in there.

So Little Amy thinks May is too quiet, too, Yan Hua thought.

"What the hell?" Frog shouted.

"It's May," Yan Hua said.

"What's going on with her now?"

"Open the door!" Little Amy shouted. She wasn't knocking anymore; she was banging.

"I have to work in the morning," Frog muttered.

"Why don't you check on what's happening?"

Frog didn't bother answering. He put his pants on, a shirt. Whatever his intentions were, Yan Hua didn't know. Or care. All she could focus on were the scenes her mind conjured. Of May: slumped in her chair with a bottle on the table. Of May: standing on her window ledge, looking at the street and ready to jump. These were gruesome images informed by the violence she saw at the Workers' Cinema, a violence she'd caused. But that was a memory for another time. Because right as Frog was about to exit their room, she heard May's door open.

"What the hell's wrong with you people?" May shouted. "Why won't you let me sleep?"

"Amen," Frog muttered.

He groaned and rifled through his pants for a cigarette. Left his wife to go smoke over the toilet. For that, Yan Hua was grateful. Because now she'd have ten minutes to herself.

Ten minutes to think and remember.

THAT YAN HUA, THE ONE WHO FOLLOWED SHUN-ER EIGHT times in eight months, told city developers that a group of men were planning to block the demolition of the Workers' Cinema. She was an informant: one who spoke in a fugue state, who didn't realize the weight or the significance of her words. Months earlier, she'd come to the men—one tall, the other short—because of a sign glued to her factory's wall. It talked of the alleyway that housed the cinema, and the city's plans to convert that neighborhood into a road. Next to that sign was another one, which complained of the landowners who refused to sell their land. "For the sake of progress," the sign said. "A better Mawei and a better China." The sign looked home-made, but the address on it, in case anyone had "concerns or infor-mation," led to this office. Where there was a watercooler and a crowded fish tank. Large plants with red envelopes hanging from their branches, and a Western-style toilet in the bathroom. A mod-ern yet Chinese-looking office. The first time Yan Hua entered it, she said: "My husband goes there."

When the shorter man cocked his head, she added, suddenly flustered: "The theater in the old part of town."

"You mean the Workers' Cinema?"

She nodded. She was wearing the same disguise as when she followed Shun-Er to the cinema. It was how she accessed the "other," fractured side of her, *that* Yan Hua, and how she sum-moned the courage (or perhaps it was hate?) that allowed her to betray her husband. Allowed her to smile calmly when the tall official—looking her up and down—asked if she was a man or a woman.

Yan Hua couldn't recall the specifics of how she came to work with these men. She knew she was involved in their schemes, and she knew that they'd given her a box, containing a gold coin, to thank her for her work. But because she acted under the guise of "*that* Yan Hua," she was able to shield herself from remembering the nastiness that transpired. She couldn't remember (more accurately, she refused to remember) the scheme where a man was hired to burn the cinema down. She couldn't remember how she'd heard about it, and she couldn't remember how she'd refused to tell her husband about it, who could've died in the flames. Thankfully, the plan failed, and Yan Hua continued informing on the cinema men. She followed Shun-Er there often, rifled through his belongings, allowed the hate to fester in her chest every time she discovered some small but irritating keepsake of his lover's. A comb with hair wrapped around its teeth, a charm from a folk god's altar. It was the discovery of the charm, ultimately—the yellow pouch with the pink sand in it, the withered petals like cracked bones, and the word "love" scrawled over its ruddy fabric—that allowed her, finally, to hand over a piece of paper to the city developers.

The paper had a date on it. A location. And, at the bottom, a description of Shun-Er.

She wrote it all down so the hired thugs, when they showed up, wouldn't hurt him.

NINETEEN

THE NEW CHINESE settling on East Broadway discovered a city that was missing its color. Aside from a sign here and a door there, everything was gray, black, brown, dirty, and brick. Storefronts with blue awnings were treated like rare and unusual flowers. So were the restaurants and bakeries that adorned their signs with colorful lettering. Even the boutiques were dreary. Opened by, and marketed toward, the new Chinese, they sold nothing imaginative, nothing outside the realm of the useful. The beautiful and fashionable garments came later with the fabric stores. Until their arrival, shopping was the choice between black boots or brown ones, a white shirt or tan. Anything that was cheap and wearable to work. Were the boots anti-slip? Would the soles separate and flap like loose jaws? And even if color existed (in the green of cabbage, the red of apples), it was dimmed by the drab emotions of labor. What was a red Brooks Brothers dress under the sterile fluorescence of a factory bulb? What was the significance of textures like velvet and silk if you touched them, snipped threads from them, cut-bled-wept on them, daily, all for less than fifty dollars a day?

And yet, when the new Chinese realized how bleak the city was, they sought it. Fought for it. Color. They discovered the pleasure of green when the next word was "card." They remembered the places they came from, villages surrounded by trees and hilltops, and began to terraform their new home. Arcades appeared, and in them were selections of not just red tomatoes but purple ones as well. Farmers established stalls under the Manhattan Bridge with merchandise as colorful as candy. Fabric stores opened next to toy stores, and the bolts they hung seemed a reminder of all the things their owners missed. People remembered, suddenly, that the sky wasn't a solid blue. It could be orange. Pink followed by violet, then purple, then darkness. A darkness tinged with a blue that wasn't at all like the darkness of the smuggling boats.

They remembered that darkness. At the very least, Frog did. He was crammed into a cargo boat and saw, for sixty-seven days, nothing but pitch-blackness. The exception was when someone opened a door to let in jaundiced light. It made everything in the hull dark yellow; caused dust and foul odors to erupt like spores on a dandelion. There was no bathroom, and Frog had to use a bucket as a toilet. Most days, he abstained from solid meals to ward off seasickness. When he was bored, he talked to the other travelers; imagined what life would be like in America. "Hopefully it's more colorful than this boat," Frog joked. Because everything in the hold was sepia-toned, even the Dawn dish soap he used as body wash, and he had to remind himself that the liquid he scrubbed into a lather was, in fact, the same blue as the ocean. Upon arrival in America, the first thing he did was search for color. In the texture of money in his wallet, in the name of the card that would eventually grant him freedom. Afterwards: in clothes, food, and later—in 1989—the blushing face of the woman he learned to call "wife."

THEY'RE WALKING DOWN EAST BROADWAY ON THEIR DAY off. Yan Hua wears a black pea jacket while Frog wears a red puffer coat. They look inside storefronts, at the rich displays of ginseng, candies, stationery, hair dyes, and phone cards. A woman outside the East Broadway Mall sells candied hawthorn, and Frog buys one. Not for its taste, but for the excuse it gives him, the explanation as to why his wife won't hold his hand. She can't if he's holding groceries and a stick of candied fruit; she can't if it's cold out and neither husband nor wife is wearing gloves.

"I want to stop here a moment," Yan Hua says. "I need cold medicine."

"You're not sick."

"You're not hungry, and yet there's meat in your bag."

Yan Hua and Frog spend their one day off running errands. The other six are crammed with work, sleep, gossip, and nothing but. A routine of shopping followed by temple-going is often accompanied by doctors' appointments, phone calls to China, and aimless walking. But the walking is pleasurable, more pleasurable than it used to be. East Broadway, with the passing of every year, has become a place that Frog can claim as his own. American signs disappear behind Chinese ones. Restaurants selling village food open, as do job agencies with clerks speaking dialect. And inside the East Broadway Mall, a mess of kiosks providing services to the new Chinese have opened, services that no American business wants to, or can, provide.

"What took you so long?" Frog asks when Yan Hua returns.

"It's busy in there. You can see for yourself how busy."

"But ten minutes?"

"Don't exaggerate," Yan Hua says. "You could've come in with me, you know."

They continue browsing the storefronts as they walk, leisurely, toward their apartment. While Frog searches for knickknacks in the window displays, Yan Hua plays with her hands, apparently deep in thought.

"To tell you the truth, I ran into someone in the mall today."

"I knew it," Frog says. "Who?"

"May's husband."

"Kevin?"

"We didn't talk. The mall was too crowded from Thanksgiving."

"Since when do Fuzhounese people celebrate Thanksgiving?"

"But he did see me. I know he saw me because our eyes locked." Yan Hua is quiet a moment, then says, "There was a man next to him."

"Did he look like a fag?"

"No. I didn't catch his face—he never looked at me. Kevin whispered something in his ear and they walked away."

YAN HUA LIED. THE TRUTH WAS, KEVIN SPOKE TO HER. OR, more accurately, Yan Hua spoke to Kevin. The thing that caught her attention was the man standing next to him, his skin resembling the surface of a coin. She only saw part of his profile, but he looked familiar to her. He was wearing a hat pulled low, but he looked at

Kevin like a child at a new toy. His was an experienced gaze: one that tucked itself away the moment Yan Hua approached. She wanted to see the man. She wanted to make sure he wasn't who she thought it was.

"Yan," Kevin said. His friend had begun to leave, escaping through a side exit.

"Is that your friend?" Yan Hua asked.

"No. Yes." He chewed his lip, then became angry. "No. He's not my friend."

"It's okay if he is."

"How's May?"

"She's working, she's eating, she's surviving like the rest of us."

"Does she need money?"

Hearing Kevin's pitiful yet defiant voice made the anger churn in her belly like heat. She planted her feet on the ground, stuck her lower lip out.

"You did a shitty thing to her," she said.

Yan Hua said the right thing at the wrong time. Kevin's face reddened before darkening, transforming into the peeled flesh of a plum. He raised his hand, and his breaths became shallow; his eyes flickered with hatred. But no words came out. For a moment, Yan Hua feared he was going to strike her. For a moment, she flinched and stuttered. But a second passed, then another, and afterwards, Kevin's face was different. The thing Yan Hua referred to as "falling into a rift" had entered his expression.

"You don't understand," he said.

"I do."

"You don't understand."

"My ex-husband did the same thing you did."

Kevin opened his mouth to speak, but the sounds that emerged weren't his. Drop-jawed, the man was speechless, and his body became like that of a puppet, erupting with the voices of the mall. Clerks barked prices from kiosks. A woman introduced a new medicine to a man in Mandarin, and the man haggled back in dialect. Babies cried in strollers, and the children of the storeowners ran around, laughing in whatever language came first. Dialect, Mandarin, Cantonese, but never English. Never, never, in the East Broadway Mall, do the people speak English. At an especially noisy moment, loud enough to muffle the evil in Yan Hua's mouth, she spoke.

"He was a faggot. He was a faggot and he left me the same way you left May."

APARTMENT 4A OVERLOOKS THE SLUMS OF EAST BROADway. The street leads directly to the mall: an ingot-shaped building with bricks the color of honey. The Manhattan Bridge sits above the mall, hat-like, and every few minutes, a train passes by. Rattling windows, disrupting conversations, and causing children to cover their ears. A week ago, in the mall's basement, Kevin and Yan Hua met to discuss a secret more private than their thoughts. They waited for the other to reveal the hidden layers of themselves, layers that, in this crowd of shoppers, would never be seen. But instead of their truth, they spat out their anger. Their loneliness and their regret—though not to each other. Kevin and Yan Hua released their anger into the air, causing the mall that usually smelled of plastic to be infused with the stench of secrets.

At first, the stench was subtle. Then, when Yan Hua spoke to Kevin, it began to saturate the air like pollen. That morning, the shoppers turned their heads to make faces at each word she spoke. An old man scrunched his nose when Yan Hua whisper-yelled about how her dead husband had betrayed her. Then, when Kevin spoke of the secret loves of his life, the man's daughter puckered her mouth, like she'd sucked a lemon. "My ex-husband did the same thing you did" was a fist that punched nearby shoppers. "He was a faggot" slapped innocent heads, and the sentence that followed ("He left me the same way you left May") was as forceful as the rattling of passing trains. Yet in the middle of it all was a pair of tiny, overworked bodies, each trying to suppress the hurt that shot out of them like a lash.

"I'm not your ex-husband," Kevin said.

"I never said you were. I'm saying you're May's."

"You don't understand."

"And you keep saying that."

"Until now, I lived like one of those fish they sell on Canal Street. Trapped in a bag and drowning—yes, drowning—in its own filth. But now . . ." Kevin's voice trailed off. "Now . . ."

He paused, shifting his gaze from the floor to Yan Hua's face. The harshness in her features angered him, but there was also a quiver, a flash of emotion, animating her mouth. A minute later, the quiver traveled to her chin. Kevin released the pressure in his hands. Both had been balled into fists and seemed ready to strike at anyone daring to approach. But his anger faded at the sight of her trembling chin. It faded into exhaustion and sadness and, later that evening, guilt.

"I have nothing to prove to you," Kevin said. "I'll visit May and give her some money if she needs some. But to you I have nothing, nothing at all, to prove."

BUT KEVIN KEPT SEEING YAN HUA IN THE EAST BROADWAY Mall. It wasn't just proximity to Apartment 4A. No, the mall was indispensable if you were a new immigrant in Chinatown. Called dirty, backwards, and illegal by the establishment Chinese, the East Broadway Mall was a culmination of all the things the new immigrants brought to America.

For instance: a restaurant that sold peanut noodles in plastic bags. For a dollar extra, you could add some flat meat wontons and listen to the waitress while she talked about her hometown (which was also probably yours). Who died this year? Who hadn't? Who got smuggled to America? And had the police ever released the immigrants caught on that fishing boat? (They had.) Her gossip, faster and more reliable than the news, traveled through the mall like the murmurings of fate. It entered barber shops, wove through candy stores, ruffled the collars of shirts in empty boutiques. Then, like a spirit seeking a body, the gossip moved downstairs: past the escalator that once ate a shoe off a toddler's foot, past the jewelry store that rented more rings than it sold, past the balding head of an old man who sewed with the lights off, past the office of the sleeping acupuncturist, and knocked (once, twice, three times) on the bathroom door.

Inside were three friends—May, Little Amy, and Yan Hua—who spoke to each other from their stalls.

"I don't think he's here today," Yan Hua said.

"He better not be," Little Amy said. "I'll knock him dead if I see him."

"He *does* come often, though. I saw him yesterday and the day before that."

"Can we stop talking about Kevin?" May asked. "The way you two go on, it's like *you're* the ones getting divorced."

May recovered from her heartbreak the same night Little Amy knocked on her door. There was no discernible cause. She simply snapped like the band she used to tie up her hair. In the following weeks, while Yan Hua argued with Kevin, May was out looking for jobs. She continued to eat spoonfuls of Argo when she was nervous (her pica was awakened and would remain until her death), swallowing two before speaking to the owner of a nail salon. Thank God she did, because it softened the hurt of the "no" she heard. The "We want our apprentices to be younger" accompanied by the shoulder turn mean enough to cut steel. That very evening, she accepted a position at a Cantonese bakery, and today—on her day off—she was having a girls' day, gossiping with her roommates in a bathroom that reeked of mothballs.

Three toilets flushed, one only halfway. Unlike everything else in the East Broadway Mall, the restrooms were in disrepair. The walls leaked water while half the faucets didn't. There was no soap. No paper towels, and the hand dryers were useless; they released cool air weaker than an infant's cough. This was the only place in the mall the immigrants didn't like to visit. Every other square inch was magical to them. East Broadway was an extension of their homes. You could send money to your parents here, from a place called the Little Fuzhou Express. You could buy cassettes of Chinese music and load your phone cards with extra minutes. Neither May, nor Yan Hua, nor Little Amy could afford international calling, so they sent tape-recorded messages to their families. In them were stories, pauses, laughter, and sometimes nothing at all.

This month, May's message was filled with the sound of tears. She shared nothing about her life and told her mother Kevin was starting a new job across the country. She didn't mention his infidelity and sent the tape in an envelope filled with trinkets. A bracelet the color of mutton fat, some earrings, a quarter, and a brooch with a feather glued on it. She then went with Yan Hua and Little Amy to eat noodles and get haircuts. The women's restroom was a tiny detour in what would soon become a tiresome day, but May glimpsed a premonition peeking out from one of the mirrors. She told Yan Hua, then Little Amy, but neither of them saw what she saw: a series of scratches that spelled out the word "faggot."

"Maybe they permed your brains along with your hair," Little Amy said.

"A sign's a sign," May said. "That's what my mother used to say."

"It's all in your head."

But Little Amy was wrong because Yan Hua started seeing them, too. Signs and premonitions. A body that resembled Kevin's trailed the corner of her vision, causing Yan Hua to move in strange directions. She walked down one corridor, saw Kevin's double at the end of it, then made excuses as to why she had to go down another. At the noodle shop, she saw reflections of his hands (pale and clenched, with hair on the knuckles), while smelling the stench of evil secrets. And what she thought was the ghostly noise of tears was actually that of a thunderstorm. The deluge arrived without warning—people didn't have time to raise their umbrellas—and the East Broadway Mall was quickly packed with damp, dripping bodies. Looking up from the table, Yan Hua watched May search the crowd for her husband. Little Amy watched, too, though she did so with a more relaxed expression. But nobody saw him, and this caused Yan Hua to feel strange. She was surprised at herself. It made sense that May should look for and see signs of Kevin, but why did she? Why did the image of his double cause a bird to flutter in her chest? Yan Hua considered her reasons. She made excuses, hated them, and listened tremulously when May spoke in a tiny voice.

"I think I see him."

"The only thing you should see is a psychiatrist."

"No, Amy, it's him. Look. Look behind you. That man."

May pointed at someone who looked nothing, Yan Hua decided, like Kevin. But then he came closer. He came closer and Yan Hua realized the mistake she'd made. The man didn't look like Kevin because the "Kevin" Yan Hua had imagined was Shun-Er. Although she'd seen him many times this week, she'd somehow replaced his face with her dead husband's.

"I want to leave," May said. She looked close to tears. "Can we leave?"

"You and Little Amy go ahead," Yan Hua said. "I'll pay the bill and wrap things up."

She walked over to Kevin when May and Little Amy left. He was watching them but pretended not to with an embarrassed expression.

"Was that May?"

"Yeah. Why didn't you say hi?"

"I don't think she wanted me to."

"She didn't."

"I can pay for your meal," he said.

"How generous of you."

There was no more animosity between them. Just shyness and something akin to embarrassment.

"No," Kevin said, reaching for his wallet. "Let me do it. I've been working a lot lately."

"How's your lover?"

". . ."

"I'm being serious, Kevin."

"He's good."

"I remember," Yan Hua said. Softness entered her voice—a softness that surprised even herself. "I remember how my first husband wanted to talk about him. His lover. I could see it in his eyes: a certain kind of glow and eagerness . . ."

"Why are you telling me this?"

"Because now I realize how lonely it is not to talk about the people you love."

"It's lonelier to talk about the people who don't love you back."

Yan Hua raised an eyebrow, then nodded.

"Where are you going after this?" she asked after he paid for her food.

"The church. There's free English classes there."

"Will your . . . Will he be there?"

"No."

"Are you two still together?"

"No."

TWENTY

OLD SECOND IS running through the bus depot. Past chairs filled with tired bodies, over bags sitting next to dancing feet, into a restroom with a scratched mirror, and out through doors that lead to East Broadway—a street where, minutes earlier, he was savoring the heat of Kevin's body. The two met when Old Second was new to this country, outside a wedding banquet that Kevin was attending. Made reckless by wine, Kevin had approached him with a cigarette wagging between his fingers and invited him to step outside. Old Second hadn't meant to cruise that day, and he wasn't planning on developing a crush on another married man. But he was young and excited by the worth of his body; pleased by the fact that he, a jobless stranger in Chinatown, could be desired by someone whose beauty was literally slanted.

Kevin's face was split down the middle, with one side smiling at the other. He was handsome if you stared at him from the right, strange if you stared at him from the left. That evening, standing outside the Eldridge Street Hotel with his body obscured by shadows, he'd looked like a thug to Old Second. But his movements were shy and rehearsed, resembling those of the men who frequented the Workers' Cinema.

Look at how he began his courtship, at how he took his first step toward Old Second. They examined each other: watching eyes to see where they roamed and wrists to see how much they limped. Was Old Second staring back at Kevin, or was he watching the drunk women laughing across the street? When Kevin offered up his cigarette with an air of brotherly nonchalance, did Old Second smile, or was he scowling? For seven agonizing minutes, they spun around each other, dancing a delicate dance that meant happiness if they were on the same page, violence if they were not. It was the exact same performance Old Second had seen and been part of as a young sissy in Mawei. He knew that accepting another man's cigarette meant that you were going to hit a home run. Which he might've that night, had Old Second not remembered the coughing fit that came with his first cigarette, all those years ago with Shun-Er.

"I don't smoke," Old Second said. He was older now, wiser but still nervous, and took a gamble by smiling at Kevin. Whose face, in that moment, was going through an entire journey: at first grinning to mask his confusion, then frowning and crestfallen.

"But you don't have to leave," Old Second said. He extended his arm and held Kevin's wrist. "I'm the same as you."

"I don't know what you're talking about."

Both men were sweating and trembling. And both men, despite how they acted, were soft, lonely, nervous, and desperate.

"I like men."

"Yeah, well." Kevin's frown had an ironic slant to it. One that twitched until it became a grin, then a giggle, then a laugh, loud enough to smash his anxiety to pieces. The fear exited his body then. He fell forward into the street, allowed his face to collapse into Old Second's. They were childish with their affection. Generous, too, and hungry for it: snaking their bodies in the night's blistering shadows until strangers, watching from afar, began to whisper. Like a pair of thieves, their hands rifled through each other's clothes, hoping to catch something beyond the sour stench of sweat mixed with cheap perfume that hung in the air. A strip of goosefleshed skin, for instance. A deciduous patch of hair, a precancerous mole on the neck. And finally, when Kevin leaned forward to give Old Second a kiss, it was to the sound of applause radiating from the hotel's banquet hall. Afterwards: the distant voice of Kevin's wife, who had left the building to search for her husband.

"Let's take a walk," Kevin said. "It's noisy here. Don't you want to take a walk?"

OLD SECOND TOLD BAO MEI ABOUT THE KISS RIGHT AFTER it happened. She would've found out anyhow, seeing the sudden change in his behavior. The new but poorly hidden spring in his step. The way he started dancing (yes, dancing) through the halls of the Eldridge Street Hotel. They were recently "married," both for convenience and to guard Old Second from suspicion, but they understood each other, knew each other's baselines. And the excitement Old Second wore like rouge on his face was enough for Bao Mei to pull him aside, ask with bated breath if he'd come into good fortune. Did he find a job at the work agency? More importantly, would that job hire the both of them, queer husband and false wife, even though Bao Mei knew that this wasn't likely (or even possible)? But no, the thing that came out of Old Second's mouth was a spine-shivering revelation that brought Bao Mei almost to her knees.

"It was outside the banquet hall, near the hotel's entrance," Old Second said. "A man close to your age approached me with a cigarette . . ."

"First of all, I'm not that much older than you. Second"—Bao Mei paused for a deep breath—"are you sure you want to go down that road? After what happened to us?"

"Are you saying I shouldn't date men?"

"No, I'm asking you to be cautious, take things slow. Is he married?"

"He told me he wasn't," Old Second lied.

"And what about your job search?"

"He said he'd help me look tomorrow."

"And you're sure, absolutely certain, that he's not married?"

"Why would he lie about something like that?"

"Shh," Bao Mei said. "You're shouting. Keep your voice low."

But he couldn't. Excitement took hold of Old Second's body, and every word he uttered seemed insufficient, a weak substitute for the emotions rambling in his heart. He wanted to run around the room, to jump and throw a ball in the air, to kick a trash can over. But because it was late at night, he had to settle for a leg tremble: a childlike rocking that animated first his left foot, then his right one. Meanwhile, he talked in circles about "what happened last night," his lips loosened by juvenile love. It was the same love that allowed him to skip over and erase his crush's flaws. Like, for instance, Kevin's mossy teeth. His beer-rotten breath, masked poorly by the cigarettes he smoked. Most dangerous of all: the men's lack of chemistry outside their touching, which seemed hungrier than it was deliberate.

But Old Second needed those feelings and clung to them like a baby to a bottle, though he knew this was a temporary balm to soothe the aches of his past. Bao Mei heard his voice and understood this as well. It was why she allowed him to continue his rambling, releasing a sigh only when she heard how serious Old Second was about meeting his lover. They'd made the plans already: twelve p.m. tomorrow at the East Broadway Mall. They'd have lunch and check out Kevin's apartment, when nobody would be home. Not Kevin's roommates and not his wife.

IN THE BATHROOM OF THE BUS DEPOT, OLD SECOND DIPS A tissue into sink water before wiping it across his forehead. With a comb, he itches the crown of his scalp, scratching until a pair of bothersome memories fall away like debris. Old Second is deliberate when he presses lotion into his skin. He's careful about not rubbing too hard, about not causing redness in his cheeks and forehead. And while the hand dryer turns on and off, he snakes his head around, making faces until he is satisfied with his appearance in the mirror. It's a slow but necessary ritual, one that causes the bus depot's other patrons to bang their fists against the door. Which is what happens now: shocking Old Second out of his reverie and reminding him that his bus is about to arrive. *Finally.*

For months, he's been working as a prep cook in Parsippany, away from Bao Mei and the man who causes him to run around in public. He returns to East Broadway once a week to visit them, splitting his time evenly between his wife's home and Kevin's. Old

Second's is not an unusual life, and his journeys to and from the city are common among the new immigrants of Chinatown. All of his coworkers travel in the same way, and judging by the look of the bus depot's other passengers—asleep or sipping Ovaltine with rheumy red eyes—it's likely that they perform a similar ritual as well. One that begins with waiting, in the morning, for a Panda bus. The places they wait in are liminal and strange. If it's six a.m. and you see a group of Chinese workers holding travel bags outside an Asian supermarket in rural Parsippany, or if it's seven a.m. and you see the same thing in Albany, Syracuse, Boston, or even Providence, don't clutch your purse. They are harmless people—their only desire is to go home.

One they can stay in for no more than a few hours. Afterwards, they must return to the bus depots and wait, the way Old Second does, until the evening bus whisks them back to their worksites. And today's wait is obnoxious. The buses are late, and the ticket sellers are rude about it. The delay is so prolonged, in fact, that the excitement that once animated Old Second's body has transformed into a pair of sobering memories.

The first is of Bao Mei: sitting on a mattress in the basement studio she calls home. She can't find work because of her dragging foot, and she's begun decorating her room with cheap but colorful items. There are the flowers she's taped to the wall. Free calendars, both from nearby supermarkets, hang beside them on thumbtacks. Job postings litter the bed, as well as notebooks crammed with sloppy letters. Bao Mei writes in them, but she never says what about. Not wanting to reveal the low-down details of her life (which sometimes include secret rendezvous with silent men), she instead asks Old Second about his: laughing at his jokes, crying at his miseries, and frowning when he talks about Kevin. Which happens quickly today, Old Second being so deep in his feelings about love. He spends hours chatting to his wife about how his newest relationship makes him feel. Which is uncertain. Annoyed (because that's what Kevin is), giddy (because other men make him feel that way), and, yes, guilty, too. Old Second understands that Kevin has a wife. He understands, too, that Kevin is planning to divorce her, that the two are working their way through a separation.

"I didn't want that to happen," Old Second says. "I never asked him to leave."

"Weren't you the one who said he was single?"

"He lied to me. Plus, I didn't see a ring on his finger."

"Do you see a ring on mine?"

"Our arrangement is different. But Kevin's—his is similar to . . ."

"Shun-Er's."

Old Second shrugs, coughing.

"That's what you were going to say, right? Just come out with it. You're worried that this is a repeat of our past. That what happened in Mawei will happen again here."

"Not quite."

"Then what are you afraid of?"

I don't want hurt his wife, Old Second thinks.

MORE TROUBLESOME THAN HIS FIRST MEMORY IS THE ONE that follows. It causes Old Second to dance like a maniac, his trembling lips pushing back a grimace.

In it, he walks with Kevin along the East River, both men drinking tea from paper cups. Kevin's voice is buoyant. Lively and odorous with rot. Each breath forms steam between them. He suddenly declares that he's moved out of his apartment, that he can start living his truth as a gay man in America. What's better: Old Second can join him. There's a cheap place on Eldridge Street, the two can stay there together, become a couple with no one to criticize their actions. Never mind that Old Second works in New Jersey ("Just find a new job," Kevin says), and never mind that he's married to Bao Mei. These are nonissues in the world Kevin lives in, a world that Old Second, since the fall of the Workers' Cinema, has grown wary of, despite yearning for it.

Because even though he understands how juvenile his love is, and that his feelings for Kevin are purely physical, Old Second still wants, *needs*, male affection. At the same time, he's afraid of it. A barrier has been erected around his heart, and though he can look past it like clean glass, he finds that there are certain thresholds he can no longer cross. Dating a man is fine. Kissing, loving, having sex with him in the shadow of his wife's ignorance—that's fine, too. But the moment the man says he is leaving his wife, the moment he asks Old Second to move in with him and abandon Bao Mei, a coarse piece of sand lodges itself in his brain. He can ignore it in Kevin's presence. They laugh about the possibilities, about what life could look like in East Broadway. Is it a small apartment or a big one? Will they have wooden chairs in the dining room, and will they have a bathtub? One that can fit the both of them: their bodies lying sandwich-like on a bed of lavender bubbles?

"So you want to do it, then?" Kevin asks. "You want to get a place together?"

In response, Old Second smiles so hard his face hurts.

"You can look for a new job. There's lots of them in the city. Might not pay as much in the beginning, but—"

"What about my wife?"

"You can leave her," Kevin says.

These are the words that bother Old Second. He's no oyster; the grain of sand in his head does not transform into a pearl. Instead, the foreign object continues to irritate, causing his consideration for Bao Mei to bloom alongside his growing dislike of Kevin. Both are latent, quiet as a breeze rustling through combed hair. When he's with Kevin, Old Second can savor the worth of his own body. He can appreciate and yearn for the impossible, and therefore sacred, touch of another man's fingers wrapped between his. But now that he's away from him, he starts to remember all his lover's bad traits. Earlier today, when Kevin pulled him in for a kiss, he had to turn his head to the side, away from the rot that hid behind Kevin's teeth. And when Kevin was talking about his (*their*) plans for the future, he became irritated when Old Second expressed apprehension. He sucked his teeth when Old Second said, "I'll think about it," and his eyes glowered, became hateful, when Old Second brought up the possibility of Bao Mei moving with them. Because why did he have to leave her? She, who didn't bother anyone, who advised Old Second on his relationships with gay men, and who was struggling right now—she kept saying she missed her brother, who'd stopped speaking to her—why did she have to be tossed away because Old Second had a crush?

Old Second considers his wife while the bus pulls up outside the bus depot. He continues thinking about her as he gets on the bus, his dancing feet suddenly leaden. When he sits down—it's crowded and he has to sit in the back, near the out-of-order toilet—he closes his eyes, gathering first his courage, then his strength.

Old Second knows the decision he will have to make, but he wonders if he will have the resolve to make it.

TWENTY-ONE

NOBODY KNEW WHAT it felt like. The lifelong nothing amplified by the loss of a friend, one whom Yan Hua had called her husband. She'd been carrying his death with her for a long time, but that day, speaking to Kevin at the mall, she realized she had nothing left to grieve. The memories were there, as were the words, but the feelings? They were gone. Vanished, just like the blood foam she spat after brushing her teeth. By then, ten years had passed since Shun-Er's death. Ten years of Yan Hua holding on to a grief she could barely access. She could tell her friends about it, and she could tell Frog. She'd say things like: "I was hurt when Shun-Er cheated on me. I was devastated when he died." But the words no longer translated into feelings. They were a plain language now: the same she'd use to describe a tabletop as dirty, a chair cushion as soft. Even with the ongoing drama of Kevin leaving May and May cracking like a fallen plate, Yan Hua discovered that the pain that used to make her cry out was nothing but syllables. A collection of sounds that came out of a mouth too numb to realize it was smiling.

It was early morning, and the radiator was rattling like a chained dog. Nobody in Apartment 4A was awake yet, and nobody would be for the next half hour. The world was only Yan Hua, dressed in going-out clothes and brushing her hair in the mirror. Its reflection revealed a spotless yet lived-in bathroom. A shower stall with a bucket where yesterday's clothes floated in soapy water. A sink surface crowded with toothbrush cups and vials of Tiger Balm, Seirogan pills, headache medicine, and blood pressure tablets. Finished with her hair, Yan Hua went about cleaning the bathroom. She wiped the sink with a paper towel, then hung it on a towel rack to dry. She wrung the clothes out in the bucket and scrubbed mold from the toilet bowl. Bending over to retrieve a dropped vial of hand cream, Yan Hua was assaulted by the sting of Fabuloso, strong enough to make her eyes water. And the moment she felt dampness in her eyes, she accepted that she couldn't hold in her laughter any longer.

But she had to. She couldn't risk waking the others up.

In twenty minutes, she'd be talking with Kevin in a nearby church. The same Kevin who forced Yan Hua's past to bump heads with her present. One in which she finally felt grief for herself. But who could she share her feelings with? Without people to speak to—*really speak to*—her thoughts felt inconsequential. Meaningless as a burp against the wind. And this was the thing Yan Hua grieved the most. Not Shun-Er's tainted and deceitful husband-love, but the way he took her thoughts into consideration. Her real thoughts, not the domestic nothings imposed on Chinese immigrant women. She didn't want to talk about money anymore. And she didn't want to talk about work, either.

Yan Hua wanted to talk about other things. Like the surprising smell of flowers in a Min An Village street market. Or, in America, the heartbreaking sight of red in the spools of sewing machines. Last night, after her girls' day with May and Little Amy, she told Frog that red reminded her of her mother, but he was too busy scratching his back to notice. He didn't care that red dye was pricier than meat in Min An, and he didn't care that Yan Hua's mother starved herself to buy scraps of red silk. Her dream was to one day own three meters' worth: enough for a blouse and a skirt. The leftovers she could use as handkerchiefs, or—if no other use was found—they could live in the kitchen as place mats. Ones she could bolt to the tables and touch for comfort. But every time she got close to reaching her goal, her husband would find the money. A bundle taped inside the rice bucket. An envelope buried with the flour. He'd find the money and gamble it away within days. And no, this wasn't easy money.

This was money made by sweeping garbage off the highways. Money made by cleaning public toilets. Money made by selling water bottles in Mawei, and money made by smashing rocks at the quarry. Where dust filled the air and the sun was white-hot. Yan Hua's mother curved her spine to make pocket change at the paper factory. By refusing pork, she lost the fat, followed by the muscle, that cushioned her wrists. All for the dream of red. This wasn't, despite what Frog said, a "silly" or "childish" desire. *No*, Yan Hua thought. It was the only thing her mother ever wanted. The only thing she allowed herself to be selfish about. She wouldn't accept the muted, meat-colored red of beet-dyed fabric. It had to be the exact red she saw in the fabric store. The exact red she'd stroked with her skeletal hands, feeling the life-giving velvet of a flower's petal.

Outside was brown and freezing, and the bored men patrolling East Broadway, walking nowhere but in circles, shot nasty looks at Yan Hua. She was late and almost running. Past streets with folks sleeping under awnings. Past old, down-on-their-luck women digging for bottles in the trash. Cold, dead air forced her hands into her pockets, and slush in the streets forced her to command the center of every sidewalk. Which was why the patrolling men hated her. Here was a woman who refused to twist her body, who refused to let the men pass. Instead, she bumped into their shoulders without turning back to apologize. Why should she? Yan Hua was busy with her own concerns; plus, her boots were brand-new, fresh as butcher meat. The patrolling men weren't cops, anyway. They were nothing but moralizers who winked at slender legs before criticizing the mothers who bared them. Men who wanted to start beef but who couldn't finish it. They chewed on it, seeking the manhood they lost by not being police officers, by not having a paycheck. But their loss had nothing to do with Yan Hua, who, running to meet Kevin in a church, was consumed by memories of her mother.

She was blind now, and mean. Too old and feeble to live on her own, she had to take a room with one of Yan Hua's aunts. One whose heart was barely large enough to accept another body in the house. The arrangement was good for Yan Hua because all she had to do was wire them money, and call twice a week from a neighbor's phone. But what was at first an easy call turned into a nightmare loaded with accusations. Requests for not only money but gifts. Her aunt made snide comments about the things other village folks owned. Tiled hallway floors. Electricity in every room. Stoves that burned gas instead of wood, and a color TV to watch Beijing operas.

"I've had a hard life, and I don't want much of anything," Yan Hua's aunt liked to say. "But it sure would be nice to feel thanked instead of thankful. To drink tea with the meals I cook, and to place a chair before the TV . . ."

Yan Hua's mother wasn't much better. She was short with her

words, impatient and rude. No doubt she was ashamed of living on her sister's charity, and no doubt she felt, since the neighbors kept saying it, that she was losing her mind. It started one morning, when she threw a nasty question into her conversation with a friend.

"So your son is going to America—are you afraid he will die?"

"What did you ask me?"

"I asked when will he arrive?"

Afterwards, when her sight faded, her madness became a rejection of the world she could no longer see. She'd wake in the middle of a summer night and put on a jacket. Then she'd go outside and sit at the bus stop. Shivering, really shivering, until a neighbor found her in the morning. She'd remember, then, that the famine was over, and that her husband was roasting in hell like the selfish pig he was. And once, when Yan Hua asked about the red silk, she lied. Spoke in a voice issued from another woman's throat.

"No, I hate that color. I've always hated it. Red is what whores wear."

Yan Hua didn't want to argue, but she couldn't help but remember how her mother would skip meals and work extra jobs for the sake of red.

"With what eyes would I see red with?"

"You're not *that* blind, Mama."

"How do you know? Am I your mother or are you mine?"

"You can still touch the fabric. And Third Aunt can describe it to you."

"There you go again, doing things nobody ever wanted. Like how you married that man and how you killed him, too."

"What?" Yan Hua asked. It was the first time her mother had said this to her, and the shock of it—the venom of such casually spoken evil—made Yan Hua sit on the floor.

"I said 'Like how you married that man.'"

"No, the other thing you said."

"I didn't say anything else and don't you tell me otherwise."

KEVIN WAS LATE. AND FOR THIRTY MINUTES, IN THE TIME IT took for the sky to turn blue, Yan Hua waited outside the Chinese church. Trembling, excited, worried, and alone. If you saw her, you would've thought she was one of the women roaming the streets. Because she muttered stories into the wind. Her only audience was her shadow: too long and too thin to expose the hateful nature of her clothing. Her jacket was a hair too short, as were her jeans. Cut hideously above the ankles, they revealed a dry and freezing line of flesh: ghastly in its paleness. Her boots, despite being brand-new, were ridiculous. She bought them because they were cheap, and she didn't care, not at first, that they were as pink as pork belly. It was only after this thirty-minute wait, wherein she did nothing but tap her feet and rehearse her ideas, that she noticed. She took a sideways glance at the nonsense on her feet and shrank.

She wanted to be taken seriously. To be more than an immigrant haunted by her past. More than a woman who split her heart for a gay man who did nothing but listen. To: her stories about childhood, her stories about her mother, her stories about seeing a girl-student painting by the Mawei City piers. Yan Hua still remembered that girl. How young she was. How long and deft her fingers. She painted, while nobody but Yan Hua watched, a landscape that could only be described as far away. There was a sunset and a crimson swallow, like blood from a cut finger. It was small, the swallow, but its details were vivid. Each feather seemed deliberately placed, as though by an act of God, and Yan Hua remembered the girl's gentle and serene expression.

"Why don't you start painting?" Shun-Er had asked.

It was an offhand question, but he'd been serious, and his actions that evening confirmed it. Because suddenly paintbrushes had appeared in her room. Two of them, and three colors of paint: red, white, and yellow. Lacking the money for more, Shun-Er added a fourth color by mixing charcoal with wheat starch, then water.

"That's how my mother used to make makeup," Shun-Er said.

"You're crazy. Absolutely crazy."

"If we have beets, we can boil them, make pink and purple. You can paint flowers with them: white ones, red ones, purple ones. But no stems."

"Or leaves."

"C'mon, paint something for me. I want to see."

He must've heard it somehow. The desire in Yan Hua's voice. Her wish to become the girl painting in the street. The girl wore fashions that were right then becoming popular. Instead of the feminine, tight-fitting clothes typical of Mawei's princesses, she wore baggy corduroy slacks and a chore jacket over a lilac blouse. Her hair was teased into a cabbage, and the makeup on her face—thin brows and a red lip—made Yan Hua salivate like a dog. She wanted that face, that calm and powerful coolness. And it was Shun-Er who urged Yan Hua to pursue it. Shun-Er who accompanied her to the beauty salon and who paid for the teased hair (it was expensive; for the rest of the week, they had to survive on noodles in broth). Shun-Er who put beet rouge on Yan Hua's face and coal liner on her eyebrows.

"My mother used to perform in the village theater," he said. "She taught me how to apply stage makeup."

"I look ridiculous," Yan Hua said, laughing.

"You do. But that's because I'm not done yet."

"Oh God, I don't think I can go to work tomorrow. Not like this."

"You can wash the makeup off if you hate it."

"But I can't untease my hair, can I?"

"I like your hair. You don't like it?"

"At the salon I did. Now I'm not so sure."

"Don't be silly. You'll be the most stylish girl in the factory."

Yan Hua had never met anyone who understood her like that. Who listened, not only to her words, but to the breath that accompanied them. The tremble and the gulp. Shun-Er could hear the inner parts of her; he could reach them and bring them out. Softly, gently, coaxing: like an adult with a shy but obedient child. But once Yan Hua's inner feelings had emerged, he went ahead and snuck into that low-down, dirty cinema. He went ahead and started dating a man. He stopped listening to her. He became sarcastic and moody. And one day, coming home early from work, Yan Hua found the same scene May did, or maybe it was worse: her husband and his lover in the bedroom, both of them trying desperately to hide the signs of their love. But no matter how quickly they moved, no matter how deftly they could put on their shirts, their socks, their underwear, they couldn't mask the toilet odor of lovemaking in the room. It wafted, hung in the air. Indicted the men like a finger pointing down from God.

Shun-Er's lack of consideration was what pushed Yan Hua over the edge. That was why she went to the city developers' office. Why she accepted their box with the gold coin. Now, having thrown the box away, she felt guilty and sat waiting for a man who was forty minutes late. Kevin said he'd show up when Yan Hua spoke to him at the mall. She said she was worried about May, that she might do something rash. But now it dawned on her, staring at her boots, that Kevin had never planned on showing up.

The sun was rising, and the church she waited in front of had started to cast long shadows. To avoid suspicion, Yan Hua had moved from one place to another. She'd pretended to read posters ("English lessons every Monday!" "Two rooms for rent, neat women only. Call to inquire.") and bought buns at a nearby bakery. Jostling past the early-morning workers, she'd made sure to glance out the windows, search for signs. And she'd made sure to buy an extra Ovaltine for when Kevin showed up, with lies and excuses in tow. She imagined she would tease him for being late. Needle and play with him a little, the way a cat does with its prey. But when she looked down to find that she'd drunk half her second Ovaltine and all of her first, she shrugged her shoulders and decided to go home.

Maybe he detected it in her: the shred of dishonesty lurking like a pimple under Yan Hua's voice. And maybe Kevin sensed that Yan Hua didn't want to talk about May at all. Because the truth, the simple coldhearted truth, was that Yan Hua wanted to banish her loneliness. She wanted someone to listen to her the way Shun-Er used to. And walking down East Broadway, she couldn't help but replay the conversation she'd anticipated in her mind. She acted it out while walking home.

I'm sick of working in the factories, Kevin. It's boring, dreadful work.

The restaurants aren't much better, sister.

I was thinking I could learn English. Maybe I can work an office job at a Chinese office. You think they'd hire me?

I don't know. How far did you go in school?

Junior high.

Then no.

Or maybe I could do nails. I'm a pretty good painter—I used to do some painting back in China. Did you know that?

I barely know you at all.

I saw a woman painting in the street once, as a girl. And I wanted to be her. I wanted to be her so bad. I did my hair like she did, my makeup, too, and my husband bought me a painting set. We only had three colors, but that was enough. That was enough back then. Now, in America, nothing seems like enough. Isn't that silly?

. . .

Isn't that silly, Kevin?

Yan Hua decided, thinking for Kevin, that yes—yes, it was. Very silly indeed.

TWENTY-TWO

KEVIN USED TO steal letters from the mailbox at Unity Church. He did it for the cash-stuffed cards folks sent to their loved ones. At first, he didn't intend to read the cards, but sometimes his eyes would wander, catching words that moved his spirit. Kevin returned the letters after replacing their money with presents (this was how he apologized for stealing). A Hot Wheels for a boy whose stolen birthday money would stretch into a day's worth of meals. Postcards for a mother who'd never left her village, let alone China. He spied on the lives of his countrymen; felt mixed emotions while reading the letters—which were really diary entries—of immigrants who couldn't read or write. They were desperate to tell their stories, however, and sought the help of six volunteers at the church, volunteers who put their words to paper.

It was a service that the church offered, and the reason they had a mailbox in the first place. Twice a week, the minister brought in activists to support her fresh-off-the-boat flock. Immigration lawyers passed out their business cards while a woman named Mrs. Ng taught classes on practical American English. "Restaurant English" was the most popular lesson, followed by "Public Transit." On Mondays, underseasoned Chinese dishes were served, and the six volunteers would offer their letter-writing services. All the immigrants needed to bring were envelopes, writing utensils, and whatever it was they wanted to say. The volunteers would help translate their thoughts onto paper, and the minister would take care of the postage.

"Dear So-and-So," Kevin read. Or: "To my dearest Such-and-Such." There were questions about So-and-So's mother (Was she playing cards still? How was her eyesight? Was it true that she fell and fractured her hip?), followed by answers, many of them lies, about life in America. Yes, the weather in New York was great. No, he didn't have his green card yet. Did So-and-So get the money that he wired last month? Gossip came after rumors, and well-wishes came after gossip. Which was vicious when it came to Such-and-Such's brother. "Tell him not to contact me anymore," Kevin read, "or I'll have to talk to him with my fists." He skimmed the rest of the letter with curious eyes and searched for money in the envelope. Finding none, he threw the letter into a wastebasket.

Letters that began with "I miss you" were immediately thrown away. Sentimental writers, Kevin discovered, were the cheapest.

Sometimes the letters included pictures of men posing in front of landmarks.

"Show this to our son," Kevin read. "I don't want him to forget what Daddy looks like."

One letter was stained by dried tears, resembling—when Kevin held it against the light—the mottled surface of a quail's egg. He skimmed its contents and saw how desperate the writer was. She worked as a server at the Golden Unicorn and had spilled boiling tea all over her hands. The burns weren't severe, but her humiliation was. Enough for her to write a letter (signed "Your Daughter") about giving up on America. Already poor, the burns left Your Daughter without the ability to earn money. She tried going to a doctor, but the cream he prescribed wasn't balm enough for the heat that lingered on her body. Now she was left with nothing but $300 and the generosity of her landlord: a Jewish woman whose kindness toward women was as stark as her meanness toward men. "I'm so unhappy here," Kevin read. "I often think about turning myself over to the police so they can send me home. Back to the village, where at least I have company. I have nothing here. All the money I've made is gone."

Kevin pursed his lips when he reached the end of the letter. Lonely, broken up with, and frequently drunk, he sought to drown out his misery with the words of immigrants—soaking it (his misery) like stale crackers in soup. He felt at ease in other people's stories. Was able to learn that his life was not singular; that his sorrow was repeated in the bodies of others. He was also—let's face it—a tremendous gossip, finding therapy in the lies immigrants told their loved ones. Kevin continued stealing money, but the food he bought with it became less important than the words he read. He discovered which people were doing well in America. Which people weren't and which people were the biggest liars. He saw taboo subjects mentioned in offhand strokes of the pen and gasped at the folks who lived double lives.

For example, there was a woman named Yoyo who missed her husband in her letters, but who came to church with her waist wrapped in another man's arms.

Then there was the man with the athlete's foot and the cat-got-your-tongue lisp. He liked to complain about poverty in his letters, but he came to church wearing name-brand clothes. Polo shirts, Tommy Hilfiger jeans, Nike shoes, a Gucci belt. Kevin could tell that the belt was a knockoff, but he enjoyed the accessory for its sheer audacity. The shameless, gold-chipped gesture at wealth. He imagined the man dictating his hard-knock life to one of the church's volunteers, all while flashing the various logos on his body. And the idea wasn't just humorous to Kevin. It was delicious.

But not as delicious as his habit of rewriting the letters he stole—secretly, and in the darkness of his bedroom. This habit was new, replacing the bottles of Heineken he'd drink, and signaled his slow recovery from heartbreak. It also became Kevin's greatest source of joy. He started with the words of a young man who wished that his mother would join him in America. There was a dollar inside, and Kevin stole that dollar to buy postcards of New York tourist attractions. There was one of the Brooklyn Bridge, another of the Statue of Liberty, and a third of the Manhattan skyline. He stuffed all three plus a packet of children's stickers (the writer mentioned a younger sister) into an envelope, then tossed the envelope back into the church's mailbox. To another letter, this one by a dad missing his son, he added pictures of toys from a catalog. Then the words: "Pick whatever you want. I'll buy it for you." Still burned by Old Second's rejection, he threw away the love declarations of male adulterers and scribbled answers to questions nobody dared ask. A cheating man might say: "I've no money to send this month, only my love," and Kevin would scribble the second half out. Exchange it for: "Because I'm dating a jobless woman."

He performed this forgery for three months, taking the stolen letters home, then stuffing them back into the church's mailbox. On the first day of his third month, he discovered a group of letters that hadn't come from the immigrants. All were addressed to the same place in Mawei City, and all were from a nameless person who, writing with an unsteady hand, called herself "Sister," "Brother," "Mother," "Friend," and "Father." Kevin was examining one of these letters when Yan Hua appeared in his doorway.

"You don't knock?" Kevin asked.

After he flaked on Yan Hua (it was an honest mistake), they made plans to meet the next time they shared a day off. This time at Kevin's apartment, filled with letters he stole and forgot to hide. A balding man who was easily rattled, Kevin lived in a cramped, dark room frosted with smoke stains. A queen-sized mattress took up most of the space, and to give himself more walking room, he stored his clothes in a garbage bag. There was no room for a dresser, or even a table and small chairs. He ate off the windowsill or the clipboard he stored behind his pillow. It was under this clipboard where he hid the stolen letters. Poorly, because Yan Hua could still see them: their thin, wide-ruled pages; their torn, crumpled envelopes.

"I did knock," she said. "I even pressed the buzzer."

"The buzzer's broken," Kevin said.

"You're writing letters?"

"No," Kevin said.

He couldn't admit the truth to her. Not to Yan Hua: a woman he called "sister" but couldn't trust. Their shared pasts allowed them to become easy friends, but Yan Hua's fidelity to May prevented Kevin from confiding in her. He had to wear the dignified armor of an ex-husband first, and the humiliation of his dirty apartment was enough for Yan Hua to wrinkle her nose. He could see it like a fortune teller with a crystal ball: Yan Hua running to May with the gossip of his living situation, followed by the gossip of his letter stealing. He heard their scornful words, their smug and hateful laughter. And it wasn't until Yan Hua moved to sit on his windowsill and a shaft of light hit her face, softening her features, that a thought entered his head. A revelation that seemed both obvious and impossible at the same time.

Without thinking, he spoke it aloud. Asked in a cautious voice if Yan Hua wrote the letters addressed to the theater in Mawei.

"Write *what* to *where?*"

Kevin's heart sank. "You didn't write them?"

"No, my mother can't read. Could you repeat where the letters are addressed?"

"Forget it, Yan. I was thinking of something else."

"Show them to me."

"All right. But just so you know, I found them on the floor of the church."

"Yes, and you happened to pick them up out of the goodness of your heart. Now show them to me."

"I'm telling the truth."

"For God's sake, will you show me the letters or not?"

THERE WERE DOZENS OF THEM. AND EACH ONE BEGAN IN the same, strikingly ordinary way: "Dear Brother," "Dear Son," "Dearest Friend," "Dearly Beloved." Yan Hua, reading through their contents with the focus of a sniper, had to stop at moments to stare at Kevin. Wide-eyed and disbelieving, she took in a balloon's worth of air when she saw the words "Mawei City." With "Workers' Cinema," she blew it back out. Place- and people-names that Yan Hua remembered were mentioned, described in a detail that made her legs shake. A tremor radiated from her tapping feet, and Kevin felt the need to ask, again, if Yan Hua wrote the letters. If not her, then who? Who else knew of these places, of these people, and who was able to remember that impossible place where men loved, and protested, and died? It would've been convenient if the letters had been signed with a name. But things in America weren't easy. They never would be for Chinese folks. And so Yan Hua and Kevin looked to the letters' valedictions, which said things like "Your Dearest Sister," "Your Mother," and sometimes a lone word: "Friend."

"The handwriting's the same. So we know it's all written by the same person. A woman."

"A man wouldn't write like this," Yan Hua agreed.

"Are you sure it wasn't you?"

"Kevin. Use your brain. Please."

"How else would the writer know about these places? The cinema?"

Is it true, then? Yan Hua wondered. *Is the past coming back to haunt the present?*

"Or maybe the letters are fake. Maybe they're fictions. Coincidences."

"Maybe," Yan Hua said.

But she knew this wasn't true. The letters, strange and impossible as they were, were "real." They came from a person who'd been to the Workers' Cinema. And if any doubt lingered in her mind, there was the mention of a name she'd forgotten. One that Kevin shrank from, pretended to ignore, and which drained the color from her face.

Old Second.

TWENTY-THREE

N HER FIRST letters, Bao Mei compares Chinatown to the night markets in Mawei. She writes that car honks are no different from the shouts of peddlers. Fruits, vegetables, toys, fish, and junk: all are advertised in a volume high enough to raze the earth. She describes the music playing in the American cars, music so loud it hangs in the air, insect-like, and compares their ground-rocking bass to the movie sounds in the Workers' Cinema. Bao Mei remembers *feeling* the movies on her cleaning rounds, a broom in one hand, a canteen in the other, her feet made shaky by the vibrations. Back then and now, she has no clue what to do with herself and pushes her thoughts away by occupying herself with chores. The stern armor she wears is a poor disguise for her fear of the future. A fear she must confront because no one in Chinatown is willing to hire her full-time: a Fuzhounese woman who walks with a limp.

It's why she's turned to writing. In the beginning, Bao Mei's letters were aimless. She wrote short and prosaic verses describing the sights in America. Homeless men begging on street corners with their better-fed pets on leashes. Sweatshop workers gossiping in Cantonese bakeries. A store that sold everything—food, clothes, cleaning supplies, medicine—in neat and fluorescent rows. Then, when she was hired to fold wonton skins at a dumpling shop, she started writing about the people around her. Her descriptions were meant to be funny, so each one carried a whiff of meanness. For example, she called her boss Ziploc Bag because he had a crease on his belly, a reminder of when he used to be fat, and his balding wife Nosferatu. Their daughters, one short and fat, the other tall and thin, were named Bamboo and Rock.

Occasionally, Bao Mei would send one of her letters to Old Second, who worked in a takeout restaurant in New Jersey. But as time went on, and as the direction of her life changed, she started to address them to her brother. Hen Bao, whose spirit stopped speaking after the Workers' Cinema was bulldozed. She felt warmth in her belly when a Chinese church, the one named Unity, offered to help its members post letters to China. Her first thought was: *At least I won't have to deal with the post office.* But then it became a project. She attended Unity Church for its social services, but now she saw that a greater possibility for her existed. A chance for her to not only remember her brother but to reach out to him as well.

"Dearest Brother," she wrote at first. "Dearest Hen Bao." Then there slipped a stream of diary entries about her new life, the fact that things weren't (and wouldn't be) going well. She was discriminated against when searching for jobs. She hated her neighbors, who poked their heads into her business and who reminisced—"like old fogies," Bao Mei wrote—almost daily about their pasts. She talked about how much she hated people who romanticized the old days. China was a source of misery for Bao Mei, and the very thought of it, of any place outside the Workers' Cinema, sent her into a rage. "It's so easy for people to forget," she wrote, "that the provinces weren't willow trees and old ladies telling stories over cards. It was its own brand of misery. It was hunger and labor and calluses on the hands: calluses that split off the fingers, fell like wax from a burning candle."

More than anything, Bao Mei couldn't stand people who regarded the past as a sacred and immutable thing. Like a sculpture you might find in a museum or a painting from some majestic, monosyllabic era: Tang or Ming or Qing. She was a hypocrite, of course, because she was guilty of that very thing. But with each letter, she'd dig deeper, remember some silly occurrence that would lift her mood like a tailwind. She saw the faces of the men in the theater. Each and every single one. She remembered how they reminded her of Hen Bao, whom she imagined as being a part of those men. It was corny, and she'd never admit this, but she believed that her brother's now silent spirit lived on inside them. Inside their lives, which, despite the destruction of the cinema, continued. Went on and on and on, the way hers did, and Old Second's, in a part of the world that tried its hardest to suppress their being. And gradually, as she moved from working three days a week at the dumpling store to working four days a week at a local bakery, she decided to change the person she addressed her letters to. Instead of "Dearest Brother" and "Hen Bao," she now wrote to "Tongzhi."

The word meant "comrade" in Mandarin. But it also served as slang for gay men. A code like "Friend of Dorothy" or "sugar in the tank." And with these new letters, Bao Mei sought to alter, not just communicate with, the past. She sought to transform events by imagining lives for the men who never got a chance to live theirs.

"History," she wrote, in her final letter to her brother, "do you think I can change it? Is that possible? Do you think I can create a new future, a better one?"

TWO STREETS AND HALF AN ALLEYWAY SEPARATE BAO MEI'S apartment from Unity Church. She walks there in the blistering cold, a lukewarm Ovaltine in one hand, a purse filled with envelopes in the other. A letter sits in each one, and even the shortest imagines a new life for the gay man she writes to. She takes on a different persona in each of these letters, signs herself off as "Brother," "Sister," "Mother," "Husband," and "Wife." If the leaders of the church had X-ray vision, or if they were unscrupulous enough to claw the envelopes open, they'd see that the letters depicted a reality where gay men felt safe enough to emerge from the closet. That these letters, written by a stern woman with a grade school education (but with a remarkable facility for metaphor), were trying to re-create the love-feeling of the Workers' Cinema. Bao Mei once believed that she was writing the letters to continue communicating with Hen Bao, but now she understands that the act of writing, the act of putting imagination onto paper itself, is her brother. She deserves credit for her idea, but a deep-down part of her—the part that motivates her to walk through the cold to post her letters—believes that it's him. It's really him.

She's in a good mood while walking to the church, but the moment her task is done, her face sags. Becomes sour and rude-looking as she turns toward East Broadway. Part of it has to do with the secret nature of her project. The fact that Bao Mei, who once was burned by conspiracy, is embroiled in a scheme of her own. The average Fuzhounese person would frown at the contents of her letters. Even somebody progressive, like the volunteers at Unity Church, or the lawyers who helped her and Old Second apply for green cards. None of them would understand. None of them would believe Bao Mei's letters were the work of a sane person. Once, when an overly talkative neighbor decided to confide in her, telling Bao Mei that Old Second was not only a fruit, but a cake as well, she vowed never to speak to that neighbor again. The neighbor didn't notice, and to this day, when she sees Bao Mei on the street, she tells her about Old Second, forgetting that he is her husband, and assuming that Bao Mei is mute.

She decides to run some errands on her way home. She walks along the white side of town and stares at grocery prices until those on the Chinese side seem cheaper. At the Hong Kong supermarket, she buys a length of pork belly. A bundle of scallions, another of water spinach, some coffee grounds, a mackerel tin. She argues with a fruit seller for weighing her apples improperly, says homemaker things like: "I buy from you all the time, don't I get a discount?" Bao Mei considers the price of a bag of dumplings at the noodle shop and, afterwards, sits to rest on a park bench near Confucius Plaza, where across the street some laborers have lined up outside the bus depot, waiting for the Chinese Greyhounds to whisk them away.

Bao Mei regrets the apple purchase. They are heavy and she is tired.

The whole time, she thinks about what to write in her next letters. What possibilities she can imagine, what pasts and what futures. Uneducated and mean-looking, she's not the sort of person one expects to be an artist. These letters to a bulldozed theater in Mawei—all of them feature fictions that foreground the dignity of a queer life. A working-class one, too, as Bao Mei imagines, staring at the queue of laborers, the first sentence of what she will write next.

"Dear Brother," she'll write. "How is your husband? Is the weather good in the village? How are you dealing with the rising prices of pork?" A simple and everyday sentence, one whose shock comes from the easy juxtaposition of "dear brother" and "husband." Then, gathering ideas from her surroundings, much like how a bagworm collects junk to build a cocoon, she'll add a detail about her writing persona's life. "I am waiting on the street for the bus, which will take me to my next workplace. America is a large country and the journey from where us Chinese people live and where we work sometimes takes an entire day. It is like when we used to travel to Putian to sell peaches, and you complained all the time about the journey, but of course that is where you met Old Second."

Bao Mei takes a notebook out of her pocket, writes down the story beats she does not want to forget. Words appear randomly on the page. "Putian" comes first, followed by "peaches," then "boyfriend," then "boardinghouse," then all the rest. "Greetings" and "shoe soles." "Roach wings" and "love." Like a student, she makes sure to circle the words that'll be used to create a lasting impact. The character for "roach" is circled three times, and the "wing" beside it is underlined, accompanied by scribbles—she was testing out her pen's ink—and an arrow. The idea is to write a memory in which the brother helps a stranger, who has a fear of roaches, kill one. Friendship will happen next (this is indicated by the large arrow pointing away from "roach wing" and toward "love"), followed by a relationship. Of course nothing is set in stone: Bao Mei's ideas are susceptible to change. Maybe, she thinks, it'll be the stranger who helps the brother kill the roach. Maybe the vermin won't be a roach at all, but a rat. A poisonous spider or a house centipede (although Bao Mei doesn't know the character for "centipede"). Whatever the case, Bao Mei has her entire walk home to envision her letter. To consider her ideas and her possibilities.

She gets up from the park bench, hears the joints pop in her knees. This is satisfying to her—not the popping itself but the sound—and for the first time all day, Bao Mei smiles. Normally, she wears a self-conscious smile: one meant to hide her large gums, her rotten teeth. But sometimes she forgets, and the moss on her canines makes them glow like river stones in the sun. Brushing the nothing off her legs, Bao Mei returns home.

TWENTY-FOUR

YAN HUA STARTED skipping work to attend the services at Unity Church. Her excuse and the lie she told was that she did it for May's sake. May, who would take over Yan Hua's shifts at the garment factory, and who complained about the lower rate of pay. Yes, even though it was better than the money she made at the bakery, where not only was she forbidden to sit, she also had to wear a uniform. A hairnet that left impressions on her forehead and that Little Amy said "squeezed all the oxygen out of her brain." There was also the matter of the sores on her hands. Small, raisin-textured bumps that itched if she ignored them, bled if she didn't. An Eastern doctor told her it was a reaction to something at work, advising her to quit, but all May did was buy gloves and ointment, which she stored in the fridge for cooler comfort. She was in a terrible situation, and May's decision to cover Yan Hua's shifts was a secret relief to her. It was a relief to Yan Hua, too, who finally had the freedom to seek mercy in a church that didn't act like one.

Few believers attended. The ones who did came on a different day, one blocked off for them, to avoid the immigrants who sought nothing but a clean place to sit. The social services were a bonus, but not everyone took advantage of them. Yan Hua did by using them as an excuse, telling Frog and Little Amy that she was missing work to learn English. It was a convincing lie because it was half true: By the end of the year, Yan Hua was able to sing the American alphabet, recognize street names, and take her roommates shopping in the white parts of town. But the real reason she came was to find the letter writer.

In the letters, paused lives continued. Gay men came out of closets, shopped for rings, planned for weddings. Some left Mawei to take jobs in other cities. A factory worker who went to the cinema was now a schoolteacher in Xinjiang. Another man, nicknamed Mulan, opened a street food restaurant in Fuzhou: a mediocre one with tasty side dishes but low-quality rice. And then there was Old Second—a name that caused Yan Hua to quake with fury—who had emigrated to America. According to the letter writer, he worked in New Jersey, where there was a whole other Chinatown, a smaller but cleaner one with two streets for shopping, and a barber who came from Min An.

Over time, Yan Hua had begun to view the letters as fact. She needed them to be. Her actions and their consequences didn't appear in these letters, and this became a balm for her spirit. More than any church service; more than the release of any confession trapped like phlegm in her throat. Reading the letters made her feel buoyant. She'd often say to Kevin that she felt like she knew the person behind them. That they'd spoken before: woman to woman, friend to friend.

"That would make sense. You said you know these people."

"No, not the people. I know the place. The Workers' Cinema..."

"The one your husband went to."

"But I don't see his name here."

She didn't and never would. Out of respect and superstition, and also because it would break the realism of her stories, Bao Mei didn't write about the cinema's dead. This was a shame because part of Yan Hua wanted Shun-Er's life to continue on the page. She wanted to watch him thrive as an entrepreneur (like Ugly Mulan), or find love in a city not his own. But a different part of her, the part that whispered "jump" when she looked down staircases, would've been spooked by his mention. Furthermore, reading his name would force her to confront the hideous but obvious truth, which was that the letters were nothing but a bundle of lies. There were days when Yan Hua wanted to confront them head-on. But every time she thought she had the courage, she'd open her mouth and leave it there, hanging.

A tooth in the back of her mouth was beginning to rot, and Kevin smelled it whenever Yan Hua was moved to confess. He never heard the battle raging inside her. The *I did it, I killed my husband* that never reached her lips. It was an unusual paradox: Yan Hua befriended Kevin because she wanted someone to talk to, but now that they were close, and had something secret between them, she couldn't say anything to him. Anything that really mattered.

Instead of telling Kevin the truth, Yan Hua chose to believe in the letters' stories. She believed in them like they were her religion. Her faith. Her belief was so deep that, one morning, while she walked to work, an urge struck her, one strong as a sick man's desire for water. Without thinking, she searched her pockets for coins and ran toward a pay phone. It didn't matter that she didn't know Kevin's number, or that he didn't own a phone. All she wanted to do was speak. To a friend, to herself, to nobody at all.

What? she imagined Kevin saying.

She spoke into the phone: "I want to know who they were. To find out about these people who might've known my husband. Maybe," Yan Hua said, sucking on her bad tooth, "maybe he's alive somewhere. I never saw him die, you know. Maybe he got up the next day and . . . and . . ."

The lies had begun to taste like spoiled milk in her mouth.

BAO MEI SAW THE MAN FIRST. THEN THE WOMAN WITH THE shrewd and sneaky face. The woman was standing in the foyer of Unity Church, wearing a purple jacket with a high collar, a fake Burberry scarf, a pom-pom hat. The scarf obscured the lower half of her face, exposing a chilled strip of nose and piercing, watchful eyes. It was Sunday, the last December of the millennium, and church volunteers were passing out cold sandwiches. There were two kinds: ham with cheese and plain cheese, each paired with an orange and a child's carton of milk. The food was donated and would be distributed every day until supplies ran out. Although the new Chinese complained (calling it "prison rations"), they secretly thought the sandwiches were delicious.

Bao Mei was one of the people who showed up every morning. She was not a proud woman, merely a shy one, and she dreaded the possibility of a former coworker seeing her. Hence her watchful eyes. The hiding of her face behind a scarf rough enough to scrape skin. She wasn't scared of being seen as poor, nor was she ashamed of eating cold sandwiches. She simply hated the small talk that places like these encouraged, the necessary but embarrassing lies ("I'm only here because it's free") that came out of people's mouths.

Such conversations were happening throughout the line as she waited, listening and sighing and shuffling her feet.

She'd arrived at the middle of the line when the man and the shrewd-faced woman walked in. To Bao Mei they were complete and utter strangers, yet their presence sent a ripple of recognition through her body. Until she reached the front of the line, she'd believed that they were old coworkers or acquaintances from the smuggling boat. But the moment a volunteer put a sandwich in her hand, the moment she extended her wrist to reject the offer of milk, she turned around. Stared straight into the shrewd woman's face.

And remembered.

She'd seen her before, in the Workers' Cinema. A woman dressed incognito, like a man, with charcoal slathered on her face and jacket. It was a convincing disguise at first, but when Yan Hua walked past the ticket office without heeding Bao Mei's words, and when she stood before the screening room with a frightened expression on her face, Bao Mei realized that this customer was a wife. A confused and grief-stricken one, though her face slowly calmed. Bao Mei had stepped forward then, defensive and with stuttering words on her lips.

"This isn't the place for you," she said.

Afterwards, when the woman didn't respond: "People like you shouldn't be here."

It hadn't been the first time a wife had come into the Workers' Cinema. Their appearances were rare but mind-crushing; each one gave Bao Mei a migraine. The full-body kind that left her bedridden, with burst veins in her cheeks and a tingling sensation in her hands. Some of the wives, Bao Mei remembered, showed up with weapons. Hammers, curtain rods, beer bottles, a knife. They'd enter the screening rooms to search for their husbands, small and defiant men whom they'd drag out (if they could find them) or yell death threats after (if they couldn't). Others wept and stood silent, the way the shrewd-faced woman did. These women revealed to Bao Mei that the Workers' Cinema was no utopia. That this wasn't a safe space—not for everyone.

Watching the shrewd-faced woman reminded her of this fact. Despite her disguise and the stench that came off it, the woman stared at Bao Mei with a stately expression on her face. Tears were in her eyes, but they didn't fall, almost as though she was too good for them. When Bao Mei asked if she wanted to sit down a moment, perhaps drink some water, the woman turned away. And while Bao Mei stared at the stooped curve of the woman's back, the defeated, sack-crumpled shape of it, she understood, finally, the horrible contradiction that breathed life into the Workers' Cinema. Yes, it was a place for love, and yes, it was the only place where a certain kind of man *could* love. But it was also—was it not?—a place for betrayal. A place where wives were lied to. Where wives were humiliated, though of course they couldn't show it. They had to continue living dignified, proud, and pretend-happy lives. To live otherwise in a place like Mawei would've insulted them.

Bao Mei remembered all of this at Unity Church.

She saw the shrewd-faced woman and noticed that her expression was completely unchanged. Perhaps "barely" was a better word, because the wildness that once commanded her lips was now hidden by lines deepened by laughter. That plus the hint of a mustache, the sight of which made Bao Mei chuckle. She almost said hello to the woman. Not to remind her of their meeting, but to . . . but to what? There was no reason to dig up the done-and-dirty past, no reason to fulfill the useless nostalgia she felt. She had a desire to say "hello," but no courage or justification to do so. At this, she walked out of the church, where she was met by the wind: sharp as a wolf's fangs. *It would've been weird anyway*, Bao Mei thought. Weird and uncomfortable and perhaps even mean. Thoughtfully, carefully, Bao Mei made her way to the bus stop, her church rations swinging in a plastic bag on her elbow.

As the saying goes: We should leave the bones in the graveyard alone.

YAN HUA COLLECTED COLD SANDWICHES AT UNITY CHURCH. She took English classes and attended holiday mass when hot meals were promised. But she never saw Bao Mei there again. The one time it happened, Yan Hua didn't feel a lightbulb flash above her head. Only the mild heat of shame as a woman stared at her from afar. She assumed that the woman was judging her for taking the charity of a religion she scorned. If only there had been an exchange, then Yan Hua might've recognized her as the stranger who offered her kindness at the Workers' Cinema. The one who limped and asked if she wanted a seat and water—from a bottle instead of tap. But maybe there wouldn't have been a spark of recognition had such a meeting occurred.

Because the truth was, she only remembered that night in bits and pieces. Some memories, like the walk leading to the cinema, were as clear as the bottled water that was offered to her. Others were murkier. How had she gotten home? What did the woman tell her? Did Shun-Er pursue her? Did they argue afterwards, trading tired, quiet, furious words in their way-too-tiny bed? Yan Hua wondered about the past, not knowing whether to be frustrated or thankful for her opaque memory. The one thing that stood out was a memory of longing: one that shook Yan Hua to her core. It was a selfish longing, unspeakably selfish.

All Yan Hua wanted was for the Workers' Cinema to shut down.

She came close to telling Kevin about it, like the time he asked if Yan Hua had "really been okay with Shun-Er going to the cinema." They were sitting on a park bench, watching teenagers play handball. Kevin carried Bao Mei's letters with him as a pretense to hang out.

"What do you mean?" Yan Hua asked.

"The way you talk about him, about the place. You don't seem angry about it."

"I am. And was. It's that a lot of time has passed."

"You've forgiven him."

She paused. "Sure. It's hard to stay angry at the dead."

"You said he had a lover?"

"Yeah."

"And they met in the theater."

". . ."

"If it were me, and my boyfriend did that, I'd want to kill the other guy." He laughed like it was a joke, but she didn't. She simply looked at the letters and sighed.

The truth was trapped like a pebble in her shoe.

TWENTY-FIVE

AS THE SEASONS passed and later the years, the new immigrants of East Broadway continued to invent themselves in the slums of Chinatown. Street signs appeared with Chinese as well as English characters, and white men selling knockoff bags learned to yell cusswords in Fuzhounese (before getting replaced, in the early aughts, by Chinese men yelling cusswords in English). Residents filled their fake wallets with real dollars, and quarters were pressed into the hands of bus drivers, the Chinese ones who took laborers from one Chinatown to the next. Gone were the days when sweatshop workers had to fuss with their MetroCards on the subway (many had moved to Brooklyn after 9/11), counting minutes and searching the windows for signs of their stop. They discovered the pleasure of a highway without traffic, of headphones in the ears and a window with a Gowanus view. A woman's leg nudged her neighbor's, asking him for more space, and sometimes this action stirred up a conversation. A pleasurable and banal discussion about the price of meat, the blandness of watermelon, the sales at Macy's.

Then summer came, and what could beat the feeling of entering an air-conditioned factory? Of a Coca-Cola from the fridge of a bakery? Of a prep cook's smoke break under the shadow of an awning, his respite from the heat of a sweltering kitchen? Hurricane season came and went, and the new immigrants learned how to hoard supplies from Costco. They pitched in for membership cards, tossed toilet paper and Poland Spring crates into their carts. Afterwards, they'd share a pizza in the food court, their awkward, English-shy tongues ruining orders and generating laughs. Prejudice angered and amused the new immigrants, and this was no contradiction in a place like Chinatown. No, it was the simple truth, the reality of living in a place where four or five city blocks belonged to them, and nothing else. Not the next street, where the American clothing stores were located, and not the park that stood beneath the shadow of the county jail, where years or even months earlier, they stood in a closet-sized room with only the orange of their jumpsuits for comfort, and where their brothers, sisters, cousins, nephews, and neighbors waited, praying for a quick release.

Yet they built this place.

They named East Broadway "Little Fuzhou" and suppressed the feeling that they were foreigners. The Americans were. English was scorned by immigrants trying to harness its patterns, and their friends laughed at the joke-like nature of its alphabet. *J* looked like a fishhook, but the letter had little to do with fishing. *Y* was a fork in the road; *F* was a rake. Perhaps they should've paid closer attention in Mrs. Ng's class, because every so often they'd have to leave the safety of their bubble. They'd find themselves in the situation that Yan Hua was in, in the summer of 2002. She and her two friends, trailed by Frog, were standing like geese in the middle of the Costco food court. She'd asked for a pepperoni pizza but had gotten cheese, and she was debating whether to ask for an exchange.

Frog pretended not to care. He was a man who had no problem nagging his wife in private, but who was meek as a lamb in public. Not wanting to be part of a scene, he stood away from Yan Hua while she asked the cashier for her correct order. The very sight of which made the heat rise in his belly. He couldn't abide prejudice toward Chinese people, but he didn't have the courage to confront it head-on. All he could do was lip-sync his wife's English, as though he were talking to the cashier himself. The same cashier with the braces and the impatient demeanor, who Frog was certain had laughed at him earlier, for grabbing a handful of ketchup. Her open dislike of Yan Hua embarrassed Frog, making him hateful. But because he didn't have the tools to attack the cashier, he decided to attack his wife instead. First while sipping Fanta in the Costco food court, then in the twin-XL bed they rarely made love in. He mocked the *R*'s Yan Hua tucked into her "hellos" and the way she counted to three but not to four (she could not pronounce her *F*'s). He put a mask in front of his words, made faces to show people that he was joking. But there was a bite under his breath. A nastiness, certain as the cashier's boredom.

("Count to four!" he'd say. "You're so good at English, Yan Hua. So why don't you show everyone how well you count to four?")

Yan Hua felt the bite but pretended not to. She made excuses for her husband. But one day, in a fit of anger so severe it made her *calm*, she peered deep and carefully into the well of her affection.

Only to discover that it had dried up.

"She's like a cow," he said. "No brains. All mouth and udders."

"All right," Yan Hua said, laughing along.

"And look at her belly, look at the size of it!" Frog reached under the table to poke her, but Yan Hua had shrunk away, a reflex that transformed itself into conscious movement when he tried again, this time with an *I'm just teasing you* look on his face. "Her belly's like a pregnant woman's. Look how she stuffs her face!"

"Maybe she *is* pregnant," Little Amy said. She thought the entire exchange was a joke, because what belly could Frog be talking about?

"I'm not."

"She can't even order a pizza, you expect her to take care of a child?"

"You're still eating that pizza, aren't you?" May asked. Her voice was quiet but meaner than what Frog was used to. He began to stammer.

"I like meat on my pizza."

"Then ask for some yourself. If you have so much to say, why don't you go up to the counter, ask the cashier for some pepperoni?"

"I was just joking," Frog grumbled.

"He was just joking," Yan Hua said. But she tapped May's foot under the table, a gesture neither women knew the meaning of.

~

THERE WAS A TIME WHEN YAN HUA HAD LOVED FROG. NOT dearly, and not in public, but the love was enough for her to soften her skin with Vaseline, applying it to the places Frog touched. These were her hands, her cheeks, her clavicles, her inner thighs. On special nights, she'd substitute the Vaseline with baby oil, heating a small amount in the microwave before applying it to her skin. The smell was Frog's first hint that she wanted something. The second was the lacy strap of underwear peeking out from under her pajama bottoms. This was the only "cute" pair of underwear she owned. The rest, which she bought in bulk from the vendors at the mall, were dull colors. Anything extravagant would've gotten her unwanted attention, so she settled for the plain, the cheap, the convenient, the simple. Except once, when a slip of the hand (but was it really a slip?) led her to choose a striped, lacy pair, more suitable for a schoolgirl, which she used to signal her desire.

He'd put the underwear in his mouth, chewing it and savoring the baby oil smells that struck him in the nose. Frog was a tender man in bed, and a giggling one, too. Confident in his sexuality, he understood and even invited the humor that came with intimacy, laughing tenderly at the mishaps that lovemaking invited. He grinned when strings of fabric got stuck in his teeth. When a kiss in the wrong spot put a bitter taste of oil on his lips. When the shock of her thigh skin (soft as baby flesh) caused the moisture in his mouth to disappear. He'd reach for a water bottle on his desk then, drinking it while Yan Hua watched the apple bob in his throat. She was quiet when they made love. Motionless. And most nights, she kept her eyes closed. But her breathing was quick. Loud as the spasms that caused Frog to release his final and hideous roar.

Afterwards, they'd lie together. Shiver or sweat under the covers and talk.

It was a love Yan Hua guarded. Not out of fear or jealousy. Instead, she acted out of instinct. Out of a village girl's conservativeness, one passed down by her mother (and which felt as natural to Yan Hua as tea leaves in water). She didn't want strangers seeing her act like a schoolgirl in public. Yan Hua was too grown for that. Plus, grown women didn't blush at the pleasure of clasping a husband's hand. They didn't smile when a husband leaned forward to convey a secret message in their ear. In Yan Hua's world, men could "give" love in public, whereas women could only receive. Adding complexity to this mindset were her memories of Shun-Er: how he betrayed her and how she betrayed him back.

Those memories came and went, and Yan Hua experienced their potency in waves. Some months she was haunted by them and walked around like a woman possessed. Other months she fell into a depression that she brushed away, as if feelings were nothing but a trail of ants marching across her body. There were months, too, when she didn't think about Shun-Er, months when she could push him aside, cram him into some cluttered or dark corner of her mind. But these periods never lasted. In fact, by the time Yan Hua started hunting the woman who wrote letters to gay men, these periods of quiet had disappeared. Completely. And, along with them, the nights that smelled like baby oil.

At first, Frog was understanding. He was a pleading man, but he wasn't forceful. And though he might've spent one or two mornings pressing his firmness against Yan Hua's back, he never forced her to do anything she hated. He might ask and he might wheedle, but he accepted that no meant no, and that a man's integrity was one of the eight Confucian virtues. But his patience had a limit, and when he crossed that limit, he grew careless with his words. It was during these times that Frog's breath would develop its rotting stench.

"I want to get dentures," Frog said.

"Close your mouth," Yan Hua said. "I can see the problem, there's no need to show me. Plus, your breath stinks."

"It's not a matter of money, it's a matter of time. I don't have any."

"Ask your boss for a vacation."

"Not every job is like yours," Frog said. He was not over the rudeness of the Costco cashier and tossed in an extra sentence, one meant to hurt and humiliate. "I don't get to sit around on my ass all day doing nothing."

"Who said I do nothing? You better watch your mouth."

"Unlike yours, *my* boss would fire me if I asked for a day off."

Despite his complaints, Frog knew that his was a better job than most. It paid decently and the worksite was local. Plus, his boss was a laughing man who didn't yell at his workers, who didn't knock them down to build himself up. Sure, he might expect you to do the work of two men, and sure, he was known to let folks go without notice. But he never cursed at them. The most he would do was tell them to leave, to go home and never come back, but Frog—whose gratitude to the man verged on worship—believed that he did so with regret in his eyes. It was an unfounded belief, one built on a gesture of kindness that had knocked Frog off his feet when he was first smuggled to America. Years ago, he'd asked his boss if he could work seven days a week instead of six (to repay his debt more quickly to the Snakehead). His boss, instead of agreeing, simply gave him a raise.

The raise was not a large one. You'd laugh or be shocked if you heard the amount. But to the young, single Frog, the raise was life-giving. It brought in enough money to lift him out of poverty, changing his status from destitute to simply poor. For the first time in his life, he had the freedom to buy frivolous things. Sides to go with his meals. Nike shoes and socks from the American stores. Later, when Yan Hua arrived, Frog received a second raise, followed by a third, the last one decent enough to purchase a Coach scarf for his wife. The thing he wanted most, however, was three days' vacation so he could replace his rotten teeth, a request that wasn't fulfilled until his fifteenth year at the noodle shop.

He'd lost his left canine by then, and the replacement was a short-term, back-alley fix: pale and small. Seeing it for the first time next to his big yellow teeth caused Yan Hua to laugh and hiccup and slap her knees. She called her husband "bicolor corn," giggling as he play-argued with and tickled her. The joyful payback of a husband who was too grown and too childish at the same time. This was back when their baby oil nights were dwindling but alive, back when Frog could expect the balm of his wife's desire at least once every two weeks. Now he was lucky to kiss her once a month. Her factory job was gone, but a friend at the Unity Church—Yan Hua wouldn't say who—had introduced her to a company that sent you beads to make bracelets, which you then returned for a check. She did this every day with May and Little Amy, complaining at bedtime about the aches in her hands.

Frog endured a marriage without love for what seemed like no time at all, until one night, while talking to his wife about vacation days and teeth, the knowledge that a full year had passed struck him with the force of a sledgehammer. The figure dazed him. Made him wonder if his math was wrong. If he'd miscounted the hours, the days, the weeks, the months. To calm himself, he left the room with a pack of cigarettes, a bottle of water. And the moment the door shut behind him, fear began to creep up Yan Hua's spine. She realized, right then and there, that to maintain the peace, she'd have to forfeit a part of herself to her husband. Something in his mouth suggested it. She saw a firmness there: a deep-rooted, no-longer-suppressed male impatience—the very same one that allowed husbands to demand, fathers to punish, boy-children to bully. All in the name of love. The sight of him frightened her so much that she started searching for the baby oil. Not finding it, she wondered if plain Vaseline would work. She changed her underwear. Worried, with trembling hands, about whether she could still do it, whatever "it" was. She walked to the suitcase Frog used as a dresser and unzipped it, though for what reason she had no clue. Perhaps to search for money, money she'd steal and leave the city with. The radiator hissed, encouraging her. Minutes later, it began to bang, fighting for center stage with the beat of Yan Hua's heart, and eventually winning after twenty minutes had passed and Frog hadn't returned.

HURT BY THE ABSENCE OF HIS WIFE'S DESIRE, FROG TURNED to flirting with the women around him. He didn't realize what he was doing at first. Then, when he did, he denied the flirting by calling it "small talk." He laughed too hard at the jokes of female co-workers. And when they offered him their attention, he spoke about things like philosophy and religion. He never expected anything to go further than a friendly rapport. Perhaps a smile followed by touching hands. To the stocky and rough-skinned waitress who teased him at the noodle shop (making his heart tremble but not flutter), Frog mentioned that his wife might as well have been a radiator and not a woman. "All she does is lay next to me in bed, sweating and complaining about me sweating." And though the friendship with the waitress fizzled into nothing, the possibility that desire could exist outside his marriage made Frog dream.

After the rough-skinned waitress, he moved on to the cashier at a local bakery: a shy but talkative woman who lowered her eyes to prevent people from noticing how crossed they were. Then Little

Amy, though she put a stop to his advances with a look so fierce, it was as if she'd burned him. His cowardice prevented any act that was too forward, any conversation that was too lewd, but he discovered that his love-desire could be satiated by many small and simple kindnesses. A smile over here, a handshake over there. Giggles made hummingbirds descend like angel wings over his head, and the attentive gaze of a friend, whether male or female, made the child in him kick his legs with happiness. It turned out that physical touch wasn't the only thing Frog craved. He wanted joy, plain and simple. The joy and the conversation of a wife not consumed by letter reading, a wife not obsessed with a phantom.

So, when he fell into the bathtub that night—the night he discussed teeth and vacation days with Yan Hua—with May naked on top of him, the first emotion Frog felt was shock. Surprise that the flirting he believed was innocent was actually selfish after all. Regardless of who did what or who acted first, the reality was that his wife's friend had begun to kiss him. Yes, right there in that small, cracked tub, with the laundry dripping detergent water over their bodies, which were twisting like hogs in mud. One minute she was on top; the next minute he was. Panting. He wondered how it happened, since, of all the women he spoke to, May seemed the least interested. She withdrew into herself after Kevin left and was the subject of strange looks. Observing her from afar, Frog thought she was muttering to herself, or speaking in tongues. But the reality was that she had to chew on things to keep from falling apart. In private it was cornstarch, but in public she had to settle for rubber bands or hair ties, jacket lint or the blunt ends of toothpicks. Her withdrawn nature kept Frog at arm's length for a long time, but earlier that day, after returning from Costco, their fingers grazed beneath the rushing water of the sink.

The touch was accidental, but when it persisted, Frog was forced to call it *secretive*. Afterwards, tender and warm, though the latter might've come from the steaming sink water. She looked away from him, a toothpick wagging in her mouth, while he considered the possibilities of this strange, bird-thin, and birdlike woman. He remembered her sass at the Costco food court, how she leapt from her seat to defend Yan Hua from . . . to defend Yan Hua from what? Frog's bantering? His rash anger about the cheese pizza? Standing next to May and sensing her body heat, Frog wanted to tell her things he refused to tell his wife. Did May know (she must, he realized) what it was like to share nights with a spouse who ignored you? Who ignored her husband in favor of some words on a page? And who, when Frog told her there was no more baby oil, shrugged and asked, as though words couldn't cut people to the white meat: "What do we need that for?"

Frog blinked and discovered that there was a lump in his throat. If he wasn't careful in dislodging it, he'd begin to cry, and what good would that do? He stopped himself from speaking for a moment, measuring his breath instead.

"Yan Hua's going around town with Kevin," Frog said.

"I know. I've seen them before."

"You knew?"

"Everyone does."

It was a nothing conversation, and Frog didn't put any stock into it. Nor did he interpret any meaning behind the strange looks May gave him. Now, suddenly, here they were: naked and kissing in a bathtub too dirty to sit in. Gnats hovered in the space above May's head, and Frog, wanting to be playful, swatted at them. But she did not smile. Instead, she kept her eyes locked on his and said, cautiously, "You'll disturb the others." It was then that Frog woke from his stupor. It was then that he saw, under the dim lights of the bathroom, his wife's best friend in all her variable, too-familiar forms: haughty roommate, abandoned wife, sneaky sister. God, look at how ugly they were! How their bodies bristled with goose-flesh, gathering dirt and foul odors in the unscrubbed bathtub; how, upon discovering the emptiness of their desire, they'd begun to make moral excuses for their actions. And yet, Frog considered, their love had been satisfying. Not even satisfying (that was the wrong word) but *satiating*: like eating a slice of bread to stave off the afternoon hunger. He understood, however, that this was a one-time event. The moment he stood up, he understood that May had used him. Their meeting wasn't accidental. Thirty minutes earlier and consumed by anger, he'd opened the bathroom door and saw her sitting under the dripping laundry. Not beckoning but not repel-ling, either. Plus, there was that towel she was sitting on: that dirty dough-white towel with the dampness in its fibers spreading like flowers. Why hadn't he left? Why hadn't he closed the bathroom door and returned to the room where his wife was? And why (he looked into May's eyes) did this woman want to hurt Yan Hua so badly?

Now, he thought, laughing to himself, he'd have to leave for real.

Not just the bathroom but Yan Hua altogether.

"I'm going out for a smoke," Frog said.

May reached for a towel and began cleaning herself.

"FROG TOLD ME YOU WERE GOING AROUND TOWN WITH Kevin."

"You've seen him? Frog?"

"This was three days ago."

" . . . "

"Is it true, then? Are you going around with Kevin?"

"We take English classes at the church. He's gay, May. We're *not* dating."

"So how come you never told me about it?"

"I thought you knew."

"Not until your husband told me."

"He's not my husband anymore."

"Did something happen between you two?"

Yan Hua was quiet. From the look in her eyes, May could tell she knew nothing.

PART III

TWENTY-SIX

BAO MEI KEEPS dish soap in a Poland Spring bottle. She combines it with sink water, careful not to let the mixture foam. Afterwards she grabs a ball of steel wool, scraping it soft and easy against a wok covered in sauce. The food she makes is meager. Flavorless, because she never learned to cook, and oil-free, because Old Second has problems with his heart. He takes pills and walks around to steady its faint murmuring, though nowadays, he has no choice but to stand in front of a window—looking. He listens to music, but he owns only one CD with one song burned onto it. "Woman Flower": a love ballad slow as the rain dripping down the window. The dripping causes people on the street to think that Old Second is crying. They see him sometimes as they stroll along East Broadway with takeout bags and rolling luggage in their hands, the latter noisy against the quiet of a litter-strewn street.

People are leaving Chinatown. What started twenty years ago with 9/11 and the mass closings of sweatshops has continued, accelerated, in fact, in this era marked by illness. Workers' motels have shut down, and their remains have been carved into condos.

Doctors operating without licenses have grown old or paranoid, and the few who remain work in "offices" with broken elevators. They can't compete against the medical plazas with the bi- or tri-lingual receptionists. Nor can they compete with the doctors who can take in white *as well as* Chinese clientele. Locals agree that the East Broadway Mall is a shadow of its former self, an oyster with its meat scraped out. The only storefronts that remain are a barbershop, two market stalls, and a basement restaurant. Gone are the dim sum parlors named Palace where immigrant grooms once kissed their brides to too-loud, way-too-loud music. Gone, too, are the clothing stores where factory women rediscovered color. In their place sit "trendy" restaurants and boutiques—businesses that the younger generation have argued, good-naturedly, "will revitalize the dying neighborhood." But who is it being revitalized for? Do the original immigrants of East Broadway, the ones formerly called "new," want to drink seven-dollar bubble teas? Do they want to eat corn dogs stuffed with cheese, never mind the hassle of having to take a Lactaid pill every time? As one local sternly notes: "The new businesses are nothing but buckets of piss to douse a fire with!" (To which his neighbor responds, shaking her head, "We've got to move on with the times, old friend. And the mochi donuts are quite nice with tea . . .")

Of course there are some old businesses that still stand on East Broadway. People, too: many of them elderly and used to a certain way of life. Too practical for nostalgia, they look upon life's mysteries with a subtle shrug of the shoulders, as if to say, *What's coming will come.* But in the meantime, they continue to shop at the immigrant clothing stores. They continue to drink Ovaltine at the bakeries named after flowers, scoffing at the foods people eat with their eyes rather than their mouths. They recognize that Chinatown is declining and hear the people who say there's no good reason to come here. Brooklyn has cheaper housing; Flushing has better food. And the new-immigrant hubs that used to define East Broadway are gone now. They've closed or relocated or are hanging on by a thread, snipped at last by the pandemic's arrival.

When lockdown began, Old Second saw no one but youngsters roaming the streets. Mask-wearing but otherwise unrestricted; their movements made limber by their youthful bodies, the loud clatter of their skateboards. Chinatown was their playground. He saw tourists taking pictures of empty roads and shuttered storefronts. Watched as elderly folk, not adept at ordering online groceries (and not trusting them, either), walked with fear animating their gaits. There was a market down the street from Old Second's apartment. Leaning out the window, he could see the spaced-out lines of people waiting outside it. Sometimes they spoke, causing joy to course through their bodies—the specific happiness belonging to a bored and lonely group of people. How good it was to see a friend. How nice it was to hear familiar speech. Even small talk could bring joy, if the pitch in the voice was welcome enough. But when lockdown ended three weeks ago, Old Second refused to join the people he watched: the old folks, friends, and neighbors made childish by the pleasure of a simple daytime interaction.

And he still refuses, to this day.

While Bao Mei dilutes Dawn at the sink, Old Second stands at the window, sweating while Chinese war dramas play on his wife's phone. He watches them on YouTube and doesn't know how to skip ads. Instead of learning, he asks Bao Mei for help, or otherwise listens to the Allstate commercials that interrupt the flow of his muzak. It's all background entertainment anyway. He likes the sound of the shows, how sometimes they knock loose a memory or two.

The Projectionist used to play a similar genre of film at the Workers' Cinema, and it was to the rhythm of machine-gun fire, the boom and thunder of land mines, that the theater men twisted their bodies in new and loving ways. Old Second clings to that period, the memory of it, because life in America, especially in recent years, has begun to frighten him. It's not a question of belonging, of assimilation or not. No. Old Second's main issue, now, is his inability to disregard pain.

There's so much of it. So much that it blinds him, makes his fingers go numb. Once, he woke with a tension in his right hand. That was twenty years ago, when Old Second worked as a chef in New Jersey. A period when $2,000 a month was enough to make immigrants forfeit the use of their arms and legs. It was his first job in America. Not only that, he'd found a boss who was friendly. Generous. One who called him "friend" and not "faggot," "brother" and not "sissy." But the problem remained that Old Second suffered from tension in his right hand. And that problem continued when that tension transformed into a tremor that crawled up his shoulder. Ultimately, his tremor transformed into a numbness that made him drop a wok full of broccoli, splashing himself with hot oil. He lost consciousness and woke with burns that would later dry into barnacles on his face and body. But he didn't wake up in a hospital bed. His boss, worried about that day's profits, about the legality of hiring a man without papers, simply laid Old Second out in a storeroom. He put cold water and cream on the burns, but nothing was balm enough to excuse the question that was posed to Old Second when he opened his eyes.

"Are you good to work this afternoon?"

"Yes," Old Second had said. "I think I am."

"I can put you on prep duty if you need."

"I'm good."

"Or dishwashing."

"I can handle the wok. I was just dizzy."

Scared of a demotion, of his $2,000 a month becoming $1,500, Old Second insisted that he was strong enough to work. And he did—that afternoon and that night as well. Yes: Even though his boss watched him wince in pain; watched him twist his burnt, soon-to-be-scarred hands away from the wok's heat; watched as he dunked his right arm into a bowl of defrosting shrimp to take the edge off his hurt. Three days of wincing passed, of balm on his face and body, before Old Second's boss gave him a day off. And even then, it was given with the caveat that he was not to have one the following week. And what a stressful day off it was: trapped in an apartment with neither company nor heat, and with the only food being an old Burger King meal that wasn't his. Hoping that nobody would miss it, he warmed the food in a microwave when, like a jolt of lightning, he considered the possibilities of living with Kevin.

We might've had a future together, Old Second thought. *But now I'm stuck in this cold, lonely, and mean place.*

Being young at the time, Old Second assumed he could handle pain. Because at first, he was able to ignore the wok's heat. The way its flames, like tendrils, stretched toward his burn marks, licking them. But the loneliness of work life plus the nonchalance of his boss cut Old Second down like a tree. Standing before the microwave, he was reminded, suddenly, of his childhood. Of the day when his brother exposed Old Second's man-love to his family. Old Second considered the idea that, had he only suffered his father's anger, had his punishment ended with a slap and a night's worth of kneeling, he might've never left his home. He might've never gone to Mawei and gotten involved with the cinema men. But then his mother had to go and spit her hatred out like vinegar on him. As a teenager, Old Second could handle pain and meanness, was able to shrug both off without tears. But he was a different man in America. The pain was fine, but the disregard in his boss's voice when he asked if Old Second could work after fainting . . . the callousness left an impression on him. An impression that blocked him from realizing, until he saw the wet spots on the counter, that he was crying.

TWENTY YEARS LATER, OLD SECOND HAS EVEN LESS OF A tolerance for pain. Yet, because there's so much of it in America, he decides to forfeit his reality for something safer.

Memory.

He remembers tenderness. Love and sneaky laughter. Bao Mei indulges him at first, and they speak every day about the cinema's past. But then Chinatown begins to die, and a group of youngsters comes to their door, asking for a picture. Something strange happens then. Something unbelievable that Bao Mei can't tell Old Second.

Somebody messaged her on WeChat.

A woman who says she is Shun-Er's widow.

TWENTY-SEVEN

SHE GATHERS WHAT she needs and leaves Old Second by the window. Downstairs, and faced with the light of a winter sun, she puts on sunglasses. A fake Burberry scarf and a pom-pom hat. These plus a grim smile serve as Bao Mei's armor. She takes comfort in knowing that few people will recognize her beneath her layers. That her journey's purpose, hidden from Old Second, will remain private until she decides it's not. Will Bao Mei discover the truth today? And what, if the truth exists, would it look like? A thing with feathers or a creature with scales? These are the questions she asks as she scrolls through Yan Hua's WeChat profile, reading statuses, watching videos, and snorting at memes.

She is the same woman—of that Bao Mei has no doubts. The one who split her heart at the Workers' Cinema, and who once stood in line for sandwiches at Unity Church. The face is the same—small, girlish, sharp around the jaw (but round everywhere else)—and now Bao Mei can attach a name to it. *Yan Hua*. She is a nail tech, apparently, and takes pleasure in her craft, often posting videos of herself painting landscapes on people's nails. They are beautiful, the nails, but Bao Mei finds them gaudy and unsuitable for proper women. Plus, there is the matter of the videos' music: a grating collection of noise that Bao Mei can only describe as childish. And "childish" is the word she uses for Yan Hua's pictures, many of which are selfies with unfunny captions, or group photos with rich-looking but tacky friends.

Why am I so annoyed by her? Bao Mei wonders. And what, more importantly, is she afraid of? Is she worried that Yan Hua will disrupt her calm and static version of history? Is she concerned that Yan Hua's words will destroy Old Second's memories of the Workers' Cinema?

We're old, Bao Mei thinks. *There's no reason to dig up graves like this.*

The time for that was years ago. Decades. And Bao Mei, at fifty-five, is stuck in her ways, Old Second as well, and any truth that changes the past, or alters memory, would sink in their bones like snake venom in blood. She finds such changes unwelcome, rude as the way Yan Hua sends her first message. Not with a greeting, a word hello, but with a sentence ("I am Shun-Er's widow") that makes insects crawl up Bao Mei's spine. Afterwards, as if to answer a question nobody asked, Yan Hua writes: "I saw you in a photo album and recognized your husband's face. I'm in Brooklyn and would like to meet over lunch or dim sum."

Dim sum? In a time like this? Bao Mei thinks.

But she puts on her scarf anyway. Her pom-pom hat and her surgical mask. Walking down a street full of shuttered storefronts, she thinks about the life Yan Hua has built in America. She's envious of how easy it looks on WeChat. Along with the nail art videos, the selfies, and the group photos with friends, Yan Hua shares pictures of vacations. There she is: standing with two girlfriends in front of Niagara Falls. In the next shot, she leans over a railing and pretends to slip, her face warped into an expression of mock fear. She stands with arms akimbo in front of fancy restaurants, takes pictures of sushi arrangements and too-rare steaks ("I can still hear the cow mooing," one caption reads). Yan Hua is a frequent attendee of weddings but doesn't seem to be married herself. She doesn't have a husband or children and doesn't like posing with boyfriends for pictures.

Bao Mei arrives at the East Broadway Mall, where her thoughts shift toward finding a bus. One sits by a park near the dry goods market, and before entering, she loops a second mask over her face. Immediately, she's met by the reality that a trip to Brooklyn is five dollars, a fact that angers Bao Mei. Why does she have to travel in the first place? Why can't Yan Hua take into consideration the difficulty of a jobless woman making her way out of Chinatown?

Bao Mei is capable of conjuring mean feelings toward Yan Hua, but the truth remains that she cannot—is unable to—hate her. She can be mad, and she can be fearful, but hatred sits like a weak ember in her chest. Eager to flare up but refusing to. Perhaps there is something in Yan Hua's status updates, the funny-yet-lonely captions accompanying the homecooked meals she eats. "They call this," she writes, referring to a picture of sweet-and-sour squid, "a two-person meal at the store. Thank God women have two stomachs!" Or maybe it's that half of Yan Hua's clients, the ones she posts pictures of, are girlish but stern-looking men. They stand in positions that probably look good to their mothers, but all Bao Mei can see is the gaudiness of their nails. The patterns like bird plumage, the gradients like unstirred coffees, and afterwards (as she lowers her eyes): the way their left or right hips jut out just so, as though their thigh bones have popped out of their sockets. Standing next to the men, always, is Yan Hua, smiling or laughing, her eyes shimmering with pride.

"Look at these fun avocado nails I did for Kevin," she writes. "He loves them and thinks they're perfect for summer. If you're interested in booking an appointment with me, you can text me at the number above."

The picture has only one like and it is Yan Hua's own.

THE TRUTH IS, BAO MEI HAS TRIED TO ENTER THE BEAUTY industry. Not out of passion or artistic intent. She simply figured it was easier money. Her left leg has been stiff since childhood, and the nerves in that ankle, in that foot (and sometimes those toes), feel raw as a fresh wound. On rainy days, the pain is so bad Bao Mei has to count to ten before pushing herself off the bed. Once, she counted to fifty and there was moisture in her eyes, though she couldn't tell if it was from sweat or tears. It's hard for her to stand for long periods, to walk without a limp entering her gait. Tired of the jobs requiring her to do both, Bao Mei accompanied a friend to a beauty salon that advertised jobs for young women. This was eighteen years ago, and the boss man only hired Bao Mei's friend, telling Bao Mei that she was "too old to work there." He said, in any case, that he was only looking to hire one girl, not two. So Bao Mei left and sought the employment of another salon, where she was told the same thing by a woman whose jowls could've touched the floor, the nasty hypocrite. At the third salon, Bao Mei tied up her hair and filled out her eyebrows before entering. And because life had a good sense of humor, she was immediately offered a position. Ha. Ha.

Unfortunately, Bao Mei had trouble making money there, on account of the owner's shady practices.

"You're an apprentice," he told her. "We can discuss your pay after you learn the ropes."

But what ropes could Bao Mei learn if all she was asked to do was wash people's feet? Smelly feet, hard feet, soft feet, beautiful feet—enough feet to make a ceiling cave in, enough feet to cover the length of a marathon. When she was asked to clip a customer's nails, the owner stared at her so nastily that Bao Mei couldn't help but shake. Not out of fear, but from anger. Because why did he treat her like she was a child? Why, if the owner wanted her to learn the ropes, did he want her to buy nail supplies from him? Why did he insist that she pay for the nail polish she used for practice, and why was she told to wash feet, sweep floors, clean the basement every single day?

Bao Mei quit after four weeks, earning only eighty-six dollars in that entire period, all of it tips from white folks too stupid to realize they'd been cheated. And that was one thing Bao Mei couldn't agree with those "Save Chinatown" youngsters on: the idea that Chinese folks were only exploited by white people and the wealthy; that they didn't sometimes do the exploiting themselves.

Bao Mei remembers how her brother used to say she had a martyr's complex on account of her stiff leg. He wasn't totally off the mark—Bao Mei was told the same thing by the owner at the third salon. The only thing Hen Bao left out was her fondness for the misery of others. She embraced their pain, held it close to her chest like religion. And while she can't say she's wished unhappiness on others, unhappiness is what forced her to come into her own. When her brother died and her father became useless, Bao Mei had to step into both their shoes, taking on the roles of daughter, sister, dreamer, negotiator, grown-up. She wore every hat but that of a grieving child. She dreamed, however, and her brother shared messages with her from a beyond that seemed within arm's reach. And that was when Bao Mei discovered the pleasure, evil as sin, of being a relied-on woman. Of being a shoulder on which people cried or placed their burdens.

It was why she worked at the Workers' Cinema for five years. Yes, she loved that place, and yes, she believed that her brother's spirit "lived" there. But equal to her love was Bao Mei's pleasure at discovering how much the theater men needed her. They called her sister, madame, friend, sometimes even wife. Bao Mei was able to listen to their problems and comfort them; she was able to feel useful rather than used. Did Yan Hua understand the pleasure of that feeling? The addiction of realizing that, contrary to the taunting words of your childhood, you are a useful woman, someone not defined by the scraping sounds of your dragging foot?

Bao Mei is still childish like that. Despite the frown on her face and the sharpness in her eyes, she likes to comfort others, and the pleasure she receives is richer than blood. Perhaps that was why, when she first saw Yan Hua's profile, she bristled and became mean. *She does not need me*, Bao Mei thought. *She is not contacting me because of something I can provide or something that I can take off her chest.* In fact, the opposite may be true.

Yan Hua may be offering something of herself to Bao Mei.

TWENTY-EIGHT

YAN HUA'S APARTMENT is small but filled with light. Good-luck plants sit next to good-fortune ones on the windowsill, casting shadows while dropping leaves. In the living room, standing next to the sofa—its cushion backs torn and fixed with duct tape—is an ironing board. A basket of laundry and a spray bottle. Moments earlier, when Bao Mei walked into Yan Hua's apartment, kicking her shoes off but refusing slippers, she said, "You are doing laundry." Afterwards, as though remembering her manners and where she left them, a blush enters her face, followed by a small child's shyness. She swings a bag in front of her body and thrusts it toward Yan Hua, whose lips can't decide if they should curl upward or down. They twitch instead, and when she discovers the fruit inside, she smiles. Or believes that she does.

"Lovely home," Bao Mei says.

"It's too small," Yan Hua says. "The kitchen and the bathroom. They're tiny."

"It's perfect for two people. How many bedrooms do you have?"

"Just the one."

For a while they talk like this, unfamiliar but friendly, discovering (in the crumbs and crevices of their words) the surface facts of each other's lives. Meantime, and with a cat's lightness defining her steps, Yan Hua shows Bao Mei the pride of her apartment: an L-shaped bedroom with windows spanning the southern wall. It's decorated the way she once tried, when she lived with Frog, with every surface covered with tablecloths, a bed with matching sheets, flowers in fancy vases, and pictures on the walls. There are nail utensils in a box on the dresser, and swatch sticks, and polishes in every color. Bao Mei paces the room, politely smiling at furniture pieces but secretly finding them hideous. She can't hide this well, but either her host doesn't notice or she doesn't care. Yan Hua's lips flap like a car's motor and her voice is cautious.

She isn't married, Yan Hua says, but she has been. She doesn't have children and finds the sight of them tedious. In the past, she's had health problems: a breast cancer scare followed by high blood pressure. Pre-glaucoma as well, and migraines so serious they sent shockwaves down her fingers. But now she takes pills and works at a nail salon in Bensonhurst—is Bao Mei familiar with that neighborhood?

She isn't but nods to prevent an explanation.

They've moved to the sofa and sit on opposite ends of it, watching TV but also each other. Their lips are twisted and resemble sickles. Neither woman is bold enough to speak about why they're meeting, why they're here. Neither woman wants to take the first step into the dark and dirty past. And as the light in Yan Hua's apartment transitions from gold to orange, as her well of small talk begins to run dry, she—not knowing what to do next—decides to examine her visitor's nails. To Yan Hua's surprise, they are long and well maintained, perfect canvases for the art she's been meaning to practice. A lightbulb flashes and she clears her throat. Once, twice, three times, until out she comes with it: not with the words that she meant to say, when she first messaged Bao Mei, but the ones that would lead her to them.

"Is it all right if I paint your nails?"

Bao Mei shrugs. And pushes her left hand forward.

IT IS THEN THAT THEIR POLITENESS DISSIPATES. IT IS THEN that the women discover, begin to understand, the rifts in each other's minds. Like how one woman is stern but soft as belly meat on the inside. How the other pushes buttons with a smile on her face, feigning shock when people snap at her, cobra-like. Yan Hua prods her visitor gently. She massages Bao Mei's hands with flaxseed oil before snipping her cuticles like she's tearing fibers off an orange. In a gravelly voice, she asks questions about her favorite colors, explaining at the same time the nail art she wants to create. The procedure is very professional: Yan Hua's expert explanation of what a topcoat is, the way she handles tools shaped like ancient artifacts—both cause Bao Mei to see her companion in a different light. But during her speech, a rude question sneaks out, fast and revealing Yan Hua's intentions.

"Your husband couldn't come today?" she asked.

"I didn't tell him I was coming."

"Is he ill?"

"In a way."

Yan Hua looks up from Bao Mei's hands to stare at her face. A flicker of recognition enters her eyes, one accompanied by a spine

shiver that disrupts her movements. *Who is this woman?* she wonders. Because Yan Hua doesn't know all the things that Bao Mei
does—yet. Two days earlier, when they were talking on WeChat,
she'd discovered basic details, some of them lies, about Bao Mei's
life. The shock of these details hasn't sunken into Yan Hua's mind.
Until now, as she examines Bao Mei's features for the source of her
recognition. Has she seen these creases before, beside Bao Mei's
eyes? What about her eye freckles, the way the bulb of her nose is
tipped with a bump the texture of a pearl? They sit close to each
other, close enough for Yan Hua to hear the pause in Bao Mei's
breath when Yan Hua asks:

"Do you know the kind of man your husband is?"

"Do *you?*" Bao Mei asks.

"I'm asking you."

"I know that he is an old man now. And that he has worked
thirty years in the restaurant industry. He has damaged nerves in
his fingers on account of a beating by thugs." (*A lie*, Yan Hua
thinks.) "Arthritis and other health problems. And yet he's worked
all these thirty years, every single one without a break."

"What about before then?"

It is at that moment, in the space between Yan Hua's question
and Bao Mei's response, that Yan Hua realizes who this woman is.
Where she's seen her before, and where she's heard her stutter—
soft as the flapping of wings.

"We've met before," Yan Hua says. Anger, bold as a fist, causes
her once cautious smile to widen into a sneer. "You were at the
Workers' Cinema when I came in that night."

"I worked there."

"You were complicit."

"I worked there," Bao Mei says again.

"You saw me dressed like a soldier with charcoal smeared on my face. Not just charcoal but mud, sweat, leaves, and tears. And not once did you try to stop what was happening. You didn't think to search for my husband; you didn't ask him or anyone else to take me home. You thought a seat and a drink of water would be enough before you shooed me out the door."

"I didn't 'shoo' anyone."

"To your credit, you had sympathy in your eyes—"

"I don't want your credit. But don't lie on me and my name."

"—but it was the wrong kind of sympathy. Dead wrong. You saw me as a cheated-on wife and not the woman that I was. One with autonomy. Wants, needs"—Yan Hua twists the cap off a bottle of gel topcoat—"and limits. And that night I was testing mine. I'm no idiot. I knew what my husband was doing with your husband. But before I entered the theater that day, I thought to myself: Everything will be all right if he comes home with me. If he can show me that he cares. But you didn't think to grab him for me. In your sympathy, your desire to view me as a pitiable woman, you flattened me like a pancake."

"How was I supposed to grab your husband if I didn't know which one he was?"

"Just like that: You flattened me . . ."

"Was I supposed to barge into every screening room with your picture and a flashlight, asking men if you were their wife? Come on now. We didn't have cell phones back then."

"But you could've asked. You could've asked me. Instead, all you said was 'This is not the place for you.'"

"It wasn't."

"That's for damn sure."

Bao Mei sighs. Yan Hua has been doing Bao Mei's nails

throughout their entire conversation, pausing only once to get a heated point across. She's finished applying the glossy topcoat, and now they're done: ten cool-toned, holographic nails resembling the scales on a mackerel's tail.

"Is that why you asked me to come today?" Bao Mei asks.

"Keep your nails under the UV light. Don't move them."

"So you can scold me?"

"No. That's not the reason at all."

"Why then? If you want me to apologize, then fine. I'm sorry. But what is my 'sorry' going to do for you? What is my husband's?"

"You've got it all wrong," Yan Hua says.

OLD SECOND WATCHES, CATLIKE, AS HIS WIFE EXITS THEIR apartment. Bao Mei doesn't tell him where she's going, and at first, he doesn't think to ask. But the frequency and length of her absences have sparked his curiosity. Standing by the window, he peers down at her: at the orange jacket on her back, the thin and flapping Coach scarf around her neck. It's windy today. And the darkness of the afternoon sky tells him that a storm is coming, and that his knuckles will ache tonight. Walking to the toilet, which he has to grunt to sit on, he wonders, uneasily, where Bao Mei got that orange jacket. And that Coach scarf: raggedy as a torn kite, but unfamiliar and therefore new to his rheumy eyes.

Has she found a job?

No, she would've told him if she did.

Did their unemployment applications finally go through?

It's possible. But she would've told him about that, too.

He removes the thought of his wife being reckless with money from his mind. If anything, Bao Mei isn't reckless enough—just look at the meals they eat. Steamed eggs for breakfast, microwaved hot dogs for lunch, sliced potatoes and onions from the Jewish food pantry for dinner, canned goods from the church (no longer named Unity) for a snack, and any fruit she can scrounge up for dessert. She isn't a seamstress, but she sews up the holes in her shirts. She doesn't like luxury goods but buys the fake versions from Canal Street, claiming she prefers those styles anyway. And suddenly, in a labor desert, you're telling me this miserly woman buys a brand-new jacket and a hundred-dollar scarf?

No, Old Second thinks. *There's no chance of that happening. Unless* . . . (He pauses his thoughts to focus on standing up.) *Unless she has a lover.* A sugar daddy, as the Americans say. And this thought brings Old Second so much pleasure that he chuckles and slaps his knees, heaves phlegm from his heavy, heavy throat. A new feeling, similar to childlike wonder but not quite, erupts from his body as it dawns on him—not for the first time, but rather *again*— that his wife is her own person. That she has her own mind and body to consider, to be selfish about. Not everything revolves around Old Second, and thank God for that, because look at how he's been acting these past months. A quiet, doddering companion to a woman who might've experienced things of her own. Past-things, today-things, future-things, but things outside the history they have shared and talked about. Obsessively.

Early in the pandemic, when Old Second and Bao Mei lost their jobs, Bao Mei decided to collect recycling on the street. She'd exchanged her bottles and cans for thirty-eight dollars, which she tucked away for emergencies. Old Second never tagged along on those walks, but his wife always came back with amusing stories: youngsters arguing with each other at the park, riffraff in the white parts of town, gossip from friends or neighbors. He'd appreciated these tidbits and was surprised when Bao Mei stopped going on her recycling trips. There was a reason, perhaps a troubling one, but Bao Mei didn't talk about it and Old Second didn't bother to ask. He was already slipping into the past by that point, and though they still spoke frequently, their conversations could not extend beyond a certain line in the dirt. Uninterested in the present, he decided the only painless way to live was to dream of the past. Until today: when his notice of Bao Mei's absences transformed into curiosity about her life. And perhaps a little fear—fear that his only companion would abandon him for the grass on the other side.

Maybe she's collecting recycling again, Old Second thinks, hoping a little. *I never understood why she stopped in the first place.*

He decides to ask her when she comes home.

He returns to the window, where he waits for her jacket to appear.

WELCOME WORDS COME FASTER THAN THE KNOCK OF BAO Mei's fists when she stands outside Yan Hua's door. Some days, nicer ones, the door will simply hang open. Yan Hua wears blue jeans and a pajama top, plastic sandals and a puffy coat. Despite her extravagant life on WeChat, Bao Mei quickly discovers that Yan Hua is cheap, that she doesn't leave the heat on (if there are no guests) or even the lights (if she can help it). Hence the chill of the first few minutes whenever Bao Mei visits her "friend"—a word she uses cautiously, and only after Bao Mei's fourth visit, during which Yan Hua dyes her hair.

They are easy with each other now. Frank and a little rude.

Perhaps there's some truth in that saying about secrets and strangers: How one comes out more willingly in the presence of the other. Yan Hua and Bao Mei have begun to lay their stories beside each other's—comparing notes, experiences, pleasures, and miseries. The only subject they avoid is Yan Hua's decision to contact Bao Mei. She hinted at it during their first meeting but couldn't come out with the truth. And though she wants, each time, to remove that stone called guilt from her chest, she realizes that she can't. That for some reason she likes this woman sitting in her kitchen or her living room: shrewd and combative, downright mean sometimes, but always with sweetness hidden in the gravel of her voice.

It's the kind of voice that can scrape your skin off. That leaves you raw or burning if you're not careful (and sometimes even if you are). And yet how nice it feels against Yan Hua's back as she adds highlights to Bao Mei's hair.

"You want me to paint your nails while the dye sets?"

"Long as it's not whatever you did last time," Bao Mei says. "Looked like a dog was chewing on my fingers."

"I didn't think it was that bad."

"Then why didn't you snap a picture for your social media?"

They laugh a little. Slap a knee or two. The radiator, recently turned on, has begun to bang and hiss. There is a mildew smell in the air, and tea going on the stove.

"Does your husband notice your nails?"

"Nope. And if he does, he doesn't tell me. The old coot doesn't do anything but sit beside the window nowadays. Remembering and sighing."

"He like your new coat?"

Bao Mei shakes her head. "The last time he noticed anything was when I got him some goldfish: two itty-bitty things from an old man down the street. He gave me the tank, the fish, and fish food, and told me that they were siblings, brother and sister. It was in the beginning of the pandemic, and I'd sold enough cans and bottles to buy that idiot a present. But I carry the tank home and he starts grumbling! Just like how I'm about to start grumbling if you don't steady your damn hands! Are you dyeing my hair or my cheeks?"

"Sorry."

"He complained about having to clean the tank, about feeding the fish and changing the water. 'Fish die easily,' he said, and asked how much I paid for them. I told him five dollars (which wasn't far from the truth; they were fifteen) and he seemed to settle down a little. I remember thinking at the time," Bao Mei says, laughing, "that I'll never do a nice thing for him again!"

"My second husband was like that," Yan Hua says. But she bites her tongue, deciding to wait until Bao Mei is finished.

"My husband grumbled for a few days. But he was fascinated by those fish. He watched them like a child and asked me, sometimes, to watch them with him. Even though all they did was circle each other, or look out the glass, or flap their gills when it was time for food. And of course, though it happened sooner than I expected, they started to get sick. My husband, may God strike him down, started looking at me with this *told you so* attitude in his eyes. Acting like he never cared about those fish when in fact he really did. Because when they died—it was in the morning, my husband wasn't even awake yet, I discovered them floating and flushed them down the toilet—he let a sob escape from his throat. No tears: only a sob like a frog's croak. Afterwards, nothing. He said he was tired and moved a chair beside the window. And he's been looking out it ever since."

"My second husband was like that," Yan Hua says again.

She and Frog reconnected on WeChat last summer. He lives in Texas and runs a PokeBowl business with his wife: a tall and dark woman with eyes large as plates. They have three sons together (all resembling the wife), and the eldest goes to NYU, a medical student. A strange fate, considering how often Frog rants about the COVID vaccine, sharing anti-science articles on his timeline. The only other things he says to Yan Hua are "Happy New Year" and "Happy Birthday," the latter a surprise, since he never said it when they were married.

"He criticized things just to hear my disagreements. Not in a malicious way. In fact it was kind of endearing. Childlike. For instance, he'd say something negative about the food he cooked, something about it being too salty or too oily. And he'd sit there, waiting for me to tell him no, that his cooking was delicious. Sometimes I'd mess with him, especially if it was one of my favorite dishes. Sometimes I'd tell him I hated the meal and pretend to spit it out. He'd laugh then, and so would I."

"Why did you leave him?"

"I didn't love him."

"That's no reason to leave someone."

"Why not? What better reason can you have to leave your spouse?"

"They stop providing for you. Or they beat you. Take your money. Gamble and drink."

"I'm not old-fashioned like that. If I don't love someone, I won't stay."

"You're not afraid of being alone?"

"Alone is better than a loveless marriage."

". . ."

"Wait twenty minutes for the dye to set in. Then you can go wash it off . . ."

"I think nothing's more frightening than being alone," Bao Mei says.

"I'm not alone. I have friends."

"Because what are you going to do? With all that feeling in your chest? Who's going to help you carry it?"

"Myself."

Bao Mei looks at her, about to talk about her brother. But she stops herself.

Another time, she thinks.

WHEN BAO MEI COMES HOME, AND OLD SECOND—WEARING a playful smile—asks her why she's stopped collecting bottles and cans, Bao Mei says:

"Because a man at the recycling plant told me to go back to China and if I didn't he promised he would kill me."

TWENTY-NINE

B AO MEI ISN'T trying to be nasty. Her words, blunt but not mean, are born from the horrible truth Yan Hua revealed, hours earlier and in a room gilded by sunlight.

Bao Mei doesn't remember the buildup to Yan Hua's confession. Nor the way her own face twisted when the first of those words struck her in the ears like an uppercut.

"I have to tell you something."

IT CAME OUT OF HER LIKE A CRY FOR HELP. AN INTERRUPtion uttered urgently, like the gasps of a man choking at a party, or the cries of a swimmer drowning in a lake. Yan Hua's voice had taken on an element of strain, and it cleaved in half the story that Bao Mei was trying to tell. Which began in the following way:

A year after the protest at the Workers' Cinema, when she and Old Second first started living together, Bao Mei received a message from her father. It was about Hen Bao. Apparently, he'd been pestering Bao Mei's father in his dreams, asking for money in the afterlife. Bao Mei's father had gone to a priest about the dreams, and she told him that Hen Bao's burial had gone terribly wrong. Something about being buried on the wrong date, under poorly performed rites. "If this wrong isn't righted," the priest had said, "your son's spirit won't be put to rest. He might rise out of his tomb." The threat was so large that she was willing to help Bao Mei's father out for a steep discount. Bao Mei had objected to this at the time. She, being a member of the younger generation, believed that the priest was up to something sneaky, that what she said was a load of superstitious bullcrap. But you could not voice such opinions in a rural village in China, especially if you were a woman with a limp.

"So we exhumed his body," Bao Mei said. She spoke with her eyes closed, with sweat dripping from her forehead to her chin. Her knees knocked together like loose change in a dryer. And look. Look at the strain in her mouth as words fell out of it like rotten fruit. How could she explain the shock of seeing her dead brother's body? The horribly incorrupt state of it, as though he were buried three days and not yet three years earlier?

"His teeth had grown. His hair and his nails as well. His belly was protruding like a pregnant woman's, like he'd been eating in his grave, and there was a scowl on his face. At first, I thought the scowl was a trick of the light. An illusion stemming from my exhaustion at work. But then the priest, pinching her nose, said something about how we arrived 'just on time.' She said if we'd exhumed my brother any later, he would've started eating people. I didn't react to this because I noticed that there was a mark on Hen Bao's face. A welt more horrible than the stench permeating the fresh, mountainside air . . ."

It was precisely at this moment, in the space between the words "mountainside" and "air," that Yan Hua snuck in her confession. It happened so fast that Bao Mei could barely register that Yan Hua had said anything. No, not at first, and not while she was struggling to describe the odor of her brother's corpse. The smell, however, was nothing compared to the reminder of what she'd done to Hen Bao's face, of how she'd pinched his cheek while he was lying in his coffin. That reminder was too much for her. It was dizzying and sent her into a fugue state, and this was when she finally registered that Yan Hua had spoken.

"What did you say to me?" Bao Mei asked.

"I wanted to tell you the first time we met, but I couldn't. I was not brave enough. I thought I'd tell you the second time, but . . ."

"But what?"

"I did not expect us to become friends."

BAO MEI DIDN'T BELIEVE YAN HUA AT FIRST. AND BECAUSE OF that, she was able to finish her story, talking low about how the priests prayed over her brother's grave. Wrapping Hen Bao's body in two layers of sooty white fabric, they moved him to another grave site. One closer to the foot of High Mountain, to where Bao Mei's ancestors once lived. Afterlife money was burned, and the ashes were blown into the stream locals had named River. And that would've been the end of the story, had she told it right after it happened. But she's since learned that, just as the past can alter the present, the present can also alter the past. And the buildup of her memories allows Bao Mei to focus on two sentences the priest spoke.

The first sentence indicated that Hen Bao, because his spirit had been put to rest, would stop bothering his father for food and money.

The second was spoken to Bao Mei with a hint of sorrow in the priest's face (or was it a twitch?). She said that Hen Bao wouldn't speak to Bao Mei again. At the time, she didn't realize that this meant he'd stop visiting her in her dreams, that his spirit would stop attaching itself to hers. And because she was dealing with the fallout of the cinema protest, Bao Mei failed to notice the lack of Hen Bao's presence—having assigned her melancholy to the death of the Projectionist.

"It was only later, when I was in America, that I realized. When I understood that something was missing. Like when you wake up one morning without your sense of taste. It's why I eventually started writing letters at the church. Those stories that he told me about gay men, those squalid and impolite dreamers who wanted nothing but to live without fear. To love and be loved back. I wanted to re-create them. And I wanted . . ." She paused, her mouth suddenly taut with fear. Yan Hua's confession had finally started to sink in.

"What did you say?" Bao Mei asked.

"I didn't say anything."

"No, earlier."

The sun was bright still, in Yan Hua's apartment, but clouds had begun to billow outside her window, promising bad weather or at least some rain. But none fell and there wasn't even a strong wind to speak of.

"Were you serious when you spoke those words?"

Yan Hua nodded. "I informed on the protesters. On my husband and his lover and . . ."

"And me."

"You were there?"

The revelation, which at first seemed unreal to Bao Mei, quickly became mundane—like a toddler spilling juice on the carpet. A stain would be left behind, perhaps a matted patch of fabric, but it was nothing a little baking soda couldn't fix. Or, in Yan Hua's case, a long list of justifications. She said that she didn't know she had it in her. The normal Yan Hua certainly didn't. But *that* Yan Hua, reeling from the nights she followed Shun-Er into the cinema, did.

Yan Hua believed that her "informing" was what resulted in the destruction of the Workers' Cinema. Why else had the cadres given her that box with the gold coin—the gold coin and the money she would use to purchase her passage to America? But according to Bao Mei, the city had been going after the cinema for a while. She said the cinema would've been torn down regardless. She remembered conversations with the Projectionist about building code violations and how he'd been too stubborn to fix things around the theater. In hindsight, it was a rather decrepit place: full of roaches and creaking stairs and leaks in the ceiling. And even if they did fix the place up, the government would've taken the land anyway. All this was spoken in a tone meant to comfort, meant by Bao Mei—a woman so shocked she didn't have time to be angry—to stop the tears like dust tracks on Yan Hua's face. "So it wasn't your fault," she said. "What happened would've happened anyway."

Her comforting was confused but genuine. She didn't sneak unkind words into her sentences, didn't make sneering faces when Yan Hua walked to the bathroom for tissues. A seed of discomfort sat like a stone in her chest, but Bao Mei attributed the sensation to the sight of a crying friend. She hated this feeling and tried not to let it show. It was only when she was going home, when Yan Hua was being overly kind with her send-off, forcing fruit into Bao Mei's hands and a red envelope packed with several hundred dollars, that the anger began. The sadness, the tiredness, the need to sit down.

"Are you all right?" Yan Hua asked.

"It's my migraines. I just need to sit a moment."

"You can lie down in my bed."

"No," Bao Mei said, a little coldly.

You've done enough to me.

Because yes, perhaps the cinema would've been demolished anyway. It was inevitable, Bao Mei believed, since the government was involved. But Yan Hua's act—that changed everything. *How did she know that we were going to protest?* Bao Mei wondered. *Who gave her this impossible sliver of information?* If Yan Hua hadn't informed, perhaps the men wouldn't have been beaten. Perhaps Shun-Er and the Projectionist wouldn't have had to die. And more hateful than these thoughts was Yan Hua's attempt at deflecting blame by assigning her actions to a different self. Bao Mei spat phlegm into a garbage can when she realized that.

It was you, she thought, staring at the rusty streaks in her spit. *It was you and you alone. Don't give me that "different Yan Hua" shit.*

While Bao Mei had to deal with a broken-down theater and a boyfriend too tired to live, Yan Hua received a gold coin. A free ticket to America. She didn't have to be smuggled on a boat; she didn't have to beg for, then get rejected from, beauty salon jobs. And now she was trying to pay off Bao Mei's hatred with gifts and money.

"I wanted to tell your husband," Yan Hua said. "That's why I messaged you. I didn't know you were involved. But my first instinct was to tell him, to confess, because of everyone involved—it was cruelest to him. The thing I did."

But what about me? Bao Mei thought.

"You don't think I should tell him?" Yan Hua asked.

"I don't know."

"Do you think it'd hurt him to know?"

"I think so."

The bus on the way home encountered traffic, and Bao Mei had to close her eyes, press her head against the seat in front of hers, to keep from vomiting.

NOW SHE IS TAKING HER JACKET OFF AND BEING RUDE TO her husband. Bao Mei can't help herself. All her energy is focused on the balls of her feet, thick and tight from walking so long. She wants to sit, but the chairs in her apartment, even the futon, are too far away. One step forward would be impossible, let alone ten. When Old Second responds to her rudeness with a fragile smile, when a strap from her purse catches on the handle of a door, a coldness trickles down her spine. Afterwards, heat. She decides to give it up. All of it: her manners, her armor, the weight on her shoulders. Admitting defeat, she sits on the floor, falling gracefully like a dancer at a performance. Old Second laughs when he sees this. An awkward but playful grin appears on his face as he sits down with his wife.

"It's not too cold down here," he says. "Thank God for spring."

"I was a little dizzy. I'll be up in a minute."

"You want some water?"

"No," Bao Mei says. But her arm is outstretched.

"I didn't know about the recycling plant," Old Second says. His tone is suddenly serious, and Bao Mei realizes how long it's been since he's shown interest in any topic but the past. Not that she's in the mood to appreciate his focus right now. Her expression is normal, but her thoughts are disorganized. She can't decide, gulping down water, whether she should tell her husband about Yan Hua's confession. A part of her thinks that she should. Because how nice would it be to hand her burden to someone else? To be selfish for once, and held up by hands that aren't her own? In a way, she tried it when she shared what happened with the crazy man at the recycling plant. Thoughtlessly, yes, but it was a cry for help. One answered by her husband's misdirected and too-tardy interest.

All I want, Bao Mei thinks, *is to sit for ten minutes without worry. Ten peaceful minutes.*

"Did you see him today?" Old Second asks. "That . . . man?"

"No, I'm tired, that's all."

"Where did you go?"

"A friend from childhood, we recently connected on WeChat. I've been visiting her. She lives in Brooklyn Chinatown."

"Is that who did your nails? And gave you that jacket?"

She would bury the truth after all. The relief of her decision is enough to soften her hard and cracked feet. In three sentences, perhaps even two, she could place her burden onto Old Second's shoulders; watch his face crumble like a too-dry dough. But she chooses to lie. About how she's known her "friend" since childhood. How the two of them worked in the village paper factory. Her mood lifts as she combines lies and truth, talking low about how that "friend" has done well for herself. How she owns a nail salon and has a son who goes to NYU. And the more she lies, the more she buries Yan Hua's revelation.

"Is she married, this friend of yours?" Old Second asks.

"Yes, but I've never met her husband. Only the son. He's short as a stool and about as thick as one, too."

"But NYU?"

"I don't mean thick in the head. I meant his body shape."

Are Bao Mei's lies a secret fantasy of hers, something she wants for herself? She isn't sure. She isn't sure of anything at all. All she knows is the relief of telling lies, the relief of having a tiled floor beneath her crisscrossed feet. Like burn balm to a fresh wound. She understands, suddenly, why Old Second has spent all those days remembering by the window. He wasn't being foolish. *He was surviving.* Protecting himself from a reality that could knock you clean off your feet. Plus, it feels nice to sit like this. Nice to let go of everything and concern yourself, instead, with lies and memories—the latter so sweet they attract ants.

"You're not sitting by the window today," Bao Mei says.

"I was. Earlier. But then I saw you walking down the street."

"And?"

"I was curious where you've been."

"Are you satisfied now?"

"No," Old Second says. "Because now I want to know what knocked you off your feet."

And I want to know what placed you back on yours, Bao Mei thinks.

Instead she says, a sudden sharpness in her voice: "Can't a girl be tired without people questioning her about it?"

THIRTY

ONE MORNING, WHEN Yan Hua arrives at the nail salon, a tongue-sucking noise escapes her mouth. Irritation has settled in her stomach, causing it to bloat. Like gas or foul breath, and Yan Hua has plenty of the latter—catching whiffs of it when she wears her surgical mask. May is there, and the hello they exchange is quick. Wordless and with no indication that they've known each other for twenty years. Perhaps this is to be expected, mornings being the best time to wear a chilly expression without the danger of customers seeing. They can be quick to take offense, quick to accuse the girls of bad-mouthing them in Chinese. And that's because the girls do, sometimes, and because their expressions, on bad business days, carry something like the devil in them.

It happens to May a lot. Her face has gotten pouchy with age, and the natural setting of her lips causes her to look grouchy. Plus, she mutters to herself and chews on things, most notably the scrunchie she uses to tie up her hair. Today, while Yan Hua cleans her workstation, May munches on a plastic spoon dipped in cornstarch. Her phone is in her other hand, and she shares gossip with Yan Hua and her own husband, a man named Bun with little importance to this story, and whose life can be summed up with an occasional snort. He's the kind of man who loves his wife but disagrees with everything she says. You can see it happening now, him smirking with hidden pleasure at the vaccine news, then adding, with an air of self-importance:

"Let the Americans get their shots first. We don't know what's in it."

May ignores him, lets him rattle on. She's a newly converted Buddhist (despite her habit of eating *and* starting beef) and refuses to engage with anyone who annoys her. Contrarian husbands sit at the top of her *do not disturb me* list, followed by misbehaving children and difficult customers. To make her cold shoulder more apparent to her husband, she begins to wave Yan Hua over, to talk to her friend in a buoyant voice.

"Look at what Little Amy's doing," May says.

Yan Hua makes a face that neither encourages nor discourages conversation. It's clear that something's on her mind—she's not someone who reacts tepidly to gossip. Especially talk about a friend who's moved away. A friend who, after the arrest and deportation of her husband (*What was his name?*), eloped with a white man to Wisconsin. She's lived there ever since, with her kids, her stepkids, her dogs the size of bears. And even though Yan Hua looks bothered, she still examines the photo album May shows her: of Little Amy decorating Easter eggs with a long-eyed, sullen-looking boy. Yan Hua chuckles then, wondering how Little Amy, who seemed the most critical of white folks, ended up where she is.

"When's the last time you spoke to her?"

"Chinese New Year," May says.

"Did she do anything with her family?"

"They went to a restaurant. We spoke briefly; she said she was busy."

"I bet."

"And she has a habit of sticking English phrases into her sentences," May says, rolling her eyes. It's clear that she finds this habit stuck-up and unnatural, the same way she finds Yan Hua's nail art videos stuck-up and unnatural.

"I'm glad life worked out for her," Yan Hua says.

Her voice is friendly but flat. Ever since her last meeting with Bao Mei, Yan Hua has been fighting to maintain control over her emotions. Every task, even small ones, has required a tremendous amount of effort. Yesterday, it took her hours to prepare a meal that, in the end, wasn't worth the trouble. She poked at it (scrambled eggs and onions) until it went cold, then dumped the entire thing in the trash. *What went wrong?* she wonders. One minute, she is making a confession and asking for forgiveness. She is buoyant when her confession is received kindly, but Yan Hua's joy at being understood is betrayed by the realization that Bao Mei has rejected her.

There was one final voice message, however. One that Yan Hua clings to, for her own foolish salvation.

"I am not coming because I am sick with fever and migraines. Tomorrow I will stay home and perhaps the next day as well. I'm sure that my husband will leave the dishes for me, the cleaning, for when I am better."

Bao Mei's voice was loud. She sounded like a car engine, like the rev of an old and damaged truck. But there was humor in her voice and a note of disbelief—*How could I, of all people, have gotten sick?*—that Yan Hua responded to, laughing. In three messages, she told her to feel better. That she had nail art ideas and wanted to try them on her feet. Bao Mei's lack of response surprised Yan Hua, but it wasn't until the third day of silence that she chose to follow up with a message. When seven days passed, she tried again, sharing memes, videos, and food photographs with clumsy captions. "Messed up on the eggs again," she wrote, describing a crab omelet (Bao Mei's favorite). She compared stewed chicken feet to her customers' nails and joked about putting acrylics on them. Each message was ignored. Later, when the realization hit—that her plea for forgiveness had been rejected—a burning filled Yan Hua's chest. Hurt, clenched tight like a fist, caused a hideous thought to enter her head, and to satiate it, she'd return to Bao Mei's final message. Yan Hua played it again and again, until Bao Mei deleted her WeChat account and there was nothing left to listen to.

She's not responding because she's sick with COVID. Because she's in the hospital. Because she's dying or already dead.

Yan Hua hoped, a desperate and deep-down hope, that illness was what kept Bao Mei from answering her calls. That it wasn't the thing Yan Hua knew to be true. Which was that her confession and need for forgiveness had driven the two women apart. Irrevocably.

⤳

MEANWHILE, IN BROOKLYN CHINATOWN AND EAST BROADway, Flushing Main Street and Elmhurst, life, or the slow but cautious swing of it, has started to return. You see it in the kicks of children swinging on swing sets, the nonchalance of office workers handing their vaccine cards to servers. Uncertainty sparkles in the eyes of mothers who wonder, seated with their children at buffets, whether they should remove their masks when using the restroom. It seems rude to do so, ostentatious to not. Perhaps they should take a cue from their husbands, who allow theirs to slump on the trains as they return (sleepily, reluctantly) to their office jobs. Where a cough into an elbow now elicits a look and little else. No rudeness from the receptionist whose husband makes more than her on unemployment, or snide jokes from the manager who will, in less than a year, be terminated for storming the Capitol.

Infection statistics are tracked and shared by people crusading on social media. A hypochondriac studying computer science at City College calculates the infection and death rates, allowing himself to be comforted by both (his mother, waiting to see a doctor about a lump in her throat, is less enthusiastic). Restaurant owners construct sheds for outdoor dining, and tourists take food photographs in them. And although some Chinatown businesses, like the dim sum parlor named Palace in the East Broadway Mall, the job agencies on Eldridge Street, and the workers' motels in hidden alleyways, have shuttered for good, others, like Yan Hua's nail salon, have started to take off. Customers are returning at a steady stream. Some are regulars who say things like "Long time no see!" while others, new to the neighborhood, smile shyly behind their masks.

Stimulus checks are mailed out. Unemployment funds appear in bank accounts. Somewhere, a jobless father leans against the door of his one-bedroom apartment, thanking a god he doesn't believe in. His intentions are sincere, his relief as well, but it's hard to root for this man because he tips poorly. He takes his daughter to Yan Hua's salon once a month as a treat, waiting on a bench cushioned with beauty mags while Yan Hua applies polish to her tiny, fussy hands. May's nickname for him is One-Dollar Tip and sometimes Yan Hua's Lover. And even though Yan Hua rejects his advances with boredom in her eyes, he keeps returning to try his luck. Until one day, stressed from overwork, from the thought-pain-reality of Bao Mei rejecting her apology, Yan Hua snaps, cursing at the man in a Chinese so vehement, it crosses the language barrier.

The loss of the man is no trouble to Yan Hua. She has no time for nonsense—the salon is overcrowded with customers anyway. Some have to be turned away since Yan Hua and May are the only workers. They've talked about hiring help, about taking on apprentices to aid with eyebrow and lip waxing. But August turns to September, and business declines, slowly, like the wilting of a flower you forget to water. And during that decline, more changes happen in the city's various Chinatowns. For example: The carving out of immigrant fashion boutiques into COVID testing sites. The steady movement of Chinese businesses online, aided by social media influencers. The proliferation of food banks, where white people with friendly eyes give groceries to Chinese people with mean ones. As May's husband notes, his voice sentimental as a ballad: "The Chinatown of our youth no longer exists."

"You mean the one where we lived in poverty?" May asks.

"And were exploited by assholes like you," Yan Hua adds.

She says this as a joke, but Bun gets offended. He remains silent for the rest of the afternoon. *And yet*, Yan Hua thinks, *the man is right. Chinatown* has *changed*. She thinks about the places where she used to live, about the place where Bao Mei and her husband, who speak no English, *must* live. When was the last time she went to a Chinatown that resembled the East Broadway of 1993? A Chinatown that maintained an old-fashioned sense of seclusion? As time passes, Yan Hua's loneliness for Bao Mei turns to wonder. Becomes genuine curiosity about the world she's left, and that Bao Mei is still trapped in. Has Bao Mei gotten her unemployment money? Or is she working again, with Old Second, in the Golden Unicorn restaurant? If not: How can Yan Hua help? How can she reach out with new intentions?

A tricky idea, small and uncomfortable as a stye, wedges itself into her mind. But it isn't until the early holiday season, when business picks up again, that she can suggest it to May.

"I have a friend looking for a job," she says.

"Part-time?" May asks. "Is she available now?"

"Yes," Yan Hua lies.

"Can she do eyebrows?"

"Yes."

"I hope she's not expecting too much," May's husband adds. "We can't pay too high."

"I'll find her tomorrow," Yan Hua says.

EAST BROADWAY IS LOUD. YAN HUA CAN HEAR ITS TRAIN sounds from the next street over, through earbuds that echo her breathing. She walks with a slump in her shoulders and a crook in her back; features honed by years of bending, years of looking through dollar store glasses at customers' nails. These are necessary actions at the salon, where she and May have worked for twenty years. Yet hers is the kind of gait Chinese elders used to criticize, calling her posture impolite before reaching out with a sun-scorched arm. Why? To slap the stoop out of her back, of course! Before it becomes permanent, before it marks her for the sneak that she is.

She's been one her entire life: following Shun-Er to the Workers' Cinema, informing on him to the authorities, and creeping—with her fake papers, her secret identity—from China to America. She was sneaky when she told Frog she loved him, and sneaky again when she explored Chinatown with Kevin. Who, by the way, is working in a Japanese restaurant in Albany. Yan Hua speaks to him once a week on WeChat, and these conversations create yet another opportunity for her to be a sneak, since she can only do so behind May's back. Then, today, there is the fact that she's loping around in East Broadway, searching for Bao Mei and creating excuses for herself. Excuses for why she made her selfish confession six months ago.

The problem is that Yan Hua, while not a selfish woman, considers her feelings before those of her friends. She doesn't think about the effects of her confession on Bao Mei, nor the reality that the cinema crackdown would continue to haunt those who survived it. All she yearns for is the relief of forgiveness, the relief of knowing that her actions as a young girl weren't *that* bad. But that relief didn't (and would never) come, because the moment she confessed her wrongs to the one friend she thought would understand her, a barrier was erected between them.

Maybe I should have left the past alone, Yan Hua thinks. She sighs, playing with a receipt in her jacket pocket. *Maybe Bao Mei would've asked about it herself. Maybe she would've been more comfortable, more receptive, if I'd let her take control of her history. And maybe*—a heat sensation runs down her spine—*I'm not the person I think I am*. One who is kind. Patient and sincere. Wanting to express her goodness to her friend, Yan Hua buys some gifts for her along the way. Fruit from the vendors next to the bridge, Asian sweets from the Hong Kong market, and a pair of boots that she thinks Bao Mei would appreciate. Yan Hua convinces herself that she's doing this out of the goodness of her heart. That, once she arrives at Bao Mei's house, she'll help her to apply for rent assistance. Unemployment and EBT. Her motive, she tells herself, is to move forward with her friend.

Why, then, is Yan Hua not walking to Bao Mei's apartment? Why does she circle the streets of East Broadway, weighed down by heavy gifts? Is she afraid of meeting her friend, afraid of a second rejection? Or is she being truthful when she tells herself that there's plenty of time in the day? The afternoon that bleeds into evening?

THIRTY-ONE

KEPT SECRETS CAN wear a woman out. Like depression or anger, except the tiredness starts in the bones. Bao Mei was surprised to discover this, to learn that locking a confession in her chest could cause her to sit down and not get up again. She wanted to say, *Help me*. She wanted Old Second to put her back on her feet. But either the muscles in her throat wouldn't work, or she—after feeling the coolness of the floor, the relief of having it catch her like a lover's arms—decided it was better to stay there. And after a while, with her husband staring at her with that silly, uncertain look on his face, her decision became permanent. Sure, she'd move when she needed to, to the toilet and the bucket she called a shower. But her life, now, was lived on linoleum panels and waxed wood floors. She ate her meals "down there" (that was what she called it) on plates Old Second set down—not like for a dog but with chopsticks and paper towels. She was clean, she ate regularly, and she changed her clothes every two days. But the worry that once sat in her eyes, vacant like an ancestor's final photograph, quickly transferred to her body, sinking it and making her appear hollow. In her cheeks, her wrists, her hips, and (most visibly) her legs.

Everywhere but her belly, which ballooned like a pregnant woman's.

The food Bao Mei ate refused to stick anywhere but in her midsection. Clothes began to droop, to hang in the arms and legs. To keep a pair of pants on her body, she had to wear them above her hips, sometimes to the point where they covered her ribs. Pouches appeared beneath her eyes, and the flesh around her mouth began to sag, like the jowls of a bulldog. Only her eyes glimmered, reacted to the things Old Second did.

Unable to hold anger for Yan Hua, she had no choice but to direct it toward her husband. Who tried, in the early days, to pick Bao Mei off the floor. Not physically but rather with soft, gentle urgings: "I ran the bathwater for you." "I've put extra cushions on the couch." "Do you want to try this bamboo dish I cooked?" But her grunts followed by glares made him back off. In hindsight, perhaps he should've been more persistent, used harsher words. Because now they had two broken people in their home: one too afraid to go outside, and another who refused to leave the comfort of the floor.

"Did something happen to you?" Old Second asked. "Did somebody do something?"

They were folding wontons out of a metal bowl on the floor. The bowl had a meager amount of meat in it, and the wonton skins were freezer-burned. Food was scarce, and it'd be another week before the youngsters who ran the mutual aid delivered more groceries. Half of them would be foods neither Bao Mei nor Old Second knew how to eat. Chickpeas in a can. A box of corn grits. Macaroni elbows and a pouch of Kraft cheese powder.

"You can tell me, you know. You can tell me anything."

At first, they would throw the strange or rotting food items away. They were choosy with their lettuce leaves, with the brown spots on their onions. Whole potatoes would be tossed for being too soft, for daring to develop sprouts. But as time passed and their food supply dwindled, husband and wife had to, at Old Second's urging, become more courageous with their meals. It was funny in the beginning. They discovered new combinations of ingredients. Hot dogs in the scallion pancakes. Chickpeas cooked with sugar. Kraft powder in the soup (this one had failed—Old Second thought it would be like chicken bouillon). For a month and a half, they enjoyed their poverty on the cold but comfortable floor. And, to Old Second's credit, he *did* make it comfortable by setting down pillows and layers of blankets. He even moved the TV off its stand so that they could watch it better, "down there."

"Even if you're seeing someone. We're not husband and wife in *that* way. You can tell me if you're seeing someone."

"Pass me another wrapper," Bao Mei said.

They spoke about how poor they'd been as children. About siblings sneaking the first food off their plates and getting beaten—hard. One time, during an especially cold winter, a pond near Old Second's home had frozen over. And even though he lived in a village without magazines or TV, he and his sisters knew that they had an obligation to skate on the ice. *Like the Russians and the Americans.* So they did: sliding around on flat, homemade shoes and pulling each other down, laughing. How nice that laughter felt. How warm the sensation of held and sweaty hands. Even dinner tasted better that day. The soup that was nothing but scallions, two eggs, salt, and hot water seemed like something offered at a nice hotel.

Old Second's stories helped Bao Mei to develop a second, late-blooming affection for her husband. But words, as you and I both know, do not fill the belly. They do not ward off hunger, especially the kind so deep it rattles your bones. And as time passed and the food supply went from dwindling to nonexistent, the couple couldn't help but fall into a tense quiet. Their unspoken questions bubbled to the surface. Like foam, like scum, like dead or dying fish.

"You said you were visiting a friend in Brooklyn. Okay, fine. I believe you. But what is her name? How have I never heard of her before?"

"Are you going to pass me a wrapper or not?"

"It's not my business," Old Second admitted. He passed his wife a clump of wonton wrappers, freezer-burned and sticking together. "But I want to know what happened. About why, when you came home that day, you fell to the floor."

"I'm not allowed to sit on the floor? You're sitting on the floor."

"We're running out of food."

"The aid people are coming in a week. Actually, six days."

"This is all we have!" Old Second yelled. He pointed at the bowl of meat filling, the tray of wontons beside it. Afterwards, he moved toward the kitchen cabinet. Inside were some dusty potatoes and a bag of flour. A few dried mushrooms and some powdered Kraft. Grunting, as though with a tremendous effort, he hobbled over to the fridge, opening it to reveal six eggs and some wilted scallions. The freezer he left alone, since the contents would disprove his argument (a bag of precooked chicken sat in there, disappointing and untouched).

"Looks like enough to me," Bao Mei said.

"Have you seen yourself lately? You're bones. Nothing but skin and bones. You look"—he held up a dishrag—"like this. Like a worn piece of fabric."

"You can buy the groceries yourself, since you feel so strongly about it."

Old Second's face crumpled. He was afraid of going outside, of stepping beyond the boundaries of his apartment. It wasn't just the sickness that was floating around. Old Second was bothered by the meanness of strangers, their laughing looks and their hidden intentions. Years of working in America, in takeout restaurants and dim sum parlors, had Old Second convinced of one thing, and one thing only: the nastiness of other people. He remembered how his first boss, the one he called nice, didn't take him to the doctor after he fell and burned himself. He remembered how casually Kevin asked him to leave his wife. And then there were the stories. Of Chinese people getting pushed, punched, and blamed for the pandemic. What would he do if something happened to him? He barely spoke to anyone, even neighbors. Bao Mei was the sociable one, the one who returned with fascinating stories about what So-and-So did at the park, what Such-and-Such talked about during mahjong.

"You know I can't go outside," Old Second said.

"Why not? You've gone outside before."

"You know I can't," Old Second repeated.

He was about to justify himself, to whine and plead his case, when his wife's phone rang, flashing with a name he couldn't read. But what he *could* read was the panic in Bao Mei's face. The animal ferocity that took over when she saw him extending his arm, reaching to grab her phone. Old Second's intentions weren't sneaky. He was simply closer to it, and *she* (lunging at him) had been sitting on the floor. He'd planned to give the phone to her, to toss the thing like a white flag to his wife. A simple, perhaps meaningless act of reconciliation. But she'd gone ahead and lunged at him, snarling like a low-down and dirty dog. She'd almost stood up in the process, but weeks of sitting had weakened the muscles in her legs. All she could manage was a violent toss of her body—overturning, in the process, the bowl of wonton meat on the floor.

"Don't touch my phone," she said. Breathing heavily, she grabbed it from Old Second and declined the call.

"The doctor's office," Bao Mei said after a minute had passed. She was trying to make the situation appear lighthearted, to make a joke out of everything. But the strain showed on her face. And her breathing was heavy when she added: "You know how they bother you about your health checkups? About coming in so they can put gel on your belly, a needle in your arm?"

"No. Actually, I don't."

"Well," Bao Mei said.

Silently, she scooped the wonton meat back into the bowl.

THE MONEY TREES DIED FIRST. AFTERWARDS THE SNAKE plants with their bent and rotting leaves. A jar full of bamboo stalks clung to life for a bit—lasting until April—but they, in the end, began to wilt. Old Second tried to revive the plants by moving them from one window to another. He watered and spoke to them, brushed his fingers against their stalks to simulate wind. But it seemed as though the air in his apartment was poisonous. It choked (with the pride of a couple refusing to talk, touch, or even glance at each other) every organism in there. Even flies—could you believe that? They entered through a hole in the screen and dropped dead, instantly, into the sink. Old Second saw it happen after he woke from a nap that left creases on his cheek. He would've told Bao Mei the story as a funny joke, but she'd stopped talking to him. Sick with pride and hunger, she'd stopped talking at all.

Hers was a silence that came in stages. First, it was defined by fury. By an anger so thick, it clogged the breath that came out of her mouth. She coughed instead when she wanted to speak, glaring at her husband through narrowed eyes. When summer began and Bao Mei forgot what anger felt like, pride took over and her silence became, instead of malicious, simply annoying. She'd see smoke under a wok and let whatever it was burn there. She'd blink and smile at her husband's questions until they, since Old Second refused to speak to himself, disappeared, too. When the mutual aid people came, she'd simply look at them. The volunteers exchanged stories about her: of the strange, speechless, and skeletal woman who sat on the floor while they gave her groceries. Until, eventually, she disappeared.

That was the beginning of the third stage of her silence. When hunger deep as a cavern sank its roots into her throat, entirely blocking the passage of speech. Her breath soured and her stomach bloated with gas. Words, or the ghostlike shadows of them, fell from her mouth, dropping to the floor like acorns. Bao Mei did little but lie down now. She'd stare—when she could, when she was able to—at the TV, which played nothing but YouTube videos. Old Second didn't know how to type Chinese, so he let the algorithm take them where it did. Sometimes to cooking videos, other times to a strange-looking white woman, talking and laughing. Bao Mei didn't care either way, and her eyes flashed at whatever image was placed in front of her. Then, without warning, September snuck up on them, and Old Second realized that Bao Mei was slipping away. That her complexion had changed from egg yolk to egg white. His own fingers licked the surfaces of bowls he ate out of, but *she* did nothing but stare at the food. As though eating were a chore she was too tired to do.

He realized, then, that things had to change. That he had to go outside and look for food. If not, then Bao Mei would die and he'd be left alone: living in a country with nobody to talk to, nobody to sit with. "Outside" was a concept that terrified him. Because look at what happened there. Youngsters yelled slurs at Chinese people. They beat them up while onlookers only stopped to watch. Never mind the fact that what he'd watched could've been from years ago, or could've taken place in other cities. He only knew what his aged eyes saw, and what they witnessed reminded him of the cinema protests. Trembling, he put on his outside pants and socks.

He grabbed money from Bao Mei's secret stash, taped beneath the mattress, and rehearsed situations that were troublesome. If an American approached him, Old Second figured he could fake a conversation on his phone. If they stared for too long, he'd pull his mask down to reveal a smile. To protect himself from thieves, he hid his money in different and sometimes strange places on his body. Four twenties sat in his right pocket; another sat in his left. Two fifties (and some crumpled fives) were tucked into a secret hole in his jacket lining, the same one he used when transporting cash in the '90s, as an emigrant. When all his situations were rehearsed, and all his preparations completed, he decided to whisper prayers. The mindless sort that calmed him, allowing him to place a trembling hand against the door.

He unlatched it. Twisted the knob.

The third-floor hallway was as he remembered: dark and dusty but reasonably clean. Desiccated leaves sat in the folds of his doormat, and a neighbor—perhaps the one who fought with her husband through the walls—had left some laundry on the railing. It dripped, and the sound was like a lullaby to Old Second's ears.

Nothing bad will happen, he told himself.

Too impatient to wait for the elevator, he took the stairs, where food odors from other floors congregated, familiar-smelling and exciting his hunger. There was gentle movement in his mask, and this, if you looked closely, was caused by the continual movements of his lips. By the prayers he recited while walking down the steps. And along with the prayers were repetitions of what he would do outside. Lists of mundane chores that calmed him, made him brave.

"I will buy the eggs. The ground meat. The vegetables and the fish. I will wait in line, and when I get to the front, I will have my money ready. Nothing bad will happen to me. I will walk home and look both ways before crossing the street. I am only going one block, and if I can manage it, I will go into my wife's favorite restaurant. Order her favorite dish."

Never mind the fact that he couldn't remember what that dish was. Nor the fact that his legs were about to buckle, fold beneath his body.

Right in front of him was the open street.

THE FIRST STORE HAD DRY GOODS IN BUCKETS OUTSIDE THE window. The second had a rolling rack of jackets and sweaters, a glass door propped open with a stool. An old woman was sitting on it, eating wontons out of a quart-sized container, while a teenager— her grandson?—wrote figures in a book behind her. The third store was a bakery, and the bread smells made Old Second momentarily forget his fears. He was muttering still, and the early September sun made his back moist with sweat. When he removed his wool cap, a sap-like sensation was left behind. As he lingered outside the bakery's doors, staring at the buns, his tension began to fade.

Feelings returned to him. After months of staying inside, he remembered obscure sensations that made his feet skip instead of walk, his stomach yearn instead of grumble. Hunger could exist as a source of pleasure, Old Second realized. A source of anticipation. He remembered that flowers grew in the cracks of sidewalks; that children, walking beside their mothers, jumped over them in their imaginary games. Old Second played along after purchasing a roll cake, after a young baker's fingers brushed his own.

"Thank you," the baker said. "Come visit us again."

The fourth store was a mini mall with a Western Union in the front, a coffee shop across from it, and a lawyer's office in the back. The fifth wasn't a store at all but a prep school: its doors painted red as ketchup. When Old Second walked past, a line of children ran out, eager to leave behind the world of books.

Step on a crack, break your husband's back.

Old Second fumbled with the coins in his pocket. He recorded their weight and their sounds. Feeling whimsical, he stopped near the corner of a street to gaze at apartment buildings, allowing their crooked facades to burn in his mind. Then, as he crossed the road to look more closely at a bookstore, a pleasurable thought entered his head. Which was that he could go outside whenever he wanted. He could, if he pleased, see this all again. And when Bao Mei was better, he could take her with him. They could walk the streets and forget all about whatever had happened these past few months. None of it mattered anyway. They'd been through things. Crossed the ocean together on a fishing boat.

At the supermarket, he laughed to himself about how things turned out. For months he was terrified of the outdoors. But here he was: happy, even optimistic, among the cabbages. It was like the gods had decided to play a cruel joke on him. And that cruel joke was that a doctor's mundane advice—that a walk could do you a world of good—was true. He laughed. He thought about telling this to his wife. It would lift her mood. Perhaps he was being foolish, but what did he have besides hope?

He thought about this as he walked home. But halfway down the street, he stopped. Because there was somebody, a woman, waiting outside his building. He saw her profile and waited until she moved. She had an arm extended, as if to rap on the door. But then she pulled her hand back. She turned around. And saw him.

Old Second walked forward.

THIRTY-TWO

O
LD SECOND KNOWS that woman. Standing outside his building with her hand tentative against the door. Her name escapes him, but he recognizes her expression. Even though it is only her profile that he sees, even though she is far away. But that mousy face paired with that overconfident gait—Old Second would know it anywhere.

BUT WHAT HE DOESN'T KNOW, AND WHAT PERHAPS BAO MEI *does*, is the misery Yan Hua has gone through. The way she's tried, over the years, to offer her friends the bones of her memory, only for them to bite the bones into gristle before spitting them back up—sometimes right in her face. It's striking: how Frog, Kevin, May, and Little Amy are willing listeners until they reach the climax of her story. They coo and pat her back, frown in all the right places until Yan Hua reveals that a slip of her tongue (and later, her mind) killed her ex-husband.

At which point her friends' faces fall, crumbling like sand. Their muscles tense. They don't want to hear about Yan Hua's guilt because it's too complicated for them. Too terrifying. And because they can't face the reality that her actions killed someone, even if indirectly, they decide to pave over her words, flatten them with small talk and feigned ignorance. Until, of course, the next topic of conversation comes up. Until Yan Hua retracts her confession and blames it on a migraine, a momentary loss of her senses. Despite being her support system, they took the easier road by forcing Yan Hua to play the part of the victim. And because Yan Hua wasn't (*isn't*) brave enough to confront her shame, she decided to accept her role. For more than twenty years.

The only person who understands her is Bao Mei. She presses a torn napkin against Yan Hua's cheek when Yan Hua talks about the past, spinning words around the room like a spider's colorless silk. Bao Mei is accepting where Yan Hua's friends are not. And later, when Bao Mei sinks to the floor, it is not because of her anger toward Yan Hua (though this is what she believes at first). Nor is it because of the blame she so desperately wants to lay on her friend's feet. No: Bao Mei's sinking is the result of her regret, her belief that she could've prevented what happened at the Workers' Cinema.

This is a deadly, self-centered delusion on her part. Lying on the floor and listening to the footsteps in the hallway, to the voices and the jangle of keys, Bao Mei contemplates her actions the way a child might some building blocks. What would've happened had she approached Yan Hua with more empathy the night she entered the cinema? What would've happened had she said "Hey, girl" instead of "You do not belong here"? From the safety of the floor (a place from which Bao Mei can't fall), she imagines, then rearranges, scenes from her past. She discovers the dirty reality that her past decisions were made to protect the Projectionist. He couldn't know what the cinema *really* was. Nor the hell it could, without him knowing, transform into.

He was the sort of man Chinese people used to call "book-stupid." The Projectionist knew all kinds of trivia about movies, and he, despite only having a fourth-grade education, could take apart and rebuild machines. Yet despite his knowledge, and despite his genius with electronics, the Projectionist knew nothing about business. He refused to bribe local politicians and was quickly slapped with building code violations. He refused to renovate the hallways, with their dripping ceilings, or the screening rooms, with their hard-as-candy-and-just-as-sticky chairs. When the Workers' Cinema became a cruising spot for gay men, it was because the place had become run-down. Nobody would go there without a se-cret reason, and it was out of luck that the cinema made any money at all.

Bao Mei didn't want the Projectionist to know about the visits of the theater men's wives. It would've disheartened him, and he was under a lot of stress back then, becoming, on his worst days, a moody and childish lover. It goes without saying that he never put his hands on Bao Mei. He didn't yell, drink, gamble, or ask for money. But there were days where he would ignore her; days where Bao Mei would tell a joke and he'd stare with eyes like a dead fish, saying: "Nothing's funny, please stop laughing." Bao Mei was young at the time. And because she didn't want to lose that thin, sheer blanket she wrapped around herself—calling it romance— she decided to stand with him, to offer him her love and support.

Which meant she had to dismiss the complaints of the theater men's wives.

She lied to them. She used her status as a woman, as a sister and as a friend, to convince them that her words were sympathy. Trying to dissolve their anger, she made up false promises about talking to their husbands; scenarios where she'd convince their men to return home (fat chance!). Bao Mei convinced herself that she was doing something selfless. Something brave. She, a young woman from the provinces, was defending love! Protecting the rights of gay men to have a space for themselves! But now she understands that her actions were informed by desperate self-preservation. *My priority wasn't the protection of gay men*, Bao Mei thinks. *It was to save the Projectionist from the reality that his cinema was a dirty, immoral, and failing place.*

Hearing Yan Hua's confession made her confront the truth. She'd always known that the cinema was a utopia for gay men, but she'd neglected its other reality, experienced by the wives. And now, lying inside a nest of blankets on the floor, on a pillow too flat to support her neck, she sees the heart of the thought that prevents her from standing up. Which is that she's made a terrible mistake.

What if? Bao Mei wonders.

What if her sympathies had lain with the wives? What if she'd helped them like how she did Old Second and Shun-Er? Not in a way that would go against their husbands, but what would the outcome have been if she didn't treat the wives like nuisances: people to be hidden and, later, tossed?

***

OLD SECOND DOESN'T SPEAK TO YAN HUA WHEN SHE FOLlows him into his building. He simply holds the door open before staring back at her, a ghost he is too shocked to see. The same thing happens when he shoves a key into his apartment's lock. There's a split second where he wonders, fussing with the grocery bags on his wrist, if he shouldn't let Yan Hua in. If, instead of leaving the door open, he should turn around and slam it in her face (though not before telling Yan Hua to fuck off). But the anxiety he mistakes as hatred goes limp when he spots the humor in her eyes. The wry, simpering gladness animating her lips, telling Old Second she's happy someone has come along to let her in. Yes, even if that someone is the man whose life she ruined. A hidden wit lies in the pout of her bottom lip, and the sight of this makes Old Second want to laugh. *Thank God she's not crying*, he thinks. *And thank God she's not seeking sympathy, either.* Both those actions would've hardened Old Second's heart, causing him to revisit the dislike he holds for this woman. But because she is calm, because she is tactful enough to give him his space, Old Second wills himself to lower his guard.

"My wife's sick," he warns.

Yan Hua nods in response.

But when the door swings open, she isn't prepared to see her friend lying on the floor, wilted as a cooked leaf of spinach. Bao Mei's hair has fallen out, and her mouth, lacking false teeth, has sunken in. Patches of bulbous skin—remnants, perhaps, from a long-ago battle with cancer—run up and down her left leg. The sight disgusts Yan Hua. There's also the moist, overripe smell permeating the apartment, one that causes Yan Hua to turn around, to gag. *Like the stench of a market street after closing time*, she thinks, *or the odor of a compost bin that hasn't been cleaned.* She wrinkles her nose, scans the living room's various surfaces, all of them uncomplicated in their filth. Instead of place mats, there are old and soggy newspapers on the floor. Sauce spills that have been coated in dust. Flies cling to the walls, and large, clicking beetles walk in circles on every chair, every table. The sight of them bewilders Yan Hua, and she gasps, clamping a hand over her mouth right as Old Second tosses her a pair of house shoes.

He doesn't address the sorry state of his apartment. Nor does he, when he walks to the kitchen, seem to care about the poorly hidden disgust of his visitor. In fact, Yan Hua's attitude seems to strengthen him a bit, making Old Second puff his chest out like a bird. And when, finally, she asks him where to set down her bags, he tosses a dagger in the form of a sneer at her, across his shoulder and toward a shoe cabinet whose top is cluttered with papers.

Yan Hua walks toward it. Sets her gifts down . . . and realizes, with a start, that the papers are letters. Fake ones: like the ones that she'd read with Kevin, years ago. She's known for a while that their source is Bao Mei, but seeing the letters again, just steps away from the unlikely artist who wrote them, eases the disgust in her heart. The letters make her smile, and while Bao Mei sleeps and Old Second works in the kitchen, she riffles through them.

There are dozens of letters. Some are complete; most are not. A few are nothing but scribbles in the margins. Useful phone numbers and the names of old friends—dead, forgotten, or relocated. Yan Hua skims through them with the pleasure of a child at a toy store. She laughs at references to old jokes, smiles at the sight of familiar place-names. The last letter she reads is long, and she has to finish it at home. The start of it, however, is enough to make her feel warm but guilty. It's addressed to a sissy named Ugly Mulan in Mawei City, and it depicts Old Second's love life in East Broadway. She sees herself in the letter, and she sees Bao Mei. But Shun-Er is absent. This afflicts her with the icy heat of a migraine.

Later, she will taste the formation of a rebuttal on her lips. She will feel a thousand lashes across her back, as well as a desire to respond. A desire to alter the bleak history Bao Mei has created in her letter. But right now, her friend is awakening. Her breathing has changed its pace, and Yan Hua hears the toss of a leg from across the room. Still clutching the letter, she walks over to where Bao Mei is sleeping.

"I'm here," she says.

I've come to visit you.

THIRTY-THREE

OLD SECOND WORKS in the kitchen while Yan Hua and Bao Mei sit in the living room, silent over a bag of nail supplies. They aren't talking, and their uneasy silence is cut by the roar of a stove exhaust. Bao Mei sucks her teeth, and Yan Hua reacts by humming. At one point, she even makes a lively, though unfunny, joke about Bao Mei's situation. She understands now. Twisting the cap off a bottle of nail polish, then applying it to Bao Mei's trembling hands, Yan Hua sees that her friend's silence is the result of illness. And not normal illness, either, but one caused by a rude and uncertain shock.

Yan Hua knows because she has experienced it, too. Back then, Little Amy, Big Amy, and May had "healed" her by fluttering over her like a flock of birds. Chanting and praying and crying along, chorus-like, when Yan Hua needed to cry, then singing to her when the hurt in her chest felt thick as a heart attack. Now Yan Hua is trying to do the same thing for Bao Mei. Look at how delicately she snips Bao Mei's fingernails. Listen to how she hum-sings as she tugs away at her cuticles, pulling them off like threads. She'd come with every intention of justifying herself, of making it known that she wants to continue her friendship with Bao Mei. But now, all she wants to do is put her weapons down.

We will have a chance to talk later, Yan Hua thinks. *We will have a chance to remember our pasts and see what comes of it.*

But right now, the touch of an arm will do. A laugh that comes out of Bao Mei's throat like coughing. From the kitchen, delicious (albeit too peppery) smells radiate into the living room, causing nostrils to widen and stomachs to grumble. Yes, even Bao Mei's, who sits up in time to catch Old Second walking toward her with oven mitts and holding a bowl. Afterwards, a plate of roast duck.

"Would you like to stay for lunch?" he asks Yan Hua.

His voice is cautious, tentative as flowers in March. But his eyes are beckoning.

"I brought some food, too," Yan Hua says. "Mangoes. Do either of you like mangoes?"

Old Second nods, but he does not return her gaze.

YAN HUA'S REVISION

BAO MEI'S FINAL letter is not so much a letter as it is a story. The sentences are formed using small, sloppy characters—perhaps by a hand weakened by illness—but the world they depict is familiar to Yan Hua. It's a chimerical world. Strictly speaking, it's an untruthful one. Yan Hua feels moved by its fiction. Every word strikes her like a whip. For example, the "scene" where Old Second talks about cruising in the bathrooms at Columbus Park, and how it reminds him of the Workers' Cinema. The nostalgia of cruising makes him want to return to China, to Mawei. But is there anything left for him if the cinema's gone? The letter's forlornness is undercut by a current of stern humor, one that is distinctly Bao Mei's. And it is on this note of humor, accompanied by hope, that the letter ends. Abruptly and mid-sentence (perhaps Bao Mei had to attend to other matters that day) on a line about Old Second hoping to be married someday, because sissies like him can get married now, in America.

The ink on the page is barely visible. And when Bao Mei writes, she presses *hard* on the paper, the way village children used to. The sight of the indentations causes Yan Hua to laugh. She's home now, after her visit. It did not feel successful to her—Bao Mei fell asleep right after Yan Hua painted her nails. In the end, Yan Hua simply left: leaving her mangoes and some cash on the shoe cabinet.

But she took Bao Mei's letter with her. She folded it in her purse with the intention of finishing it. Of revising the future it depicted: warm but a little bleak. And now, feeling the flap of wings in her chest, Yan Hua discovers the act of writing, of imagining, is frightening. It causes her wrists to knock. Yet with a deep breath, she puts her pen to paper, managing to write a series of scrawling characters.

Old Second and Shun-Er will meet again, she decides. And the Workers' Cinema will be rebuilt. She imagines possibilities, battles with them in her mind. What if the government, working with the Projectionist, tore the place down only to remodel it with larger screening rooms? What if the protest had worked, all those years ago, and the Workers' Cinema was never torn down? She closes her eyes and imagines Shun-Er again . . . and realizes she cannot remember what his face looks like. Just his laborer's clothes and a skim of brown skin. A crooked eyebrow and a length of arm hair. Working slowly, she places features on his face. And with the passing of every minute, the image expands. Yan Hua isn't sure if this "new" version of Shun-Er is "correct," but he is smiling, and his hand is pointing at the open doorway of the Workers' Cinema.

Old Second will be waiting there, at the door, Yan Hua thinks.

In Chinese, she writes, "They walk toward each other."

And she sets her pen down to breathe.

ACKNOWLEDGMENTS

To Kent Wolf, for being the kindest and most formidable advocate a writer could ask for. To Pilar Garcia-Brown, for understanding— and loving—the imperfections of my characters. To Yassine Belka- cemi, for being brilliant and all-around incredible. To the teams at Neon Literary, Dutton Books, and John Murray: Gabe Pettegrew, Anna Sproul-Latimer, Jamie Knapp, Nicole Jarvis, Claire Sullivan, Mary Beth Constant, Ella Kurki, Christopher Lin, Sofia Hericson, Jocasta Hamilton, Alice Herbert, Ellie Bailey, Rachel Clements, and more—thank you for helping to make this book better. You have all changed my life forever.

To Vanessa Chan, for your friendship and generosity, and for making me howl with laughter whenever we talk. I am so honored that our books are coming out in the same year.

To Mariel Rodney, for being my smartest friend. To Mehdi Okasi, for teaching me to write beautiful sentences. To Anthony Domestico, for reading Proust with me. To Kellie Wells and Nana Nkweti, for believing.

ACKNOWLEDGMENTS

To Kukuwa Ashun, Mark Galarrita, Jackson Saul, and Saul Alpert-Abrams: You've all read pieces of this book in its infancy; and you've all helped me to become kinder, smarter, and more courageous in my writing. I couldn't have written *Cinema Love* without you.

To all the friends I've made before my prefrontal cortex fully developed: Autumn Fourkiller, Lanessa Salvatore, Kelp, Ajani Bazile, DJ Kim, Kenne Yang, Tiffany Chen, Gina Chung, Grace Liew, Jemma Wei, Emily Polson, Sabrina Pyun, Rebekah Jett, Clare Maurer, Brianna Yamashita, Marysue Rucci, and Kathy Belden. I'm grateful you are all in my life.

To Jessamine Chan, my literary auntie. To Randy Winston, who is kind and brilliant. To Yves Gleichman, for feeding me various patties at Vanessa's rooftop party. To Keziah Weir, who will someday win all the awards.

To Joshua Brandon, for being my best friend in the entire world.

And finally, to my parents: Mei Cai Yang and Chun Lin Tang, for everything. Words can't even express how lucky I am to be your son. 我爱你们。一辈子都爱你们.

ABOUT THE AUTHOR

Jiaming Tang is a queer immigrant writer. He holds an MFA from the University of Alabama, and his writing has appeared in *AGNI*, *Lit Hub*, *Joyland Magazine*, and elsewhere. He is a 2022–23 Center for Fiction Emerging Writer Fellow and lives in Brooklyn, New York. *Cinema Love* is his first novel.